Also by Dana Mentink

Spoon
to be
Dead

A SHAKE SHOP MYSTERY

DANA MENTINK

Poisoned Pen
PRESS

Published by Poisoned Pen Press, an imprint of Sourcebooks
P.O. Box 4410, Naperville, Illinois 60567–4410
(630) 961-3900
sourcebooks.com

Printed and bound in the United States of America.
KP 10 9 8 7 6 5 4 3 2 1

*To Uncle Barry, who always carried Cuba
in his heart. You will be missed.*

Chapter One

"IF I'M GOING TO DROWN, it might as well be in chocolate syrup." Trinidad Jones surveyed the contents of the food truck parked on the sidewalk of the Shimmy and Shake Shop, adding another container to the box marked 'toppings'.

"Nobody's going to drown, Trin." Juliette, one of the three ex-wives of Trinidad's former husband, pulled her bulky sweater tighter against Oregon's December cold. "That's a little bit on the dramatic side, don't you think?"

Trinidad shoved back a strand of her coily hair that defied any elastic. "Doesn't feel like it. I'm a thirty-seven-year-old divorcée with no business experience trying to sell ice cream in the face of an Eastern Oregon winter. Summer was one thing, but no one wants Freakshakes when there's snow in the forecast and Christmas lights on every house."

The panic that surfaced repeatedly during the night now rippled up her spine. How could her ice cream dream possibly melt away? The giant Freakshakes, enormous concoctions featuring fantastic toppings of doughnuts, sauces, slices of pie, and their punny themed names were hot sellers in the summer, but sales had dropped along with the temperatures. The citrusy "Partners in Lime" extravaganza, complete with graham cracker stars and an entire wedge of pie protruding from the green shake, was now officially retired along with the fall Caramel Carnival Crunch and the Yodelayheechew in honor of the departed Alpenfest celebration. There was no denying the fact that ice cream wasn't a hot commodity when Sprocketerians unboxed their gloves and scarves.

Sweat and tears along with every dime and what was left of her mental fortitude had gone into the expensive remodel to fix the shop's front wall ruined by a killer on the rampage.

"In with the good air, out with the bad." Juliette flipped her silky blond hair over one shoulder and demonstrated blowing through her glossed lips. "You expected this and you've retooled. All your holiday flavors are mouthwatering and the hot chocolate bombs are darling. People will eat them up, so to speak. Perfect for parties or weddings. They'll be a hit, enough to tide you over until summer anyway, along with the classes you've planned." She patted Trinidad on the back as they closed the rear doors of her food truck, newly repainted a fetching shade of bubblegum pink. "Just keep breathing."

Trinidad's sense of optimism was at odds with the stack of bills her old Labrador Noodles was intent on hiding under his doggie cushion. It had been so easy to be confident when the summer visitors were flocking in. Lately there was more fear on the menu than fortitude. "I sure hope you're right."

Juliette waved away her doubt. "I'm virtually always right.

We're tough women, you, me, and Bonnie. We all survived being married to Gabe, who was as bad an embezzler as he was a husband. Jail was just deserts for him, if you'll excuse the pun. That all worked out for the best, didn't it?"

Trinidad supposed it had. Gabe deeded her the storefront, Juliette a storage business, and Bonnie a piece of property that was now home for Bonnie's Sprocket Station, an adorable train-car inn.

"Plus we three have become sisters," Juliette said. "*Hermanas,* as Papa Luis would say. Awesome, right? We're like a live-action sitcom."

Trinidad wanted to board Juliette's optimism train, but her mind wandered back to the pragmatic. Had she packed extra ice cream scoops for the product demonstration that would commence later that day? Landing a gig with the Sprocket Steamboat would do wonders for her dark mood. Juicy rumors were circulating that some big spender had booked an extravagant last-minute Christmas party on the steamboat. Extravagance was unusual in Upper Sprocket, a town of barely three thousand people. As far as she could tell, the most popular winter topic was when fishing would resume in Three Egg Lake after winter let go its icy hold. Now people were all atwitter guessing the celebrity visitor's identity. She realized Juliette was waiting for an indication that Trinidad was paying attention. "Yes, good came out of the Gabe thing but…"

"But nothing. What's the worst that could happen after you survived that debacle?"

"The worst thing?" Trinidad chewed her lip and felt

the chill seep through her ridiculously yellow secondhand jacket. It was too snug for her ample hips but there was no extra money to upsize. At least Noodles would be comfortable in the jacket she'd fashioned him from a human coat. "I don't book this gig on the Sprocket Steamboat. I don't make the rent on the tiny house, and Papa Luis and I are evicted. My business will fail." She eyed Noodles, who peered at her from the doorway of her shop wearing a neck scarf of dapper red-and-green plaid in honor of the approaching holiday. "Noodles will starve and you'll be out of a job too." She paused. "And Gabe will choose to settle back here in good old Sprocket after he's paroled."

"Man. Talk about looking on the dark side of things," Juliette said with a shudder. "I went to jail for a murder I didn't commit, and *I'm* not ready to throw in the towel."

Valid point. Trinidad sighed. "Okay. You've succeeded in cheering me up. Let's grab our aprons and double-check the list. I plan on us getting there early to make a good impression."

As they were walking to the shop door, local bird-watcher Oscar Fuentes shuffled along the sidewalk, tufts of white hair protruding from under his knit cap. "Morning," he said with his customary wave. They waved back. Oscar would be collecting his birding buddies Stan Lawper and Leonard Pinkerton at the Full of Beans coffee shop, and the trio would take the mile-long trek to the Twisted Pines Overlook, their habitual destination.

"Saw the photo you posted on Instagram yesterday," Juliette said. "A yellow-breasted chat, right?"

Trinidad was impressed with Juliette's birding

knowledge, considering she proudly proclaimed she'd never been hiking except at the mall.

Oscar's round face lit up. His white mustache drooped down over his top lip like a lush albino caterpillar come to settle there. "Yes, it was. Stock photo but we're hoping to spot a real one. It would be a treasure to see it since most chats have migrated already. In the past, chats have been considered warblers, of course, and Leonard and I had a good dust-up about that because—"

"Amazing." Trinidad beamed him a wide smile to circumvent what was shaping up to be a dissertation. "You, Stan, and Leonard are walking bird encyclopedias. Want a peanut for Scooter?"

"Do we ever say no?" Oscar said.

"Fetch a peanut, Noo," Trinidad called. Noodles disappeared into the shop, a moment later arriving with a container of nuts. The dog trotted over and delivered it to Oscar, who extracted one. Noodles dutifully carried the container back inside.

Oscar shifted his binoculars to gingerly stow the peanut inside his partially open winter coat, which served as Scooter's comfy nest. Scooter, an eclectus parrot, could not fly since he'd been mauled by a cat as a chick. For twenty years, Oscar had taken him on daily outings to see the able-bodied birds so Scooter could "get his bird on" as Oscar put it. A small orange beak poked out, snagged the peanut, and retreated. Saluting them with a gloved hand to his puffy faux fur hat, Oscar continued across the street to the Full of Beans to meet his friends.

"See, Trin? If people still go birding in the winter, then they probably eat ice cream too," Juliette said as Oscar departed.

"Don't you have worries? I mean, selling your storage business and coming to work with me has to leave you wondering if you can pay the bills."

She shrugged. "Jobs are like shoes. Meant to be changed if they don't fit."

Trinidad wished she could be so cavalier, but this job, her Shimmy and Shake Shop, was more than work. It was her passion and it had allowed her to reinvent herself after the divorce and find the confidence to believe in Trinidad Jones once more. She was not sure she had it in her to try it again if the Shimmy failed. They started in on the morning chores, tidying, churning, and chopping as the minutes blended into one hour, then two.

"Hey, here's Bonnie," Juliette said as she flipped the shop sign to "Open" at the stroke of 11:00. "She told me she was coming by. I wonder where Felice is."

The other previous Mrs. Gabe Bigley was hard to miss at well over six feet tall. A former college basketball player, Bonnie rarely went anywhere without her young daughter, Felice, Gabe's only child. And even more unusual was the lack of a smile on Bonnie's face as she opened the door. At the moment, she was frowning and looking down at her sizable feet. Odd.

Before Trinidad could ask what was up, her cell phone rang, so she stepped behind the counter to answer with a "give me one minute' gesture. Bonnie and Juliette began an earnest conversation in low tones.

Leonard Pinkerton, steamboat captain and entrepreneur, hailed her with a hearty good morning that caused her to hold the phone away from her ear.

"Hello, Mr. Pinkerton. I'm so eager to show you the setup we can provide for the Sprocket Steamboat. I've got the perfect little holiday themed—"

"Call me Leonard, and I've got to postpone."

Her heart tumbled to her shoes. "Oh?" She considered all the frozen treats currently in her food truck. "Postpone, until when?"

"Later today. I sprained my ankle and I gotta go get an X-ray. Probably have a date with an ice pack after."

She blew out a relieved breath. Postponement of a few hours she could deal with. "I'm so sorry to hear about your accident."

"Let's make it five so I can ice and elevate and all that malarky. By the way, can you bring something nondairy? The client booking this shindig can't handle lactose."

Nondairy? With a silent groan, she considered the cream-rich lineup she'd painstakingly created and tested on her poor grandpa, Papa Luis, until she'd perfected her offerings. Never once had she considered having a nondairy option. *Think fast, Trinidad, or you'll lose this job.* "Of course, Mr. Pinkerton. Not a problem. See you soon." She disconnected, mind spinning like the agitator of her shake machine. "I've got approximately seven hours to come up with an interesting nondairy ice cream dessert," she announced, squeezing her palms together to contain the panic. "Not a moment to lose."

"Uh, Trinidad," Juliette started. "Bonnie needs to tell you something."

"I'm so sorry." Trinidad was already pulling up recipes on her phone. "I'd really love to talk right now, but I just have to get this done first. Can we…?"

Bonnie bit her lip. "Sure, sure. I can come back later."

"No, she can't." Juliette snatched at Bonnie's elbow and propelled her toward Trinidad. "This needs to be heard *pronto*."

Trinidad froze, scrolling finger paused. Alarm bells now warred with the anxiety in her belly as she regarded them. Noodles sensed the mood and trotted closer as he assessed what comfort might be required. His training as a service dog kicked in regularly, even though he'd flunked out of the program.

Bonnie must be sick. Or Felice. Trinidad's nerves zinged. No, not Felice. The six-year-old had become a fixture in Trinidad's soul in the year she'd lived in Upper Sprocket. "What is it?" Trinidad's voice was pitched high with fear. "What's wrong?"

As Bonnie was about to answer, distant sirens shrilled. An ambulance and police car flew up the street and around the corner. She expected to hear the sound swallowed up as they headed away from town, past the Vintage Theater toward Little Bit Road, but instead the wailing sirens persisted, lingering like a bad aftertaste. Whatever the problem, it was close.

"A medical emergency maybe?" Juliette said as the three women peered out the shop window.

Stan Lawper, the immensely proper proprietor of the Full

of Beans, stepped out of his shop. In a small town, lights and sirens had ultra urgency. It was clear that something bad had happened and probably to someone they knew and loved.

"We'll see if we can help in a minute," Juliette said. "Bonnie's situation can't wait."

Bonnie had a *situation*. The statement shook Trinidad once more. Firmly putting aside the sirens and the recipe clock ticking down in her mind, Trinidad took a breath and gave Bonnie her full attention.

Naturally pale, Bonnie was tending toward the color of whipped cream. There were smudges of fatigue under her eyes. She really must be sick. Why hadn't Trinidad noticed the last time she and Felice had stopped by for their regularly scheduled ice cream treats? Guilt tightened her stomach. She gestured Bonnie into a chair, and Noodles fetched a bottle of water.

"I…uh…" Bonnie gulped some water, shoving her white-blond braid behind her.

"What is it, Bonnie?" Trinidad said. "Whatever's wrong, we'll help you."

Bonnie spluttered after swallowing wrong. "I'm afraid this is gonna be a shock."

"I'm getting used to them." That was an understatement. Two murders in the time she'd been in Sprocket, the last of which involved a corpse in the trunk of her Papa Luis's prized Chevy Bel Air, had thickened her skin against unwanted surprises. "Go ahead, Bonnie. Please."

Bonnie swallowed, coughed some more, and straightened. "I, uh, I'm…sorta getting married."

Trinidad's mouth fell open. Married? Bonnie had been up to her lofty neck in getting her bed-and-breakfast off the ground. The antique train-car inn had survived a murder on the premises during Alpenfest the month before, but only barely. Between drumming up visitors, remodeling the old dining car, and homeschooling Felice, when had Bonnie had time to meet a man? And fall in love? And get engaged? And why did she look so green around the gills about it? Trinidad realized she was gaping like a fish tossed up on the shore of Three Egg Lake. "Wow. Well, I mean, congratulations. Who's the lucky man?"

Juliette and Bonnie exchanged a look.

Bonnie began to gnaw on her thumbnail. "Ummm, that's the thing that is a tad surprising."

What on earth was the woman stalling about? "Bonnie, spit it out. Who is the groom?"

Before she could answer, the door slammed open with a crash of bells and a gust of freezing air. Trinidad shot to her feet as a man from her nightmares lurched in. Gabe Bigley, serial cheater, felon, liar, and embezzler, stood there as handsome as the day she'd married him but a bit less debonair. His shoes were muddy, and there was a tear in the knee of his jeans, which were wet to thigh level. His expensive sunglasses were missing one earpiece and they dangled drunkenly from his face. A dark sweat jacket hung slightly off one shoulder. Incredibly, he waved. "Oh hey," he said as if he'd stopped by to ask the time. "You're all here."

Repeated blinking didn't help. It wasn't a nightmare. Gabe was really standing right in front of her. "Yes, we are all here," Trinidad managed, her voice rising to a squeak. "But what are *you* doing here?"

"Paroled Monday. Stopped to see Mom and borrowed her car to drive to Sprocket," he said. "And something really weird just happened."

Which part was weirdest, she wondered. Gabe materializing in Sprocket? Strolling in as if he hadn't wrecked all their lives? Or looking as if he'd just gone through a car wash without the car?

His eyes fastened on Bonnie, slightly glazed. "Hi, Bon Bon. I'll buy you that engagement ring soon as I get the money."

Engagement ring? Trinidad was now certain a cardiac event had messed with her faculties, but Noodles wagged his tail at Gabe and bumped her on the knee with his nose, so she figured she was still standing and conscious. She gritted her teeth. "Someone better tell me what is going on before my head explodes."

"Uh…" Bonnie started, then stopped.

Gabe held up a trembling finger. "I know exactly how you feel, Trina."

"Don't call me Trina," Trinidad snapped. "Only my friends call me that."

"Right, so here's the thing." Gabe pushed his glasses up and only succeeded in knocking them further askew. "I think, I mean I'm pretty certain, ninety-eight percent or so…" Gabe pursed his lips. "That I just killed someone."

Juliette gasped.

"What do you mean you think you killed someone?"

Trinidad toyed with the idea of slapping some coherence into him.

Bonnie stared, hands covering her mouth.

"Hold on for a minute." Gabe pointed his shaking finger at the ceiling. They waited in collective shock. After five seconds, he keeled over backward, knocking against the counter and upending a container of sprinkles that swirled around him in a kaleidoscope of colors as bright as the blood on his shirt.

Chapter Two

"HELP." THE PHONE SHOOK IN Trinidad's hand. "I need an ambulance at the Shimmy and Shake." She rattled off the address. After a few questions and answers, the dispatcher reported that help was on the way.

"He's breathing." Juliette knelt beside one of Gabe's shoulders as Bonnie perched next to the other, pressing a towel to the wound that had been concealed by his hair. "And his pulse is steady. There's a bump on his head."

Noodles licked the sprinkles off Gabe's chin, causing his eyelids to flutter.

Trinidad fought a dark sense of dread. "You wait for the ambulance. I'll be right back."

Juliette's eyes narrowed. "Where are you going?"

"I need to find out what happened."

Noodles sensed her agitation and shadowed her as she hurried along the damp sidewalk. They hopped into the sec-ondhand Subaru she'd traded in for her thirdhand Pinto and drove past the bait and tackle shop and Pizza Heaven.

A young twentysomething waved from the porch of the pizza shop and Trinidad stopped, rolling down her window. The lady held the door open with her hip, flour-dusted hands raised as if she was the victim of a holdup. "What happened?"

"I'm not sure yet."

"I have dough to knead, but I'll keep an ear peeled."

Before Trinidad got the window rolled up again, Stan Lawper raced out of his coffee shop and hurried to her car. She rolled down her other window.

"I am concerned," he said in that proper English gentleman way that harkened to his days as a butler. "If you are going to investigate the sirens..."

She blushed. "Yes, I was."

"May I join you? I have an overwhelming feeling of unease."

She gestured him in. As they drove on, she decided not to mention what had happened with Gabe until she had more facts in order. At the path into the woods that visitors rarely noticed, she turned in the direction of the sirens. The sprinkling of wild grass alongside the road glittered with a light dusting of snow. She drove underneath the canopy of trees that led to the Twisted Pines Overlook. Alongside she could hear the rushing water, a swift tributary of Messabout Creek. Stan stared ahead, silent.

Since the mile-and-a-quarter drive was narrow and twisty, she forced herself to take it slow. All the while, her heart beat faster and faster until it practically rattled her rib cage. Just before the last turn, she rolled down the window. The sirens had stopped but she could see the reflection of the red lights strobing from just ahead. Probably everything was fine, she told herself. Maybe Oscar turned his ankle. Gabe was mistaken that he'd killed someone. He was always a smidge on the dramatic side. The time he'd found a cricket in the cupboard, he carried on as if it was a biblical plague of locusts.

But the closer she came, the more her optimism waned. Lip between her teeth, she rounded the corner and jerked the car to a stop.

"Oh no." Stan's voice was strangled.

The body of Oscar Fuentes lay stomach down on the ground, cheek pressed to the earth as if he was asleep. His eyes were open, staring at nothing. There was no blood that she could detect, but neither was there any hint of life left in him.

She groaned involuntarily, and Chief Cynthia Bigley, trim and athletic in her police chief uniform, looked her way. Bigley's expression was shuttered, and Trinidad recognized it as the "cop face" she showed the world. There had been moments since Trinidad's arrival in Sprocket that she thought she might have seen another, softer side of the woman, but right now she was all business, hands on hips, directing her second-in-command, Alvin Chang, who was photographing the scene. Pastor Phil, Sprocket's only clergyman, shivered in his puffy jacket, his dog Pedro tucked under his armpit. His face was slack with shock. He must have been the one to phone the police.

With her heart in her shoes, Trinidad observed that the medic was not moving urgently around the stricken Oscar. Her instinct was correct; there was no reviving him. Stan's mouth was tight in a way that told her he too understood the gravity of the situation. She tried to blink back a sudden wash of tears as the three of them got out of the car.

Bigley finished with Chang and approached, her boots squeaking on the frozen ground. "He's deceased," she said simply. "Hit by a car that is now in the creek, abandoned. I'm guessing it happened less than an hour or so ago, but Pastor Phil just found him."

"Yes," Trinidad croaked. "Oscar stopped by the store a little after nine."

Bigley nodded and made a note. "Looks like the driver fled on foot."

Nausea overcame Trinidad, but she took a fortifying breath. This could not be happening, yet it was. "I…uh…I may have information about that."

Bigley arched an eyebrow. "I'm listening."

"A person, uh, a man, stopped in my shop a few minutes ago and confessed to killing Oscar. I mean, he said he thought he'd probably killed *someone* and since…" Trinidad flapped her arms around. "Oscar's, um, dead right here and all…"

Bigley waited patiently for Trinidad to wind down. "Who, Trinidad? Who confessed?"

She gulped. "Gabe."

Bigley blinked. "Gabe who?"

"Gabe, my ex-husband and your baby brother."

Now the chief's head cocked to the side as she stared. "What?"

"Gabe's been hurt. He collapsed in my shop, but Juliette and Bonnie are with him and an ambulance is on the way."

But the chief was no longer listening. She snapped a command out to Chang and hustled to her car. Her tires swirled the snow and mud together. Chang's face was puzzled as he continued taking pictures while the medics loaded Oscar into the ambulance.

The ambulance driver looked around. "We'll take him to Mercy General, if anyone needs to know that." Chang acknowledged and the vehicle departed.

And who did need to know? Oscar was a single man, never married to Trinidad's knowledge. His cousin, Iris Fuentes, was the new florist in Sprocket. Was there anyone to stand with her when she heard the terrible news? Maybe Stan would know. He and Oscar had been fast friends long before Trinidad moved to town.

She approached him as Noodles wandered off to sniff the shrubbery.

"Stan, I'm so sorry."

He didn't meet her eyes, looking at his well-shined shoes. The stoic Brit, a former butler and lawyer, was not a man comfortable with public displays of emotion.

"What a terrible accident. Oscar was on his way to take photos. He was on a mission to photograph a chat. I should have been with him, but we had a problem with the coffee grinder and I was assisting Meg." His sister comanaged the Full of Beans.

She put a hand on his arm. "It's not your fault. There's no way you could have known, and if you and Leonard were with him, you might have been hurt too."

Stan grimaced. "And Leonard was missing in action as well. Some friends. Oscar died alone."

A lump formed in her throat as she tried to assimilate the sight of the corpse with the man she'd greeted that morning. "He was so cheerful when he stopped by and…" She gasped in horror.

Stan clasped her fingers. "What? What is it?"

"Scooter."

Stan paled. "I forgot all about him."

The little parrot Oscar had tucked against his chest… With Oscar lying prostrate on the ground, broken and bloodied, no doubt he would have crushed the fragile bird in his fall. "Oh," she choked. "Poor, poor Scooter."

"Indeed." Stan shook his head. "Oscar was devoted to that bird."

Noodles returned, brushing against her thigh with a whine. She was reaching to pat his head when she realized what he had in his mouth. She froze.

Stan realized it too. "Good gravy."

Trinidad dropped to her knees. "Oh, Noo."

Noodles wagged his tail. From one side of his mouth protruded a cluster of emerald tail feathers, and out the other, a smooth green head. Noodles gently deposited his prize into her cupped palms.

The bird lay perfectly still, his tiny claws contracted into knots, until Noodles began to lick the top of his head. She was about to shoo the dog away when Scooter's black eyes popped open and he wriggled. "Oh my gosh."

"He's alive," Stan breathed over her shoulder.

Sure enough, when she gently tipped him upright, he fluffed his feathers and said in a tinny falsetto, "Oh my giddy aunt."

Trinidad cried while Noodles danced on excited paws.

Though she tipped him this way and that, the bird appeared unharmed. On his chest were none of the brilliant feathers like his back, only fuzzy down where he'd plucked them out. A neurosis, Oscar had told her. He looked like he was wearing soft gray pajamas, but there was no blood anywhere.

"How is it possible he's alive?" She kept her palms loosely cradling Scooter so he wouldn't hop out of her grip.

"I don't know, but Oscar would be so pleased. And Noodles is a hero for finding Scooter under the bushes." Stan patted Noodles on the head. "I am going to put a jar of dog treats on my counter for you, old fellow."

"What are we going to do with him?"

"First a visit to the vet, I think. Then perhaps…" Stan's voice broke and he cleared his throat. "Perhaps his cousin Iris might like him, to…"

To remember Oscar, Trinidad silently finished. A breeze rustled the down on Scooter's chest and he fluffed his wings. Too cold for him, she realized. She carefully settled the bird inside her jacket, leaving enough unzipped that he could peek out if he desired. She figured Oscar would approve of the accommodations.

Chang strolled up, the pants hanging loose on his skinny frame.

"We found…" she started to say when Scooter began to rustle inside her jacket, tickling her into giggles.

Chang stared. "You okay?"

Trinidad tried to answer but the bird was wriggling. She began to wriggle too, unable to stop laughing.

A look of alarm stole across Chang's face. "Are you getting hysterical, ma'am? Don't worry. Shock can do funny things to a person."

"No…it's…" she tried to say as Scooter made one final loop around inside before he settled. "The bird in my jacket."

Chang looked from Trinidad to Stan. Stan explained about Scooter.

"How did that bird survive?" Chang said.

"Good question." Trinidad controlled herself and wiped her eyes. The road beyond where Oscar had fallen was littered with pine needles and frost. Tire ruts showed where the car had left the roadway some ten yards past the accident site. "The car that struck him continued on and went into the creek bed?"

Chang nodded. "Looks that way."

"Funny how it continued past the trees first, though, before it plunged down." Trinidad frowned. "You would have thought an out-of-control car wouldn't have stayed on the road for so long after hitting Oscar."

"Pretty weird, for sure. And there's that one spot there in the snow where it looks almost like a heelprint, as though someone got out, which would mean the driver might have gone to check on Oscar, gotten back in then kept going, right into the creek."

Trinidad felt sick. Would Gabe have done such a thing? Run away from his crime? Of course he would. He'd snuck around with Juliette, not bothering to tell her he was still married to Trinidad. And he'd tricked all three of his ex-wives into believing he was an honest accountant, a salt-of-the-earth businessman with the boyish grin while he bilked his clients. If he had killed Oscar, he would have tried to find a way to escape responsibility, especially after just getting paroled.

Chang checked his watch. "Wonder where the chief went."

Trinidad didn't see any point in diving into the explanation again of Gabe's arrival at the Shimmy. "I'd better get back to the shop."

She unzipped her jacket, and Scooter periscoped his head out, causing Chang to hop back as if he was doing the Hokey Pokey.

Trinidad hesitated. "Do you need to take Scooter? You know, for evidence?"

"I, uh, I'm not a bird fan. Saw that Hitchcock movie when I was seven where the birds take over the town. Kinda creeped me out." He held out the eraser end of his pencil. "Think maybe it'd climb on here and I could get it into the back seat of my cruiser?"

Scooter nibbled at the pink eraser before biting it off and dropping it to the ground.

Chang hastily withdrew the pencil. "Uh, maybe you'd better keep him for now. Unless of course he's going to start talking and name the driver who ran them down or something. Read that in a mystery novel once."

"Oh my giddy aunt," Scooter said.

Chang laughed. "Cool, he can talk."

Stan smiled. "Not much. I believe he also says, 'wowee.' Oscar had the bird for the fifteen years that I've known him, and those are the only two things I've ever heard him say."

"Right, well, you go ahead and take him then, Miss Jones, and I'll square it with the chief."

Chang's radio squawked and he answered while Scooter burrowed further into Trinidad's jacket. She tried to remain still as the bird resumed a comfortable position. His feathers rustled but she did not have a giggling fit this time. Noodles stayed alert and attentive. Normally, he'd have dragged along his Betty the Beaver stuffed toy, but they'd left the shop in such a hurry, he'd forgotten. She was grateful her lovely senior dog was a gentle animal, a saver of souls no matter what the species. He'd been thrown out when his previous family dumped him in the shelter and replaced him with a puppy. Their trash, her treasure.

Chang ended his radio call. "Incredible. Gabe Bigley's confessed to killing Oscar?"

Stan's snowy eyebrows elevated nearly to his neatly combed hair. "Gabe Bigley is involved in Oscar's death?"

"Allegedly," Trinidad said, relying on her vocabulary from her days as a stenographer. "He never actually said specifically that he hurt *Oscar*." *Even though he'd kind of confessed to killing someone.*

Chang pocketed his denuded pencil. "Anyway, they're transporting Gabe to the hospital. I dunno what the chief's baby bro had to say exactly, but this case is getting weirder and weirder."

Trinidad couldn't agree more. "Stan, let's go back now and I'll tell you what I know along the way, okay? I'll have to drive very slowly with a bird in my jacket."

Stan gestured for her to go first. He and Noodles followed.

The day had started out with such promise. Now Oscar had been run down, her ex-husband was involved, and there was an orphaned parrot nesting above her rib cage. Oh my giddy aunt indeed, Trinidad thought as they returned to the Shimmy and Shake Shop.

Chapter Three

PAPA LUIS HAD AN APRON tied around his solid middle when she returned to her empty ice cream shop. He was completely at home behind the glistening counter, the pink-and-pearl-painted interior shining all around him and the scent of candy cane ice cream in the air.

"Absolutely terrible," he said to them both, his Cuban accent intensified with emotion. "Juliette told me when I arrived to mind the store. I cannot believe Oscar has been killed. My sincerest condolences on the loss of your good friend, Stan."

Stan nodded. "I can't quite believe it yet."

Papa's dark eyes narrowed behind the lenses of his glasses. "And to think the Hooligan is responsible."

Papa Luis had refused to utter Gabe's given name since the moment he'd learned of Gabe's infidelity and criminal activities. "We don't know for sure exactly what happened yet," Trinidad said.

Papa snorted. "What more is there to know? A man is

dead and Juliette tells me Gabe confessed. Iris will be in mourning. Her only family. So tragic."

"I didn't know you and Iris knew each other well, Papa." Silly statement. Her outgoing grandfather had made it a point to meet everyone once his loafers hit the sidewalks of Sprocket.

"Ah yes. We chat about gardening. Iris is a florist, you know, an accomplished green thumb. I have shown her my greenhouse."

The greenhouse was Papa's magnum opus in Sprocket, his second most precious item next to his classic car. He'd grown spectacular mint plants and produced several vanilla pods, known to be extremely finicky about growing "in captivity" as Papa said.

She realized she'd been so busy with her winter business plans, she had not been paying close attention to Papa's activities. She hadn't known he'd spent much time with Iris.

"I told Chief Bigley I would visit Iris later to be sure she is okay," Papa said.

"Was she very close to her cousin?"

Stan cleared his throat delicately. "There was coolness, I believe."

Papa waved a hand. "But after all, they are family. How could she not be grieved by this loss?"

And that was Papa in a nutshell. Family was everything. He'd lost his son, Trinidad's father, Manny, years before and she knew it still grieved him deeply. Her too. Daddy would have laughed in his quiet way about her exploits in the zany little town of Upper Sprocket and listened for hours with only the occasional "ah" in response. Then he'd have checked every elbow joint, coupling, and connection in the plumbing, which was his passion. Manny Jones was a plumber the way Picasso was a painter.

Papa adjusted his apron. "The chief and your sisters have gone to the hospital. They said for you to meet them there. I will mind the shop."

She looked for signs of Carlos and Diego, her high school assistants who reported early on their abbreviated Wednesdays. "Where are the twins?"

"Their mother called to say they had car trouble. This is what happens when you purchase a Toyota. A Chevy is the only way to go, I told them this, but..." He shrugged. "Youth, you know?"

With their newly earned driver's licenses in hand, the brothers had purchased a thirdhand vehicle that tended to be out of service more than in. "Anyway, they will arrive a bit late."

Late. "Oh gosh. I completely forgot." She jerked a look at her watch. Almost noon. "I've got to be at the Sprocket Steamboat at 5:00. And I need to come up with a dairy-free dessert to show Leonard Pinkerton."

"Dairy-free?" Papa held up a soothing hand. "Like no milk from the cow?"

"Yes. Any ideas? It's gotta be seasonally appropriate too. Terrible timing."

"Do not fret. Go to the hospital and inquire about the Hooligan. I will put on my dessert thinking cap and keep the place going until you return."

"You can create a dessert without milk?"

He looked offended. "Cooking is merely culinary mathematics. Have you ever known of a math problem I could not solve?"

She hadn't. Since her grandpa's days as an engineer in the copper mines in Santa Lucia, Cuba, he had not lost one iota of his mathematical prowess. When they'd papered the rear wall of the shop after the remodel, he'd calculated the necessary amount of wallpaper down to the square inch. "Whatever you come up with will be fantastic. Just try to think Christmassy, okay? Thank you, Papa."

He came around the counter to hug her, but Stan pointed to her jacket.

"Hold on." Carefully she extracted the parrot. Papa gasped in surprise, and Noodles shoved closer to get a peek at Scooter, tail whipping.

"Noodles found Oscar's parrot at the accident site," she said.

Papa's mouth rounded into an O as he took in the fuzzy creature. "How did he survive having his chest feathers stripped away like that?"

"That's not from the accident. He's a compulsive plucker. He did that to himself, and he can't fly either, but that's an old problem too, not from the crash," Stan explained.

"A bedraggled specimen."

She sighed, remembering the days after her divorce when she must have seemed a pretty bedraggled specimen herself. "I can't imagine how he was thrown free when Oscar was, uh, struck down. He needs to be checked out by the vet."

"I will take him," Stan said.

Scooter craned his neck around and started making kissing noises at Noodles, who managed to give him a tongue slurp. "We'll have to find a temporary cage for him. Do you think the chief would let us take the one from Oscar's house?"

"Probably," Papa said. "In the meantime, I can call Telly at the pet shop and ask him to bring over a cage. I will whip him up a caramel shake in exchange for his trouble. Caramel is his Achilles' heel along with comic books. You should see his collection."

Trinidad wasn't even surprised that Papa knew all about the pet store owner she'd never met. "That would be wonderful." She turned to Stan. "Bring him back here after the vet, and we'll figure out what to do until the cage arrives."

Papa fetched a clean pink towel. She bundled up the bird and handed him to Stan.

"Wowee," Scooter said, earning a yip from Noodles, who attempted another tongue swabbing.

"Stay here with Papa, Noo."

Noodles whined and let out a loud bark. Startling, as he was usually a quiet dog. He pawed at Stan's leg.

Papa raised an eyebrow. "It seems he is concerned about the parrot."

Noodles pawed again and Stan smiled. "Perhaps Noodles can come along. It's only down the block. He would be good company."

Trinidad smiled at her eager senior dog. "He does love to see Doctor Masha. He knows where she keeps the treats."

Noodles followed Stan as they left the shop.

She grabbed her keys, wondering as she hurried out what she would discover when she got to the hospital. It was possible that Gabe had been badly hurt, concussed or worse. Maybe he wouldn't survive. How did she feel knowing that? Her conscience told her she should be distraught, but she'd spent so much mental energy despising the man, her heart wasn't cooperating. In a state of confusion, she climbed into the Subaru and dialed her cell, toggling it to speakerphone.

Quinn Logan spoke over a cacophony of clangs and creaks. "Hey, Trin."

"You got the sorting machine working?"

"Of course," he said grandly. "Was there any doubt?"

She laughed, picturing her boyfriend's green eyes. It still gave her a thrill to embrace the word "boyfriend," but what else did you call someone with whom you wanted to spend every minute? An easygoing, steadfast man who was trying to patch up a deeply torn relationship with his mother, who'd abandoned his brother while Quinn was serving overseas. The complete opposite of her former husband.

"Didn't you know I'm a mechanical genius?" Quinn said.

"Which means Doug fixed it, right?"

"Right." He laughed. "But I pay him with your vanilla ice cream, so he works cheap and he doesn't mind if I take credit."

Quinn's brother, Doug, had some social and emotional issues, but he, like Papa, was a genius in his own way.

She took a breath. "I have something to tell you."

"Good or bad?"

"Bad, sorry to say."

She related the situation and found that her voice was unsteady when she revealed that Oscar hadn't survived. "And, um, Gabe walked into the shop and confessed."

"Gabe?" he blurted. "Gabe Bigley, your ex?"

"Yep. It couldn't get any weirder."

He was silent for a moment. "From all the things you told me, I knew Gabe was a jerk, but I wouldn't have figured he'd kill someone and drive away." Disgust dripped from his words. "Inexcusable."

She couldn't think of anything to say. She'd been surprised Gabe was the kind to do that too, but she'd never been able to see him clearly. Rose-colored glasses didn't begin to describe how deluded she'd been where he was concerned.

"I'm coming to the hospital," Quinn said. "Be there soon as I can get changed."

"No need."

"Yes, there is. If Gabe is back in Sprocket, I'm going to be darn sure he doesn't worm his way back into your life or draw you into his legal trouble. He's on his own in this mess."

As if she wasn't strong enough to resist Gabe's charms? An inkling of irritation tightened her tummy, but their call was over before she could figure out how to respond.

Odd sensations churned through her as she entered the hospital twenty minutes later. In a waiting room smelling of disinfectant, she found Juliette and Bonnie huddled in chairs.

"How is he?"

Juliette shrugged. "Haven't told us much yet. They're doing scans and all that. The chief was allowed in and she's talking to the doctors. No one will tell us bupkis."

Bonnie hugged herself. "Oh man. This is beyond terrible. He couldn't have run Oscar down and left. He wouldn't do that. It's not who he is."

It came flooding back to Trinidad.

I'll buy you that engagement ring as soon as I get the money. She lasered a look on Bonnie. "I need you to clear something up for me. The person you're marrying...really is Gabe? I heard that correctly?"

Juliette huffed out a breath. "She's been avoiding my questions about that, but now we can double team her. Spill it, sister. You're marrying Gabe *again*?"

Bonnie swallowed. "Ummm, yeah."

Juliette and Trinidad stared at Bonnie.

"Why?" they asked at precisely the same moment.

Bonnie twiddled with her ponytail. "It sort of...evolved."

"How would that happen exactly? The man was in jail until Monday." Trinidad realized she'd spoken too loudly when an orderly looked at her. She took a breath and moderated her tone. "Bonnie, please explain. I'm completely confused."

More hair twiddling. The waiting room furniture was too low for Bonnie's extreme height, and her knees were bent at awkward angles. "I, uh, reached out to him. You know, called a few times and then things kinda, uh, progressed."

"Progressed?" Trinidad said.

Bonnie stretched out a leg and toggled her foot back and forth. "Yeah, you know. It's important for Felice to have a two-parent home, right?"

Juliette sniffed. "I'm not buying it. You're doing great as a single parent. Felice is super smart and well adjusted. You've even tackled that homeschooling thing with your usual tenacity and bullheaded commitment. Why bring Gabe back into the romance picture? He cheated on you, remember? That's why you divorced him. And he stole from his clients too. Fine, if he wants to be a dad figure to Felice, but for crying out loud. I mean, you can't still love him, can you?"

Bonnie had divorced Gabe long before Gabe met Trinidad, and she knew there were probably many dalliances in between still undiscovered. They might find several more women eligible for their "sisterhood of exes" club. Gabe loved being in love. "Well, Bonnie?"

Bonnie looked at the shoelaces of her sneakers, the white pair since it was Wednesday. "Love? Um, sure, and things are different now."

"Which ones?" Juliette waved a manicured hand around the cramped space. "We're sitting here in a hospital waiting room because Gabe broke the law and ran over someone. Could be he's going right back to jail without passing go. Even if he doesn't, he's landed himself in a bunch of new legal trouble, and he thinks he can trot right into the Shimmy for help. How are things different, exactly?"

Bonnie rubbed her palms on her jeans and stood up. "I don't think it's the time to go into all this. Gabe's injured, maybe badly."

"And Oscar's dead and Gabe confessed," Juliette snapped. "There's no coming back from that."

Bonnie shrank in on herself before she uttered the one statement that quieted both her interrogators. "He's Felice's father," she said, mouth fixed in a stubborn line.

And there was no arguing with that. From what Trinidad knew, Gabe had sent money and the odd gift for Felice when he could as well as a shower of birthday and Christmas cards. He'd tried to participate, and that got him some credit, but Bonnie wasn't spilling everything, Trinidad thought with a pang. This wasn't the whole truth, not by a long shot.

Trinidad paced as Quinn hustled through the hospital doors. His hair was wet from a shower and he wore his customarily careless clothing, a pair of worn khakis and a Logan Nut Farm T-shirt with a slightly ripped breast pocket.

He greeted the women and clasped Trinidad in a tight hug, kissing the top of her head before he released her. "Has there been any update?"

A door opened and Chief Bigley joined them. Her brows were furrowed.

Trinidad's breath caught at Bigley's grave expression. Was it really possible Gabe wouldn't survive? Trinidad looked at Bonnie, who appeared as torn and confused as she had in the Shimmy before they'd heard the sirens.

"The doctors are reassuring," Bigley said. "He's got a concussion and a broken rib and needed scalp sutures. They'll keep a close eye on him for a while."

Trinidad felt relieved despite her misgivings. "Did he tell you anything?"

Bigley glanced from woman to woman. "This is an awkward situation."

Awkward didn't quite capture the catastrophe in Trinidad's mind.

"Gabe was released Monday. He hopped a bus to visit

my mom and borrow her car to head to Sprocket." Bigley paused. "To reunite with you, Bonnie."

Bonnie blushed holly-berry red. "Uh, yeah."

"I didn't know you two were back together."

Join the club, Trinidad thought.

"It's, ah, a sudden thing, you know, like, um, things can be sometimes."

Bigley did not look any more convinced than Trinidad, but she continued her report. "On his way to Sprocket, he stopped at a diner outside Joseph. Got to talking to a guy named Harry Fortesque who was also on his way to Sprocket by bus. Fortesque was hired to do a carpentry job on the Sprocket Steamboat to prep for some big holiday shindig there."

Trinidad nodded. "I'm doing a tasting for Leonard Pinkerton this evening to audition for the same event."

Bigley nodded. "Gabe gave Harry a ride. Near the Twisted Pine Overlook, Gabe stopped for a squirrel in the road, and he woke up at the bottom of the creek bed and Harry was gone."

Trinidad scowled. "So he doesn't remember killing Oscar?"

"Nope. Said he woke up, climbed out, found Oscar dead, probably just before Pastor Phil came upon the accident and called it in. Gabe was in a daze but somehow he must have been able to haul himself out of the wreck and make it to your store before he collapsed."

"What a story," Juliette said.

Bigley's mouth crimped at Juliette's tone. "Mom

confirmed Gabe's visit, and the diner checks out from my quick phone calls. The waitress remembered Gabe was a generous tipper."

Juliette rolled her eyes. "Always so magnanimous with the money he fleeced off people, especially if the waitress was a pretty young thing."

The comment stung, since Gabe had taken up with Juliette while failing to disclose he was married to older Trinidad. It was an inherent risk in all relationships… the shiny ball syndrome. There would always be some-one younger, firmer, newer. She glanced surreptitiously at Quinn. Would his attention be captured by a more youth-ful specimen eventually? Irritating to rediscover latent scars left by Gabe's betrayal that she thought had gone away. She straightened her shoulders. Gabe wasn't going to get into her head again, no matter what. "What about this Harry person? What does he have to say?"

"Haven't talked to him yet. There's an officer on the way to the Sprocket Steamboat right now to get his statement. Pinkerton's sister Renata confirmed on the phone that Harry showed up on foot for his job at the Steamboat about two hours ago as scheduled. He was out buying lumber so we haven't gotten the story straight from the horse's mouth yet."

Trinidad replayed her conversation with Chang at the accident site. *"Chief, the tire tracks at the scene indicated the car stopped after…er, the impact. Someone got out, maybe to see Oscar's body, then continued on."*

"Then Gabe left Oscar to die?" Quinn said indignantly. "Instead of calling for help? How could he do that?"

Bigley looked at Quinn with a warning in her eyes. "Gabe doesn't have a phone. He sold it for gas money. We don't know for sure that he's responsible."

"He confessed," Quinn snapped. "What more do you need?"

"After the impact, the driver got out. There was a vague heelprint. Then the vehicle continued on before it went into the creek," Trinidad hastened to add before Quinn could keep going. She paused.

"Gabe's good at running away from his messes." Juliette sniffed.

Quinn nodded his agreement. "Now he's a con *and* a killer."

Bigley's jaw tightened. "I can see how it would look like that, but I know my brother."

Juliette rolled her eyes. "We know him too. Very well."

Bigley held up a palm. "And he's been a jerk to all three of you, and he deserves your scorn, no doubt about it, but he did his time for stealing from his clients and he was lawfully released. What's more, he tried to take care of you all by deeding you properties and his storage business."

"That's more because we found ourselves good lawyers than a result of any remorse on Gabe's part," Juliette said.

"He's tried to take care of Felice," Bonnie piped up in a small voice. Her remark made them all pause.

"Right," Bigley said. "He's a screwup and he's weak, but he isn't an evil person." Her gaze went to Bonnie. "You must believe that if you're ready to marry him again."

Bonnie examined the ficus tree in the corner as if it was the last living thing left on the planet. "Um, yeah."

Trinidad waited for Bonnie to say more but she didn't.

"So what are you saying, Chief?" Quinn demanded. "That you don't think Gabe ran Oscar down and drove away? Because that's sure what it looks like to me."

"Yes. That's what I'm saying. Gabe can't remember exactly what happened. My brother wouldn't kill a man and leave the scene, and until the evidence proves that he did, I'm giving him the benefit of the doubt."

Juliette fired back. "I didn't get that benefit when you charged me with murder. Trinidad's the reason I'm not in prison."

Bigley's nostrils flared. "Police work isn't an exact science, Juliette. I followed the evidence then, and that's what needs to happen now too. If there's enough to convict Gabe, then he'll go back to prison. That's the way the justice system works."

"Some system."

The two women settled into a cold stare down.

Trinidad's stomach knotted. She wished she could wake up from this bad dream and find out that none of it was real. Gabe hadn't returned to Sprocket, and Oscar was still alive. Her father used to say, "Everyone wishes to bring water to his own mill and leave his neighbor's dry." She felt a stab of guilt at how much she still wanted Gabe's mill to be bone dry, desiccated, that he might be punished more for the hurts he'd inflicted. Sprocket was her town now and this was her life, the Shimmy and Juliette and Bonnie, Felice, Quinn, Papa, and Noodles. There was no room for Gabe.

Except that it was no longer the case. Now that he was

apparently going to remarry Bonnie, Trinidad's lovely, restarted life was already in peril. She felt like screaming. Wasn't there some part of the world that was a "Gabe-free" zone? Maybe she should have expected it since Gabe had grown up in Upper Sprocket. His jail sentence wouldn't last forever, and he likely had no money.

Bonnie was rocking from foot to foot, telegraphing her unease. Puzzling. She was clearly not a lovestruck woman ready to yoke her future to Gabe's again. Secrets, Trinidad thought. Bonnie wasn't revealing everything, and her obfuscation hurt. Trinidad wanted to take to her heels and run, leave the mess behind, like Gabe had tried to do. But her whole world was here in Sprocket. She looked at Quinn. And her heart had set down roots as well.

"There's another wrinkle in this scenario." Bigley paused. "I can't investigate it."

Trinidad gaped. "But you're the chief."

"He's my brother so I have to recuse myself. The county will be sending someone over to handle the case. I won't be allowed to talk to him again until they're finished interviewing him. I shouldn't have spoken with him in the first place, and I'm likely going to be censured for that."

Trinidad wasn't sure if it was a good thing or bad that Bigley wouldn't be assigned to the case. Was it a case? Or merely a matter of time before the details were confirmed and Gabe was escorted straight back into the penal system?

A doctor clad in green scrubs reported that Gabe was resting comfortably. He looked chagrined. "And I've been told there's another officer on their way over and you're not to be given access, Chief Bigley. Probably should have mentioned that to me before I let you in to see him."

"I apologize for putting you in that position. Thank you for taking care of him. I'll wait out here until you're sure he's stable and my replacement arrives."

The doctor looked relieved. "All right."

Bigley sat down in the nearest chair and pulled out her cell phone, poking furiously at the keys.

"I have to get back to Felice." Bonnie clearly didn't want to discuss her impending marriage further.

"I'll give you a ride." Juliette was no doubt intending to squeeze Bonnie for more information on the way to her train-car inn no matter what Bonnie wanted. "I'll be back at the Shimmy later, Trinidad."

Quinn took Trinidad's hand. "Do you have time to get a coffee at the Full of Beans?"

The world came rushing back. *Time. Steamboat. Desserts. Job interview.* "I'd love to, but I have to be at the steamboat at 5:00, and Papa's working on a recipe for me so I need to find out what he's come up with."

"All right." Quinn kissed her cheek. "Maybe we can catch up at dinner." They'd begun to head toward the exit when the doctor spoke again.

"Which one of you is Trinidad Jones?"

Bonnie and Juliette stopped before they cleared the exit doors. Quinn and Trinidad turned back.

"I am."

The doctor shoved a pen into his pocket. "Mr. Bigley is requesting to speak with you."

Her jaw dropped. "Mr...you mean Gabe? Wants to talk to me?" She was sure her eyes were the size of ping-pong balls. "Why?"

The doctor shook his head. "No idea. He was very insistent about it, though. I've got rounds but if you want to see him, make it a short visit, okay? Excuse me."

Trinidad was still trying to process. Gabe wanted to talk to *her*? He was the last person in the known universe with whom she wanted to shoot the breeze. She felt Bigley staring at her, and cold sweat pricked her forehead.

"You have every right to turn around and walk out," Bigley said, "but I would be very appreciative if you would see what you can do for him."

"Why should she?" Quinn demanded. "Hasn't he done enough to her? To all of them? Now he's back in Sprocket creating more turmoil."

Trinidad put a hand on his arm to calm Quinn. "I don't know how I could possibly help Gabe, Chief."

"Maybe you can't, but would you talk to him? He might remember something, a detail that could prove useful. Please."

"You don't have to." Quinn squeezed her fingers. "He doesn't get to impact your life anymore. He's made his bed and he's got to lie in it. Take responsibility for what he's done all by his lonesome."

Her gaze traveled from Quinn's angry face to Juliette's and finally to Bonnie's. She noted the glint of tears in Bonnie's eyes, her lower lip caught between her teeth.

The truth settled in a depressing blanket on her soul.

Gabe might be out of her direct sphere, but if he was still involved with Bonnie, then he was a part of Trinidad's world whether she liked it or not. Why, oh why couldn't things be easy, at least during her business funk? It was creeping up on three o'clock. Two hours before she was to meet Leonard Pinkerton on the steamboat and convince him she had a plethora of perfect frozen treats that would impress the guests for the holiday party on Saturday. Hopefully Papa was creating a tantalizing offering to fit into the lineup as she dithered.

As the thoughts raced through her mind, she realized they were all staring at her: Quinn, Bonnie, Juliette, and Bigley.

Bonnie spoke quietly. "I'd appreciate it too, if you would talk to him."

The final nail was hammered home. What would it hurt to talk to Gabe for five minutes, maybe less? She was no longer a naive woman with those rose-colored glasses. She was a shop owner who had solved two murders and carved out a path in the wilds of Eastern Oregon. Gabe had no power over her and she owed him nothing. A short chat, that was all, for Chief Bigley's sake and Bonnie's.

"I'll be right back." She let go of Quinn's hand and marched toward Gabe's room.

Chapter Four

TRINIDAD PUSHED THE DOOR OPEN with a clammy palm and approached the bed. Gabe's face was scratched, lips dry and cracked. His eyes were closed, one swollen and purpled. She should probably feel some pity for him. Her decision suddenly seemed like a very bad idea indeed. She had the fleeting fantasy that she could sneak away without waking him, but her shoe squeaked against the floor and his less swollen eye cracked open.

"Trina?"

"Don't call me that." It bounded out of her mouth before she could think better of it. *Easy girl. The guy is in a hospital, after all.* She was getting an F on her bedside manner. She exhaled. "You should call me Trinidad."

"Sorry."

He sounded as if he really meant it, but everything Gabe had ever uttered dripped with sincerity. He'd really meant it when he'd said, "I will always love and adore you. You are the only woman for me." The trouble was, he apparently felt the same for plenty of other women. But that was ice cream that had already been scooped. She refocused. "You wanted to see me?"

"I'm in a real mess, Trina, I mean, Trinidad."

"That you are." Again, the bedside manner was tripping her up. "But you're alive, so there's that."

He shrugged helplessly. "One minute, I'm driving along, and the next, I wake up in the creek after running some guy over."

"Not just some guy," she said hotly. "A very good man who was doing some bird-watching with his little parrot."

Gabe blinked. "He was?"

"Was what?"

"Doing some bird-watching?"

She noted the fuzzy look in his eyes. Painkillers, probably. "Yes, Oscar was a bird-watcher. He posted pictures every day on social media. It was his passion."

"That's so weird."

The gall. "Lots of people like bird-watching. It isn't weird just because you don't enjoy it. I never understood why you loved stamp collecting."

"No, I meant it's weird because I woke up from the accident thinking about birds. I don't even like birds."

It was true. Gabe didn't enjoy much of anything that had to do with the outdoors. Odd, she'd always thought, since his hometown of Upper Sprocket was an alpine delight that backed the glorious Wallowa Mountains. The region wasn't called the Swiss Alps of Oregon for nothing. A thought formed in her mind. "Then why did you drive that way, Gabe?"

"What way?"

"By Twisted Pine Overlook. There are more direct routes into town."

"Good question." He rubbed his forehead. "My sister asked me the same thing and I…"

"Have no idea, right?"

"Right." He pointed to his temple. "Nothing but fog up here surrounding the actual crash. And Cynthia isn't going to be able to do much for me, since she's got to recuse herself. Probably she's in trouble already for talking to me, but she went out on a limb. Hope I didn't screw up her career. It wasn't easy for her to break into law enforcement, because of her youthful hobby."

"What hobby?"

"Stealing cars," Gabe said. "She could hot-wire and boost a ride in a matter of minutes. Learned it from an uncle of ours. Uncle Finch was a gem. He was an accountant when he wasn't stealing cars."

"Did Uncle Finch teach you how to steal from your clients?" *Snarky, Trinidad.*

"No," Gabe said, guileless. "I learned that on my own. But I'm not like that anymore. I changed, but way later than my sister. She went into the army and completely turned her life around." His face shone with pride for a moment before it crumpled. "I've caused her enough embarrassment over the years, and now here we are all over again."

A police chief with a felonious brother. Though mortifying, Bigley likely wasn't the only person in law enforcement with shady relatives. The latest issue was more damning and the chief had already risked her career to help Gabe. "She'll be okay. They'll bring in a good person to replace her, and she'll make sure you get a good lawyer."

He groaned. "But the evidence all points to me, right? The car I was driving. My prints on the steering wheel. My criminal record. I'm gonna be charged with a hit-and-run and go right back to jail."

"Well…" she started.

"They probably haven't even sanitized my cell. There are probably viruses from twenty years ago living in those mattresses." His volume edged up. Always fastidious, Gabe appeared to be inching toward germaphobe status. "I mean, I only got released two days ago. It looks terrible for me." He gulped. "Unless…"

Suspicion ticked up her pulse. "Unless what?"

"Well…" He flashed her a smile. "You've earned quite a reputation. I heard you solved two murders right here in Sprocket. Got Juliette off the hook and out of jail. I'm not surprised, with your intelligence. I always knew…"

She folded her arms. "Don't try to flatter me. It won't work anymore. State your request and let's get it over with."

He reached for her hand, but she did not extend it.

"Will you see what you can do to help me?"

The audacity of this man. "You want me to help you? How would I do that?" *And why, for that matter?*

"I've got a lot of enemies. The people I stole from, women I…" He looked at her and then his comment died away. "Well, you get the picture. One lady I did the accounts for owned a fried chicken joint and she was looking to expand to a second location, but I ruined that by stealing from her. The stress made her hang up her ambition, she said, and while she was fighting me in court, some family member scooped up the spot she was hoping to buy to expand her chicken empire. She sent me letters while I was in jail that her son would make me pay someday."

Trinidad figured he'd wound down. "Like I said, you'll get a lawyer and the police will investigate. If you were framed, they'll sniff it out."

She wasn't completely convinced, however. He was right. Juliette had gone to jail for murder, and the evidence against her had appeared clear-cut. If Trinidad hadn't uncovered other information…

"You could maybe investigate," Gabe continued. "See if there's anyone poking around who might have wanted to send me back to jail. Maybe this Harry guy was hired to set me up."

She looked him square in his puppy dog eyes. "Or maybe you killed Oscar and drove away, exactly like it appears. You'll face jail time for a hit-and-run."

He flinched as though she'd slapped him. "Do you think I'd do that, Trinidad? Run a guy down and leave him there to die?"

Did she? She'd thought she did until she found herself standing two feet away from him. Gabe was a royal pain, a screwup, and morally flawed…but as much as she didn't want to, she found she agreed with his sister. He was not an evil man. Still, it wasn't her problem to save Gabe Bigley. "I am sorry about what's happened, mostly that a good person has been killed. But this isn't my problem. *You* are no longer my problem."

He sighed. "You're completely correct. I know I have no right to even ask. I've been such a jerk to you."

"And to Bonnie."

"Yeah."

"And Juliette."

"And the people I cheated, yes, like the chicken lady. Them too."

Desperation tightened her stomach. "And I can't help you anyway. I run an ice cream store."

"I know. The Shimmy and Shake Shop. Juliette told me about it. Looked super fantastic, what I had time to notice before I passed out. I'm proud of you."

She rushed on. "And it's a critical season." A time that would decide if her dream would survive or die of exposure in the frigid winter.

He nodded sympathetically.

"I'm not a detective."

Again the nod. "But you know the people here, and you might be able to pick up some evidence that could help me."

Trinidad stared at this banged-up specimen who had manipulated her right down the road to ruin. There was no way she should help him. Exactly what Quinn would have said. No. Way.

"I'm not asking only for myself, Trina, uh, Trinidad." He plucked at the bedsheets. "I need to remarry Bonnie. Should have done it before, but now it's real important, and if I'm back in the clink, that messes up our plans."

"Why? Why is it important that you remarry Bonnie? What is the urgency behind that?"

He tugged at his earlobe.

The earlobe. Funny how she recalled him doing that on the few occasions when she'd suspected he was lying toward the end of their marriage.

"Felice is getting older, six and all. She needs a father figure, and I'm out of jail now. At least I thought I was going to be living a free life before I apparently ran over a guy." His brow furrowed into grooves. "Wouldn't you think if I actually killed someone, I would at least remember doing it? But no, that's Gabe Bigley, criminal mastermind for you. Can't even remember my latest crime. Why can't I be a regular guy, a father, and a husband who stays out of jail and doesn't cheat or kill people?"

He was looking at her as though she might have an answer.

"I have no idea." His pallor changed from milk pale to blotched and red. Horrified, she realized he was starting to cry. "Oh, don't do that." She began handing him a steady stream of tissues out of the nearby box. Soon he was clutching a snowball-sized wad. "What do you remember about Harry?" she hurried to ask. "Maybe he can help you piece it together." Then he wouldn't need anyone's help, especially hers.

"Sorry." He blew his nose into the tissues. He looked as though a fresh river of tears was starting up, so she urged him to answer the question. "I remember meeting Harry in the diner. He's a Blizzards fan. Been to a bunch of games."

The Oregon Blizzards, a pro basketball team, had an immense fan base in the area. She had yet to develop an interest in the sport.

Gabe squinted, remembering. "We were talking about the Crusher."

"The what?"

"Cordell Barrone, the Blizzard's star point guard. Crusher's his nickname. He's rehabbing right now from an ankle injury." Gabe shrugged. "He's a thug, if you ask me, got lots of criminal connections from what Bonnie remembers, but the guy's talented and you can't deny it. I mean his three-point shooting percentage is—"

She cut him off before he could start spouting sports stats. Their five-minute chat was taking up more and more of her precious day. "Bonnie knows this Cordell person?"

Gabe jerked. "Uh, well, kinda. They used to be friends and all when they were in college. Dated some."

"Okay. You were talking about basketball and you gave Harry a ride and…"

"And the last thing I remember is slowing for a squirrel, but that was a mile out of town. I already told Cynthia all this."

Trinidad nodded vigorously. "And she'll pass it on to the cop in charge. That's all you'll need. The justice system will prevail, you'll see. I really need to go now. I've got a thingy… with ice cream…on a steamboat."

"I understand if you don't want to help me. I did nothing but hurt you and the girls. I shouldn't be Felice's father anyway. She deserves better." Tears sparkled in his eyes.

"Crying isn't going to help." She resisted the urge to cut

him to ribbons about the waterfall of tears he'd caused his three ex-wives.

She thought of Felice, the shy six-year-old who didn't seem to have many friends and found riches in bits of broken rocks, pine cones, and bird feathers. "I'll ask some questions," she found herself saying. "That's all. No promises."

Hope brightened his puffy face. "Really? You'd do that for me?"

"For Bonnie and Felice," she said firmly. "For them."

He beamed. "Thank you, thank you, thank you." He tried to grab her hand again, which she kept well out of reach.

"All right. I have to go."

"Will you report back later?"

She glared at him. "Gabe, if there's anything I find out, I'll tell your sister or the cops. I'm not going to be briefing you on a regular basis."

He sighed. "All right. Thank you from the bottom of my heart."

She was groping for the door, wondering what had possessed her, when he spoke again.

"Trinidad." He fingered a bunched-up tissue. "There's something weird going on in my head."

That was for sure. "You had a concussion, so things might be jumbled."

"Yeah, but I told you I woke up thinking of birds, right? Well, it was a question, kind of, that was my first thought when I woke up in that creek."

She waited, and when he didn't continue, she prodded. "What question, Gabe?"

He shot her a puzzled expression. "What exactly is a yellow-breasted chat?"

━━━━━━━━

Trinidad tried to shake off the previous hour as she hurried to the shop after leaving the hospital. Quinn had been visibly upset that she'd agreed to help Gabe. Was he angry? Jealous? Hurt? All three? Whatever the reason, he'd walked her to her car and left with only a quick hug between them.

If Gabe's presence messed things up for her and Quinn…

No, she told herself. She would not allow it.

At the Shimmy, her employees, twins Diego and Carlos, were trying to coax a few words from Scooter, now parked in a cage in the back room with sparkling food and water bowls. Noodles was stationed underneath, watching the proceedings. Papa waved to her from behind the counter.

The twins straightened when they saw her. She marveled at how they'd grown since she'd opened the shop in July, long gangly limbs, their hair cut short now that they were halfway through their sophomore year of high school. Jeans, T-shirts, and clunky sneakers completed their trendy look. Diego had even gotten new glasses and managed not to break them. Almost men in some ways, yet still enchanted by bathroom humor and awed by all the creative ice cream flavors she'd produced. Except one. Rum raisin had received a resounding thumbs-down and been forever stricken from the Shimmy's offerings.

"Oh hey, Miss Jones. How was the hospital? Did you talk

to Mr. Bigley?" Carlos looked as if he wanted to add on but his brother trod on his foot. "Owww. I wasn't gonna say anything."

"Yeah, you were," Diego said. "You have that 'I'm about to blurt' look."

She sighed. Clearly both boys knew enough to kindle their incendiary curiosity. Might as well get it over with. "Oscar Fuentes was killed, as you probably know. It's terribly sad and it's all under consideration by the police." She put a special emphasis on "police" since they fancied themselves investigators. "Gabe is in the hospital but expected to recover fully."

They both stared when she stopped talking.

"What?" she said.

"Aren't you gonna tell us that he confessed to the hit-and-run?" Carlos said.

Diego elbowed him this time. "There's the blurting thing. Mom told us not to bring it up since it was probably more proof that the man you married was a complete loser."

Carlos rolled his eyes. "Yeah, that was sensitive. Much better than my blurting."

"Your mother was right. Let's not talk about it anymore." Trinidad reached for a pink apron and tied it on.

"Are you keeping the bird?" Diego watched Scooter dance from foot to foot, whistling to himself.

"Only until we can bring him to Oscar's cousin."

"I have phoned and left a message for Iris." Papa looked over from his position behind the counter. "Perhaps we can take Scooter over to her place later after you book the job at the steamboat."

His helpful spirit warmed her heart. The morning had been a catastrophe, but she could still salvage something out of it. She knew by the satisfied look on his face that he'd come up with a dessert that would knock her socks off.

She set the boys to work chopping nuts and preparing a batch of waffle cones. The rich aroma of spices tickled her nose as she joined Papa. Proudly, he pushed a plate over to her on which was a scoop of glossy tan ice cream, studded with chunks of cake. "The mint idea," he shrugged, "it did not spring to life, so I went with another winter favorite."

She breathed in the scent of ginger. "What is it?" She took the spoon he offered.

"I call it Gingerbread Hill."

"Why?" She savored the creamy concoction with the perfect amount of spice and sweet.

With a flourish, he carefully settled a miniature gingerbread house atop the creamy mountain and added some nondairy topping for snow. "A house on a hill. I figured it would be something different, you see, unusual like your Freakshakes. The ice cream hasn't ripened yet, of course, and I didn't have time to prepare the miniature house properly. This one is constructed using some carved walls from the batch of gingerbread you had in the back and some royal icing, but given enough time, we could make the little houses look like the Shimmy with some pink embellishments, or we could even create steamboats if Mr. Pinkerton would prefer. Advertising and dessert all in one." He cocked his head at her. "What do you think?"

After admiring the tiny cookie structure, she scooped up

another mouthful of ice cream, being sure to get a bite of the chewy gingerbread mixed in with the cream. "And there's no milk?"

"Not a drop. There's a batch in the freezer. It won't have time to fully ripen, but it can get a start."

The dessert traced a warm and comforting path down her throat and into her stomach. "I think it's absolutely inspired, Papa." She threw her arms around him. "You saved me. Thank you."

He shrugged modestly, but his cheeks pinked at the praise. "I will work on a better gingerbread house model for you to take to the steamboat now that I have the boss's approval."

She raced to the back to fetch some adorable glass bowls that would be perfect to showcase the treat. Papa stuck his head in.

"Just one question, Trina." He gestured with his spatula. "This business with Gabe and poor Oscar. It is nothing for you to be involved in, right? You'll steer clear of the Hooligan, won't you?"

She wished with all her heart that she could. "I'll do my best."

It was the truth. She'd agreed only to ask a few questions if the opportunity presented itself. That was as far as she needed to go for Gabe "Hooligan" Bigley.

Chapter Five

THE LAST HOURS PASSED IN a flurry until she found herself piloting her food truck with Juliette in the passenger seat at four thirty. Noodles remained at his post protecting Scooter and Papa, and the twins were handling sales at the Shimmy.

"Bonnie won't spill her guts," Juliette said as they turned onto the road leading to the dock. "I pestered her clear back to the inn, and all she'll say about this ridiculous engagement is 'it was kinda sudden.' What'd you squeeze out of Gabe?"

"He didn't want to talk about the engagement either." Trinidad related the conversation. "He's pretty focused on not going back to jail."

"He should be." Juliette gave Trinidad the side-eye. "He asked you for help, didn't he? Avoiding the rap? The weasel."

Trinidad heaved out a breath. "Yes, but I only agreed to keep my ears open and that's it...for Felice and Bonnie's sake."

"Quinn's not going to like that one bit."

Trinidad grimaced. "I'm not thrilled about it either, but

as I told Quinn, there is no way I'm letting him suck me back into his orbit."

"He's obviously hornswoggled Bonnie. We can't let her throw her life away again, which means you and I have to figure out what is really and truly going on here. I don't know what those two are hiding, but I'm digging it up no matter what."

The conversation would have to be continued at another time. They rattled into the parking area at the end of the dock. Big Egg was the largest of the three lakes, a shimmering expanse of water fringed with sections of steep cliffs and pockets of woods. A few precious areas of rocky sand could be found around the lake's perimeter, which served as beaches for the summer tourists. The dock was home to the Sprocket Steamboat as well as a rental business for small boats and kayaks when the weather was passable. In the winter, it was gorgeously picturesque with the snowcapped mountains in the distance.

The old steamboat floated on the water like some enormous wooden sea bird, painted a cheerful white with red trim that extended to the massive paddle wheel, which was motionless for the moment. From her cursory research, she'd learned that the vessel itself was four levels tall, encompassing main, club, Texas, and sun decks, with wraparound decking on each story so visitors could enjoy a lovely view on its daily churn around the lake. As far as she knew, the upper stories were used only for gathering places, the cabins not rented out for overnight stays.

Today the steamboat exterior sparkled in the winter

sunlight, and a mild breeze teased ripples from the surface of Big Egg. Holiday lights twined around the exterior railings, which would be charming when the sun went down.

She parked the truck next to a van with a Purple Iris logo pasted on the side. Oscar's cousin, no doubt. A pile of lumber was neatly stacked on the main deck to the side of the gangplank. A sign that Harry the carpenter had arrived? Trinidad would love to get a look at him.

Juliette piloted one hand truck and Trinidad took the other.

They bumped up the gangplank and entered the lobby done in rich velvets and dark woods. They faced an ornate check-in desk, a cocktail lounge beckoned on the stern side, and in the direction of the bow, a cavernous dining room complete with a sweeping staircase that led to the upper decks. Perfect for a wedding, she thought, envisioning a bride with her voluminous skirt artfully arranged for a dramatic photo. A woman in her sixties with unnaturally inky hair coiled into a braid around the top of her head stood behind the check-in desk. Her intricately beaded earrings twirled when she lifted her head to look up at them, and her fingernails were painted with candy cane stripes.

"Welcome to the Sprocket Steamboat. You must be the dessert people. I'm Renata Pinkerton, Leonard's sister."

"We are indeed." Trinidad introduced herself and Juliette. "We're from the Shimmy and Shake, and we've got a scheduled meeting with Mr. Pinkerton."

Renata laughed and pulled a pencil out from the spot in her braid where she'd jammed it and checked off an item from the notepad in front of her. "Call him Leonard. Mr. Pinkerton was our father, and neither of us liked him very much. Thanks for jumping in on such short notice." Her smile faded. "Terrible morning around here. The police called about Oscar. Horrible. He and Leonard were such good friends. Practically his only friend besides Stan." Her mouth wobbled as if she might cry. "It's so hard to believe. That poor man, alive one minute and dead the next. And a hit-and-run? In Sprocket?"

"It was terrible," Trinidad agreed.

Renata leaned forward. "And the man who did it? He confessed, I heard."

Good thing Renata didn't seem to have gotten wind that the confessor was Trinidad's ex. "Um, there may have been another person involved. I think the police are looking into it."

Renata nodded. "They've come and gone already. Talked to our new employee."

"Harry Fortesque?" Trinidad asked.

Renata cocked her head in much the same manner as Trinidad had seen Scooter do. "How did you know that?"

"I heard around town that Harry was in the car involved in the accident and he'd been on his way here for a job." Trinidad held her breath to see if Renata would take offense at her gossiping.

Renata shrugged. "News in Sprocket travels faster than germs, doesn't it? I think the cops are done with Harry for now. Seems like they believe it's a case of bad timing." She pinked. "I, er, might have eavesdropped a little on the interrogation, if that's what it was. In my defense, sound carries in this old tub so it wasn't all pure nosiness."

"How did you hire Harry in the first place?" Juliette asked.

"Leonard asked me to find a carpenter for a quick fix before this party. I went to my class reunion last year, and everybody posted their business cards on this big wall and I took pictures. I remembered some guy was a carpenter so I emailed him. Would have been easier to check the yellow pages but we have to cheapskate everything around here and we were in a hurry." Renata rolled her dark eyes. "You want a money suck? Buy yourself a steamboat, like our father did. Worse than a hotel by a long shot. Forty-four staterooms that are completely unused, except for Leonard in his captain's quarters, which is a pretty grand name for a fleabag hovel. Anyway, Harry answered my email. He came with great recommendations, but I didn't have time to check them out. I was busy dealing with the linens when he arrived around noon."

Noon. About an hour after Oscar died. Would Harry have had time to walk to the steamboat if he'd been involved in the accident? Most likely if he was in shape. It was no more than a three-mile trek.

"Did he explain why he was on foot?" Juliette asked.

Renata tapped the pencil. "As it turns out, I kinda overheard that part too. Harry said he bummed a ride from the Gabe guy he met at a diner, but Gabe was going too fast and not paying attention, so Harry asked to get out and he walked here."

The remark surprised Trinidad. Gabe driving unsafely? She tuned back in to Renata.

"Harry had no idea Oscar had been run over. He figures that happened after he and Gabe parted ways. Shook him up, poor thing. I offered him a place to stay in one of the club deck staterooms while he works replacing the paneling in the cocktail lounge. The room's stripped bare, but at least there's a floor and ceiling and a view of Big Egg." She blew a breath out that ruffled her black bangs. "Like I said, a steamboat is a money suck but we're hoping Christmas will bring in some bucks. Good thing we've got a big spender hosting this holiday party. Total surprise when he called on Monday."

"Who's the bigwig?" Juliette said with her trademark boldness.

Renata winked. "I'm sworn to secrecy. Sorry. Don't want the paparazzi swarming the town. Most exciting thing that's ever happened to this boat." She sniffed at the supplies on the hand carts. "I smell gingerbread. Since I run this rusty tub with Leonard, can I get in on the tasting? There should be some perks to this job."

"Of course," Trinidad said. "I prepped plenty of samples."

"Perfect." Renata directed with her pencil. "Go on into the dining room. The florist is already doing her thing, but I have to call the guy who launders our linens again since the guest list keeps growing. It's a big to-do by Sprocket standards anyway." She flipped the page on her notebook. "A steamboat receptionist's job is never done."

And neither was an ice cream shop owner's. Juliette and Trinidad rolled their supplies into the grand dining area. Windows flanked the entire periphery, bathing the wooden staircase with late afternoon light. The ornate railings were twined with holly garlands that led to the upper decks. Orbiting the staircase were a dozen tables and chairs, mostly bare except for the long rectangular one that was covered in cream linens and china, a sort of prototype, Trinidad gathered. This table was decked to the nines with plates and silver, a floral display in the center.

A woman with a crown of silver hair cut into a sharp bob was peering through her purple-framed glasses, fussing with the elaborate bouquet. The red roses were intertwined with long twisty branches and sprays of evergreen and frosted pine cones. Elegant hurricane lamps glowed with tiny flickering flames that added sparkle to the table.

"Gorgeous," Juliette said.

The woman looked up and offered a tentative smile. "Thank you."

"You must be Iris. You know my grandfather, Papa Luis. He said you'd be here. We're very sorry about your cousin Oscar."

Iris's smile lingered for a moment and then died away. "That's kind of you. We weren't close, not as adults anyway, but he's the reason I moved to Sprocket in November and started my business." She appeared to take in the dining room without really seeing it. "I guess I should have canceled this meeting with Leonard after what happened, but all I could think about was how Oscar encouraged me to start the Purple Iris. The shop is everything to me."

"I totally get it." Trinidad understood completely how it felt to pour oneself into a business that became like a living entity, a child almost. Was that obsession or good business practice? She wasn't sure. And the thought of the Shimmy failing under the weight of a Sprocketerian winter? A thud of panic drummed through her nerve pathways.

She wanted to continue the conversation, to dig deeper into Iris's relationship with her cousin, but Leonard Pinkerton trundled in. An extremely stout man who wore blue suspenders to hold up his trousers, he moved quickly to reach them, though he favored one leg, which made him lurch. His robust salt-and-pepper mustache and neatly trimmed beard were at odds with his bald head. He pumped Trinidad's and Juliette's hands and sat down with enough force to set the hurricane lamps vibrating.

"Such a day. Unbelievable. Poor Oscar. To think if I hadn't taken a tumble and tweaked my ankle, I might have been right there with him."

To think…

Fortunate timing on Leonard's part. Trinidad tried to see if there was a bandage or support showing under his pant leg, but she couldn't get a good look.

Iris turned back to her flowers, correcting some mysterious floral defect that was invisible to Trinidad.

"Mr. Pinkerton." Iris's gaze was not quite focused on his face. "If the bouquet and lanterns are acceptable, I'll recreate smaller versions for the ten tables."

Leonard waved a meaty hand. "I can't tell a flower from a finch, but it looks good to me, and Renata gave it the A-OK."

Iris straightened as if forcing herself to stand taller. "And my fee, will that be acceptable as well?"

Leonard frowned. "It's a bigger chunk of change than I was planning on. Normally I'd insist on some negotiations…" He broke into a massive smile. "But since you are Oscar's cousin and all…I'll make it work."

Iris's smile could only be described as relieved. "Wonderful. I'll draw up the contract for you to sign."

"Fine. Leave it with Renata. Did you need help schlepping your things? Or maybe you'd like to see the dessert choices?"

A gracious offer that surprised Trinidad.

Iris declined, quickly boxing her supplies and exiting while Trinidad and Juliette prepared their offerings.

Leonard was instantly brusque again. "Now that we've got the flowers buttoned up, let's talk about the sweet stuff."

Trinidad sprang into action. "The Shimmy can offer three choices for the dessert buffet, Mr. Pinkerton, along with platters of cookies." Was three enough? She tried to gauge his expression, but his attention was fixed on the first sample Juliette placed before him. "Frozen hot chocolate ice cream," she pronounced. He remained stoic as he perused the scoop in front of him. Amazing, as Trinidad thought the creamy stuff looked enticing enough to bathe in. Couldn't he see the glorious sheen? The perfectly mounded scoop?

"Along with bowls of crushed peppermint, chocolate sauce, and marshmallow cream for guests to add if they'd like." She mentally chided herself for offering up an unadorned scoop. This from a woman who'd made her mark on Sprocket by concocting massive Freakshakes with everything from slices of cake to sparklers on top. Rookie mistake.

"I'm here." Renata scurried to join them. "This is the only task I've been looking forward to, and you're not going to taste without me, Leonard."

"You're always bellyaching about being on a diet."

She held up a finger. "Not another word."

Juliette added a bowl for her, and Trinidad produced a silver tray and elegant spoons from which Leonard and Renata heaped on the toppings and tasted.

"Good," Leonard said.

Renata moaned. "Are you joking? Not good, delicious. I'd eat this every day of the week."

Trinidad hastened to present the second option, Papa's Gingerbread Hill, complete with the cookie structure nestled on top. "We can make little gingerbread steamboats if you'd prefer them to the houses. The gingerbread ice cream is made without dairy, as you requested."

Leonard and Renata tasted.

"Good," he pronounced.

"He means incredible." Renata sighed. "I don't miss the milk. This is a holiday in a bowl. A triumph."

Trinidad tried to keep her excitement in check. Two for three. "And the last offering is a hot chocolate bomb."

"A what?" Leonard stared into the empty goblet she'd placed before him.

"A bomb," Renata said. "Be quiet and watch."

Hoping her hands didn't tremble, Trinidad tonged up a shiny white chocolate globe the size of a tangerine, decorated to look like a snowman, complete with orange nose. Carefully, she placed it in Leonard's and Renata's empty mugs.

"Somethin' gonna happen?" Leonard said, staring.

"Shh." Renata gestured for Trinidad to continue.

She poured the hot milk over Leonard's bomb while Juliette did the same with Renata's. The white chocolate orb slowly dissolved into chocolatey bliss, releasing the handmade peppermint marshmallows inside. A quick stir and the drink was ready.

"Voilà," Juliette said. "A magic trick the guests will adore."

Renata's clapping telegraphed her approval, but Trinidad waited with bated breath while Leonard took a sip and then another. "Tastes good." He frowned at Renata. "Think the host will like it?"

"Oh yes, but I have one suggestion that will ensure it."

"What's that?" Trinidad asked.

A bell dinged from the front desk. "One sec. I have to get that." Renata picked up her cocoa mug and scanned the table. "Can you help me carry my desserts to the kitchen freezer?" she said to Juliette. "I may be caught up for a while, and I intend to eat every teeny bite since I missed dinner."

Juliette chuckled and loaded Renata's portions onto a tray and followed her out.

Trinidad took a cue from Iris. "If you're pleased with the offerings, Mr. Pinkerton, can we discuss the pricing?"

They did. Though Trinidad's forehead was covered in a layer of cold sweat by the time they were done, she was satisfied with the results of their haggling. Especially when it might prove to be the beginning of a fruitful partnership. The ray of optimism warmed her through and through. When the contract was signed and the deposit check written, Trinidad tidied up.

Leonard, instead of leaving, sank his prodigious chin on his knuckles and gazed out at the water, bronzed by the low angled sun. "This party," he said, startling her. "It's a real boon for us. Usually it's the summer months when we get weddings and lots of tourists and such, but this is gonna lead to more holiday gigs, I can feel it."

"That's fantastic."

He did not look particularly thrilled. "Yeah, it's good, but we could do better. I'm looking to upgrade to packages, trips that include stops, not just a sail and return to dock."

"What stops?"

"Yeah, that's the trouble. The ideal spot for another dock is across the lake." He shrugged. "I guess Iris is gonna get that now."

"I'm not following. What ideal spot?"

"Oscar's place. Now that he's gone, it probably goes to his cousin." Leonard's voice was wistful.

She knew Oscar lived on the edge of Big Egg, but she hadn't known his property was anything special.

Leonard was still gazing outside at the water. "If she's Oscar's heir, I mean. I tried to get him to sell it to me a time or two, but no luck." He pointed out the window. "See that lot across the lake with the cottage on it?"

The cozy structure stood on a crescent-shaped beach that curved along the shore. The cabin wasn't very large, but she could tell that the property was prime.

"Oscar's. Nice, right? I was trying to get him to sell it to me. Oscar's property is the only area of Big Egg with deep enough water to support a dock and clear of trees and the cliffs." His eyes shone as he considered. "With a second dock, I could pick up travelers on both sides of the lake. There's a popular hiking trail back there, and it could be like a built-in ferry service. Think of the revenue. Breakfast on the steamboat, ferry across the lake and spend the day hiking, reboard for a nice dinner and return trip. I could charge a hefty fee, maybe enough to renovate a few of the old staterooms and make them habitable, which would put me in the hotel business."

"Wow. That's really an expansion."

"Small businesses have to expand or die. You're catering now, right? Because your storefront business isn't enough?"

Embarrassed by the admission, she nodded.

He gripped the sill beneath the window. "So much potential. Anyway, now it goes to Iris probably."

"Maybe she would sell it to you."

He jerked a look at her. "Think so? I dunno. I haven't quite worked up the nerve to ask, with Oscar having just been killed and all. Figured I'd feel her out first, but she's not a chatty Cathy. I heard she lives practically in a closet above her shop, so she's hankering for a house, likely. Oscar's place is small but completely renovated with a private road. Worth a couple mil with prices being what they are, and she needs the money, a widow and all, starting up a business at her age."

A widow?

He scrubbed a palm over his beard. "Anyway, I got work to do, but we'll see you on Saturday, huh?"

"Yes, sir. We'll be ready."

She finished packing up and they returned to the food truck, breath puffing in the cold air. Trinidad's nerves buzzed with excitement. "Did we really just book our first catering job?"

"We did indeed." Juliette returned her fist bump. "And it's a pretty high-profile launch to boot. Ten tables of ten? Highbrow client? Decorations to the nines? We're going to have to get ourselves some nice clothes for serving."

Trinidad bit her lip. Her nicest clothes were the jeans without any bleach stains and a blouse left over from her days as a courtroom stenographer. "I didn't think of that. What kind of clothes? Where will we find them by Saturday?"

Juliette squeezed her forearm. "Leave it to me. I'll find something serviceable yet upscale. I am an accomplished shopper."

Relieved, Trinidad reversed out of the three parking spaces she'd occupied.

"Who's that?" Juliette peered through the front windshield.

On the second level club deck, a man leaned over the railing. His close-cut blond hair shone in the waning daylight. His posture was discouraged, shoulders slumped and chin on his folded arms.

Juliette cocked her head. "Do you suppose that's Harry the carpenter who hitched a ride with Gabe?"

"Uh-huh."

"Did you believe the story that he got out of the car before the crash because Gabe's driving was bad?"

Trinidad paused. "Nope. Gabe is an all-around despicable human being, but he was a careful driver when we were together."

"I agree. So Harry is lying? Do you think he somehow killed Oscar?"

They stared at him. "I'll ask Bigley if she's heard anything more. She's off the case officially but…"

Juliette rolled her eyes. "Fat chance. She's off the case, like I'm off reality television shows."

Rumbling out of the parking area, Trinidad filled Juliette in on what Leonard had said.

"I can feel the plot thickening. Leonard wanted Oscar's property, so there's a motive. And he was conveniently not there when Oscar was struck down. Suspicious."

"And the man in the car with Gabe is also conveniently working on his steamboat."

Juliette folded her arms. "Was Harry hired by Leonard to kill Oscar?"

"I don't know." Trinidad could hardly believe anyone would want to hurt Oscar. They were supposed to be friends after all. Her work in the courtroom had shown her that people were often not what they seemed to be. "But I sure hope the guy we just booked our first catering job with isn't a murderer."

"Innocent until proven guilty, but let's keep our eyes open."

"I'm not a crime solver, no matter what Gabe thinks."

"No, but you're naturally inquisitive." Juliette smiled.

"By inquisitive, you mean nosy?"

Juliette shrugged. "Let us say you have a tendency to solve puzzles, and who's to say you won't solve this one?"

"I do. I'm here to serve desserts. I promised to keep my ears open but not to play detective. What was Renata's suggestion for the cocoa bombs?"

"Oh, that was weird. She wouldn't elaborate much on the client, though I pried as much as I dared, but wait until you hear her idea."

Trinidad hoped it wasn't something that would require hours of prep. There were only three more days until the bash.

"She asked us to make a bunch of the cocoa bombs look like basketballs instead of snowmen."

Trinidad quirked a brow. "Basketballs?"

"Basketballs."

"Well, that's odd. Gabe said he and Harry were talking about the Oregon Blizzards in the diner before the crash. Now whoever is hosting this party would want basketball cocoa bombs? Do you think that's a coincidence?"

"Maybe. I've been doing some reading, mystery novels lately. I kinda got into them after you put on your investigation hat to get me out of jail." Juliette grinned at Trinidad. "You're the perfect sleuth you know, an amateur in a wacky small town. You even have a dog sidekick. If you were older, you could totally be a next generation Miss Marple."

Trinidad guffawed. "I am a scooper, not a sleuther. How many times do I need to say that?" Her tone was snarkier than she'd realized, and she collected herself. "Anyway, you might as well tell me what you read."

"It's supposedly an Agatha Christie quote. 'One coincidence is just a coincidence, two coincidences are a clue, three coincidences are proof'."

"All right. Providing we want to take advice from someone who made stuff up for a living, what's the third coincidence?"

"Allow me to recap." Juliette counted off. "Coincidence numero uno, Gabe hits town with a basketball-loving stranger who happens to turn up at the steamboat." She held up another finger. "Gabe and our former basketballer's sister are now suddenly about to be married." Third finger. "Renata asked us to include basketballs in our dessert buffet."

"And these three coincidences are proof of what, Agatha?"

Juliette was silent for a moment. "That there's something strange going on in Sprocket."

"I could have told you that without any sleuthing whatsoever. Maybe we should focus on getting to the Shimmy and cranking out a set of basketball cocoa bombs." Still, as they drove the truck back to the shop, Trinidad found herself wondering.

It was possible that Iris and Leonard both had reasons to want Oscar dead.

And she felt sure that Harry was somehow connected.

As for the Bonnie and Gabe angle and mysterious basketball theme?

That was pure strangeness indeed.

Chapter Six

TINTING THE WHITE CHOCOLATE A zippy orange color was a snap, though they weren't nearly as cute as the snowmen and they didn't exactly scream Christmas. More complicated was explaining her actions to the twins before they left for the evening.

"Why basketballs?" Diego demanded. "Is it a clue? Who's the host? An athlete?"

Trinidad reiterated that she had no idea. "But it doesn't matter. Catering is all about the customer, and if they want basketballs, so be it. I'll handle making them. You two help Papa with the gingerbread."

Soon six sheet trays of Papa's gingerbread dough lay neatly wrapped on the counter. The shop was redolent of all things holiday by closing time as she locked the shop door after the departing twins.

Papa offered a plain piece of baked gingerbread to Noodles, who wagged his tail in double time and took it delicately between his teeth.

Papa smiled. "Funny how dogs adore gingerbread."

She watched in astonishment as Noodles trotted over and shoved it through the bars of Scooter's cage.

"No, Noo." Trinidad removed the cookie. "I know you want to share and I'm not a parrot expert, but I know they don't eat cookies." The bird jammed his head against the cage bars and Noodles managed to give him a lick that dampened his crown. "You two are developing quite a friendship." Her stomach rumbled. Quitting time, or at least a dinner break at the tiny house she shared with Papa. So tiny, in fact, she would be hard-pressed to find space for the bird chateau. "Papa, suppose we drop by Iris's house and deliver Scooter on our way home?"

"Wonderful idea." He scurried to the back and returned with a massive bouquet of yellow mums he'd grown himself in his greenhouse. "It seems a florist probably does not give herself flowers too often, and there has been a death, yes?"

"Yes." Papa had obviously spent a good deal of time thinking about Iris. Trinidad boxed up the first batch of basketball cocoa bombs, stripped off her apron, and accompanied Noodles out the door and to her car. Papa, hauling Scooter, was concerned that the cage might result in nicked leather in his precious Bel Air so they'd decided on her vehicle. Two humans, one large bouquet, a dog, and a parrot in a cage proved a tight fit. They drove to the Purple Iris, which was closed up for the night, but a light shone from the apartment above the shop. Papa and Trinidad with their accompanying animals took the stairs to the second floor and knocked.

Iris peeped from behind the curtain, then opened the

door dressed in jeans and a boxy crocheted sweater. Her glasses glinted in the porch light. "Hello, Luis. Trinidad. I'd forgotten you were going to drop by."

"We are terribly sorry for your loss." Papa handed her the bouquet. She stared at it for a moment and then smiled.

"Thank you. It has been an age since anyone gave me flowers." The smile took the exhaustion from her face and warmed her whole demeanor. After a deep whiff of the spicy mums, her gaze drifted to Noodles and up to the birdcage, and the fatigued look returned. "Oh," she said. "Oscar's bird?"

"Yes." Trinidad held the cage closer for her to see the occupant. "His name is Scooter and he's a really sweet little guy, but he can't fly and he plucks out his feathers. Kinda of a nervous compulsion." Maybe that hadn't been the right way to showcase Scooter's finer qualities.

Iris didn't seem to be showing a real interest in Scooter, nor was she inviting them in. As a matter of fact, she'd drawn back a step.

"We thought…I mean, we wondered if you would like to have him," Trinidad said.

"Me? No. I'm sorry." Iris's expression was one of mild horror. "I'm a clean freak and I don't want feathers everywhere."

"Oh, well, he doesn't have too many of them," Trinidad joked.

Iris didn't return the smile. "Oscar already asked me about being a guardian for Scooter and I declined. My place is very small anyway, and I'm in the shop every waking moment."

The perfect opening for a probing question. "Leonard at the steamboat thought you might be moving onto Oscar's property."

"Oh, did he?" Iris twitched as if she'd been given a jolt. "I'm not sure I'm being deeded the property. As I said, Oscar and I haven't been close for a while, and we didn't discuss his estate. Leonard sure is eager to know though, isn't he?"

Very eager, Trinidad thought.

Iris fingered the door. "I'm sorry I can't keep Scooter."

"No trouble at all," Papa said grandly. "We will care for the bird until a more appropriate home is found."

We will? Trinidad looked from Papa to Iris but no one offered up an idea about alternative accommodations. Now was definitely not the time for Trinidad to acquire a new pet. She'd have to think of something fast.

Iris played with the button on her sweater. "I, um, would you like to come in for coffee or something?"

Papa patted Iris's hand and waved off her offer. "We wouldn't dream of intruding." He bade her good night and helped Trinidad carry Scooter back to the car. Noodles curled right up next to the cage and applied his nose to the bars. At least he would be excited about their new roomie.

"I can't keep this bird." Trinidad spoke with a tinge of desperation. "I'm not a bird person. This is temporary, right?"

Papa nodded solemnly. "I shall put out feelers at the pet shop and the veterinarian's office." He brightened. "But perhaps Stan might want him, being Oscar's friend and fellow bird-watcher."

The subject of birds seemed to be forever circling around her today. She thought about Gabe's odd admission of his first waking moment after the accident. *What is a yellow-breasted chat?* It probably had nothing to do with the situation, but she'd run it by Stan or Leonard anyway. Papa's idea that Stan might want to take Scooter was a good one, though he certainly hadn't offered earlier.

They drove to the tiny house. Trinidad glanced at Papa as she rolled up the long gravel driveway glimmering in the moonlight.

"I didn't know Iris was widowed."

Papa nodded. "Yes, two years ago. I gather her late husband, Albert, was a difficult man, very demanding and inclined to allow Iris to work while he stayed home and watched sports on television. He left her with considerable debt." Papa grimaced. "He was no prize, that's certain." Papa extracted himself from the vehicle and carried the cage up the front walk. Noodles waggled along behind him. "No doubt her rotten ex explains her rift with Oscar," Papa added as she unlocked the door.

"Why?"

"Iris's husband, Albert, was Oscar's friend. Oscar introduced the two of them."

Oscar introduced Iris to a man who would become her dirtbag spouse? A woman could hold on to that kind of resentment, Trinidad thought with a twinge in her belly.

The only place in the tiny house that would accommodate Scooter's cage was the cubical coffee table, so that was where they deposited the contraption. It suited Noodles fine as he perched on the sofa offering licks and sniffs to their new housemate.

Trinidad washed up and Papa took his self-appointed place in the kitchen to warm a pot of *congri*, Trinidad's favorite bean and rice dish, and fried plantains, the ripe ones that he made on a weekly basis, that spoke to them both of home and family. The fragrance of the plump black beans and bacon made her mouth water. As she was drying her hands, a text flashed on her phone.

Any progress on the case?

It took her a moment to process that it was Gabe messaging. Someone must have bought him a new cell. She cycled through irritation, outrage, and resignation all in the space of sixty seconds. Replying would only encourage him, she figured, so she stuffed the phone in her back pocket as Quinn and Doug arrived. Doug stared in outright confusion at the fuzzy, half-naked bird, staying far enough away that there could be no possibility that any dander or flying seeds might touch him.

Quinn was more interested in studying her. Her pulse flickered. He couldn't be too mad about her visit to Gabe. He pointed to the cage. "Got yourself a new buddy?"

"He had no one else. Iris didn't want to take him."

Quinn laughed. "Always the rescuer."

She shrugged. "I don't know how it happens."

His frown turned up at the corners into what might have passed as a slight smile. "I love that about you, which is why I'm telling myself you're helping your slimy ex."

"It is," she hurried to say. "I truly have no fond feelings left."

He still did not look at her. "Truly?" he said, so low only she could hear.

She went to him and squeezed him tight. "Truly."

He relaxed, kissing her earlobe, but he released her with a growl. "I still think he's gonna rope you into another mess, so I'm not taking my eyes off that chump."

"Fair, but I can handle it. Don't worry."

He peered at Scooter. "I'd take him, but Doug wouldn't be able to relax around something that spilled seeds and produced dander."

They were finishing dinner when Trinidad's phone rang. Relieved that it was not Gabe, she accepted Juliette's call.

Juliette was breathless. "The beans have been spilled about the mysterious host of the steamboat bash. I ran into Chief Bigley at the gym, and she told me she uncovered the dirt. She's with me now."

An unlikely alliance. Trinidad put the call on speaker. "All right. You've got me, Papa, Quinn, and Doug. We're braced and ready. Who is it?"

Juliette exhaled a dramatic breath. "Remember what I said about coincidences? You're not going to believe this."

"Quit stalling."

"Cordell Barrone," Bigley said.

Trinidad tried to remember where she'd heard the name.

Quinn's jaw dropped. "The Crusher? The Blizzard's point guard? That Cordell?"

"The very same." Juliette's tone was unashamedly gossipy. "Can you believe it? A big star like that?"

"Why would he come to Sprocket?" As far as Trinidad knew, Sprocket didn't even have a bowling league, let alone a pro basketball presence.

Quinn whistled. "He's recovering from a messed-up ankle so he's out for the rest of the season. It's not the same team without him."

"How did you find that out?" Trinidad said.

Bigley piped up from the background. "I talked to Candy at the real estate office about any newcomers to town. She was told to be discreet, but I leaned a little."

Trinidad tried to gather her thoughts. Crusher Barrone, a celebrity sports star, had come to out-of-the-way Sprocket to host a lavish party? "So Bonnie's college friend and basketball superstar is the mystery host?"

Papa frowned. "He must have had other reasons for visiting. To see Bonnie perhaps?"

"Seems like an awful lot of expense to visit an old pal."

"There's more. He was a lawbreaker back in the day. His family has connections, or at least they did," Bigley said.

Lawbreaker? "What kind of connections?"

Bigley said, "The kind that mean your enemies abruptly decide not to testify. That kind."

"Fascinating, don't you think?" Juliette said. "I looked him up online. He's a real hottie. Tall and all muscles. Tattoos, the works."

"Why are you investigating newcomers to town, Chief? Do you think it has to do with Oscar's death?"

"Possibly."

"And aren't you supposed to be staying out of it?"

"Definitely." Bigley paused. "I'm flying under the radar."

Trinidad did not see how it was possible for the police chief to ask probing questions without being noticed. "Not very far under."

"What's the link though between Barrone and Gabe?" Quinn said.

Bigley paused. "Don't know."

But there was something in the pause that made Trinidad wonder.

So too did the three additional texts she received from Gabe later that evening.

Sorta thought of something.
Gotta talk to you.
Gonna have to be soon.

Sorta. Gotta. Gonna. If she didn't figure things out, she was sorta gonna lose her ever-loving mind.

———————

Trinidad was determined to get a jump on the workload Thursday morning. Whatever was or was not brewing in town with celebrity basketball players was of secondary importance to the catering gig. Barrone could be the Godfather himself as long as the party went on as scheduled and she got her paycheck to keep the Shimmy afloat. There were basketball hot cocoa bombs to be made, gingerbread steamboats to be constructed, and ice creams to be churned.

Dressing quickly, she climbed down from the loft with only one thought on her mind. Coffee. She'd fix it as quietly as she could so as not to disturb her light-sleeping Papa who would report for shop duty later.

Instead, she screamed and dropped her empty mug on the floor where it broke into three pieces.

Papa jerked upright from his cot and spewed off a riff of Spanish. "What?" he finally managed when he recovered his English, raising the corner of his eye mask.

Trinidad raced to the birdcage on the coffee table. The door was open and there was no feathery inmate to be seen. "Scooter," she hollered. She scanned the cushions and dropped to the floor to check under the sofa. "He's escaped."

Where could a flightless bird have gone in a house the size of a closet? She swept the drapes aside. No bird. Under the table? No.

Papa was standing now, dark thatch of hair sticking up in a glossy tuft. Fumbling for his glasses, he made it to his feet. "Noodles. We need his nose."

Of course. Noodles would sniff Scooter out immediately. She whirled to the dog's patchwork cushion. "Noo, where…?" Her question trailed off as suspicion took hold. Noodles quirked innocent eyebrows and gave her his most guileless brown-eyed gaze. She recognized the look. Guilt. Same expression he'd given her when he'd climbed in the freezer to rearrange the boxes of frozen vegetables and gotten stuck. Noodles had a passion for rearranging and tidying. He could give Marie Kondo a run for her money.

Trinidad knelt in front of the old dog and gave him a firm stare. "Where is Scooter, Noodles?"

Noodles wagged his tail and offered a lick to Trinidad's knuckles. Adorable, but she was not to be diverted. "Please, please tell me you didn't do something to Scooter?"

A tiny puff of down adhered to Noodles's lower lip. Her own mouth quivered. Was it possible her gentle lamb of a dog had killed the bird? Her stomach churned and she pushed out a breath. "It's okay, Noo. Where's Scooter? You can tell me." Had she really just asked her dog to speak?

Papa peered over her shoulder. "Aha. Mystery solved."

She followed the direction of his pointed finger where Noodles's blanket was bunched around his tummy. The fabric writhed and wriggled, and out popped Scooter's green head. He regarded her with shiny black eyes. Trinidad sagged in relief.

Noodles's tongue swabbed Scooter, and he wagged his tail as the bird snuggled between the dog's front paws.

Papa chuckled. "Noodles likes Scooter even better than his stuffed beaver toy."

Trinidad shook her head, trying to calm her breathing. "Do you think Scooter was there all night?"

"Probably. I do recall hearing a squeak of the cage door opening after you went to bed, but I thought I was dreaming."

"Well, we can't have a bird flapping around loose at night. I'll go see Stan this morning. He'll take Scooter. He has to." She eased Scooter away from Noodles and returned him to his cage where she supplied a variety of vegetables and fruits prescribed by Doc Masha and a small amount of bird pellets. Noodles waited patiently and devoured everything Scooter flung onto the floor. The bird splashed in a small bowl affixed to the bars, and Noodles watched in rapt attention. Trinidad wasn't nearly as patient as the moments ticked by until Scooter was finished with his ablutions.

Feeling like the Pied Piper, she led the caged bird and the dog to the car and drove to town. The first stop was the Full of Beans, which had just opened its doors. Trinidad left the two companions in the car with the heater on low and hurried inside.

"Morning, Stan."

He greeted her as always, neat in his apron and bow tie, but she saw the fatigue in his demeanor. Oscar was his friend, she reminded herself, and he'd suffered a terrible loss.

"Good morning, Trinidad. May I make you a coffee and tempt you with a cranberry square?"

Trinidad schooled her mouth to decline. "Absolutely," she said instead. What could a top-of-the-morning caffeine and sugar hit hurt? Desperate times, she thought. "How are you doing, Stan?"

He remained stoic, but his voice was flat, without the usual snap. "It's a sad thing, you know. I keep looking at my watch, thinking how things would be if the accident hadn't occurred. Oscar, Leonard, and I would go about our morning bird watch an hour from now, like clockwork. I keep expecting him to pop in any minute with Scooter in his jacket."

"I'm so sorry." After a pause, she added, "About Scooter. Umm, I've been keeping him at my house, and Noodles is a big fan, but I wondered if you would be interested in giving him a home."

Stan's silver eyebrows zinged upward. "I had supposed Iris would take him in."

"She's a clean freak. No pets allowed."

"Ah." He paused, frowning in thought. "It wouldn't do to leave him home, caged all the time in our condo." Stan shared a small unit with his sister. "That would break Oscar's heart. Birds aren't meant to be in isolation, especially after having such a doting owner, and I am usually in the store with Meg."

"You could keep him here at the Full of Beans," Trinidad blurted. "People would love to visit with Scooter while they drank their coffee. He might learn some new words to say."

Stan considered. "I'll have to talk it over with Meg when she gets back from visiting her daughter, but there's a formidable complication." He hooked a thumb toward a table covered by a frilly cloth upon which sat a silk poinsettia plant. Two greenish eyes blazed from beneath the fabric covering. "Bob," Stan mouthed.

Trinidad bit her lip. She'd forgotten about Bob Scratchitt, the full-figured orange cat who'd intruded into Meg's life when she was prop master for a London production of *A Christmas Carol*. Bob was a squashed-face Persian who preferred the basement of the coffee shop when the weather was warm, but in the colder months, he rose to the upper floors like a ghost. Bob Scratchitt gave no apologies and took no guff from any animal or human, as Noodles had found out the hard way when he'd attempted a friendly lick.

Bob, she suspected, would make short work of Scooter if he was ever given the opportunity. Another idea presented itself. An animal switcheroo. Perhaps Bob might enjoy the solitude of the condo due to his misanthropy. She suggested as much, and Stan promised to present the idea to Meg. There was no choice but to wait until Stan could talk it over with his sister. Her temporary roommate would remain at least for a while.

The bell hanging from the door jingled as Trinidad gathered her coffee and cranberry square. "Stan, real quick. Oscar posted your birding adventures regularly, didn't he?"

"Ruthlessly regularly. He was faithful about that social media stuff. I don't go in for it myself, but he said he had a dedicated following. He said our 'cybercommunity' would be upset if he didn't keep them apprised. I gather we were called the 'three birditos.' Leonard was appalled, but it never bothered me."

She heard a sniff from behind her. The big, bearded man she'd seen on the Sprocket Steamboat towered over her. His shoulders were hunched, hands jammed into his pockets.

"Sorry. Eavesdropping's bad, but I heard the name Oscar and I couldn't help it. That's the name of the guy who got run over, right?" He didn't wait for an answer. "I mean, talk about the wrong place at the wrong time. One minute. you're bird-watching, and the next…bammo, you're stuck on the grill of someone's car."

"Yes." Trinidad was unsure what else to say.

"I didn't know he left a pet bird behind. Sad, real sad. Poor orphaned critter. I had a parakeet when I was a kid, and when it flew out the window…" He shook his head. "Pecky never came back. I kept picturing him flying around lost. Killed me an inch at a time."

Trinidad and Stan exchanged a look. "Um, I'm sorry about Pecky." Trinidad mentally slipped on her Miss Marple girdle and gloves. "You must be Harry."

"Uh-huh." He shook her hand and Stan's. Long, strong fingers, she thought. Smooth and sinewy. "Harry Fortesque."

"You were in the car before Oscar was run down."

"Yeah, I was, but that Gabe guy is a driving terror so I got out. Didn't know what happened after that until I got to town, and even then I thought it was just some sirens. Renata Pinkerton on the steamboat told me what happened." He shook his head. "Probably Gabe didn't intend to do it. I mean, who would run down a guy with a bird in his jacket on purpose? Musta been an accident, right? Or maybe Gabe is actually a hard-core killer disguised as a geek."

"We will see what the police investigation turns up," Stan said.

"Yeah. Still though…the bird. That's rough." Harry pinched the bridge of his nose while Stan offered him coffee and pastry choices.

Trinidad waved goodbye to Stan and headed to her car. Declining coffee and treats, Harry followed her, politely holding the shop door. Interesting that he was so saddened about the situation. He might be faking, but if so, he was an excellent actor.

When she climbed into the driver's seat, Noodles pawed the window button and rolled it down. Wishing he had never learned that trick, she watched her dog shove his muzzle out the window and greet Harry, whom she hadn't realized had followed her to the sidewalk. He fondled Noodles's ears and peered around him.

"That bird's awful cute. Are you gonna keep him? At your shop maybe?"

Trinidad felt a sudden pang of alarm. Harry knew where she worked, but what did she know of this large, hairy Harry? He and Gabe were the two people closest to Oscar Fuentes before he was killed. And if she didn't believe Gabe was a murderer, why should she believe Harry's story about getting out of the car before it struck Oscar down?

"Oh, um, well, we're trying to work out another arrangement. In the meantime, Scooter's staying with me."

Harry gave her a thumbs-up. "Right then. Saw your food truck at the boat. Shimmy and Shake. That's clever." He patted the top of the car. "Gotta get to work. Take good care of Scooter." He crooned to the bird one more time before he walked away.

Such an odd encounter. Harry could be what he seemed, a sensitive bear of a man, animal lover, a carpenter innocently arrived in Sprocket who picked the wrong person to hitch a ride with. There was nothing indicating anything deceptive about Harry.

Except for one thing.

Those hands. *Long, strong fingers, smooth and sinewy.*

Why would a man who made his living with tools and wood have such baby-soft hands?

Chapter Seven

TRINIDAD FIGURED THE ONLY PLACE for Scooter's cage at the Shimmy that wouldn't break any health laws was the corner opposite the front counter, next to Noodles's cushion. No fear of a draft or direct sunlight and close enough that Noodles could track his friend's every move. She'd erected a curtain using a rolling garment rack to provide extra insurance against any dander or down infiltrating her precious ice creams. The boys had installed a plastic seed barrier as further protection. Several customers had already checked on the proceedings through the window, and she hoped they'd return later to admire the bird and order something. Might as well make the most of her short-term tenant's attraction.

Leaving the dog and bird to their mutual appreciation, she tied on an apron and began to work on the batches of royal icing that would be the glue to hold together Papa's fanciful gingerbread structures. How could her grandfather be so mathematical and imaginative at the same time?

"God gave us math so we could all be inventors," Papa

often said. Thirty-seven years later, she still didn't know what that meant, but it worked for him. When the icing was done and sealed into containers, she turned to finishing the hot cocoa bombs. The process was labor intensive, starting with melting the white chocolate that she'd tinted a dark orange and coating the half sphere molds. While they hardened, she got to work on the filling. The easier method would have been to scoot to the grocery and buy up their stock of hot cocoa mix, but Trinidad had the Shimmy's reputation to consider so she made a rich chocolate ganache out of both light and dark chocolates and let it cool. With gloved hands, she eased an orange half sphere out of the mold, then filled it with a tablespoon of the rich ganache and as many mini marshmallows as she could cram inside. After warming the edge of the top half by touching it to a heated pan, she glued the two hemispheres together before piping on basketball seams with dark icing.

"Not Christmassy at all," she said with a sigh. She'd decided to offer classes for kids to pad her income through the lean months, and hot cocoa bombs would be a draw clear into February she figured, but the thought of scads of kiddos attempting the multistep process made her pause. There had to be an easier way, a simplified method that didn't require specialty equipment. She put that thought on her mental back burner.

A sharp rap on the door startled her into dropping her spoon.

She admitted Bonnie and Felice. "You two are early birds this morning."

Felice nodded and hugged Trinidad. Trinidad eyed the

worried crease between Bonnie's brows as she patted the child. "Everything okay?"

Bonnie spoke urgently. "I, uh, I was picking up pastries from Stan's. Um, can I use your bathroom?"

"Oh sure."

"Come on, Fee."

"But I want to see Noodles and the bird," Felice protested. "And I don't have to go."

Bonnie swallowed, staring out the shop window. "It will only take a minute." She took her daughter's wrist, and in three steps, she was almost in the back. "Uh, if anyone stops in or, uh, anything, you didn't see us."

"What?" Trinidad called as another knock sounded against the door. The shadow of the knocking person completely filled the glass pane. She unlocked the door and looked up. And then up some more.

A man the size of a redwood looked down at her, brown eyes curious. His head was shaved close to the scalp, and a similar shade of stubble darkened his chin. Though he wore a jacket and track pants, the fabric strained to contain his muscular body. She had a feeling she knew the identity of the massive newcomer.

"Uh, hello," she said to his chin. "I'm Trinidad Jones. Owner, you know, of this store that you're standing in. Right now." *Smooth, Trin.*

Noodles came to sniff his blinding white sneakers, which did not appear to be laced. How did he keep them on? He didn't scratch the dog, but he smiled. At least she thought it was a smile.

"Hello." His voice was a gravelly baritone. Juliette shoved in behind him, whapping him in the tush with the door.

"Oh, so sorry. I got overexcited. You're Crusher Barrone, aren't you?" she gushed.

Now he did smile, stripping off his glove and engulfing her tiny hand in his meaty paw. "Call me Cordell. Crusher's only for on the court. And you are?"

"Juliette Carpenter. I'm a big fan. I was getting coffee and I saw you come in here."

He pointed to the plastic lid in her hand. "Looks like you forgot the coffee part."

She giggled. "Like I said, I got a bit overexcited."

Trinidad resisted an eye roll. "Did you want some ice cream, Mr. Barrone? We're not technically open yet, but if you've really got a craving, I can…"

He held up a palm. "No ice cream for me, thank you. I'm on a strict nutrition regime while I rehab an injury. I thought I saw a friend of mine come in here." His gaze drifted over the empty store.

"Friend?" *Like the one hiding in the bathroom?* "Hmm. Don't see anyone here now."

Felice's small sneeze emanated from the bathroom.

Cordell's groomed eyebrows climbed higher. "You got a ghost with allergies in the john?"

Standing behind the counter, Trinidad froze. Before she could hammer out some sort of answer, the door cracked open and a red-faced Bonnie came out. Felice followed.

"Bon Bon, there you are. Finally." Cordell closed the distance in four long strides and wrapped her in a hug that lifted her off her feet. "I've been looking everywhere for you. It's like you're invisible or something. Not avoiding me, right?"

"Never." Bonnie was breathless as he returned her to the floor. "I didn't expect to ever see you in Sprocket."

"I know, right?" He took in the shop. "This town's smaller than my limo." He pointed to his ankle. "Rehabbing, and I have business in the area like I said in my voicemail last week. It all worked out since I wanted to see you anyway. Christmastime makes me nostalgic and all that. Remember?"

She nodded. "Yes, I do. You used to have as big a Christmas party as you could manage in your dorm room."

He laughed. "Yeah. Got me in hot water a few times but Mom smoothed things out." Focusing on Felice, he dropped to one knee and shook her hand, his palm dwarfing hers. "You must be Felice. I went to college with your mama. She's a great lady."

"This is Mr. Barrone," Bonnie told her daughter.

"You can call me Cordell."

Felice smiled, exposing her missing front teeth. Bonnie put a hand gently on Felice's pink knitted cap. "Can you ask Auntie for a glass of water for me, Fee?"

Felice dutifully approached the counter and Trinidad filled a paper cup. Odd. Bonnie never drank anything but her bottled water because she said she didn't like the taste of the Sprocket tap stuff. Trying to get Fee away from Cordell?

"Actually, Fee," Trinidad added, "why don't you bring Noodles a dog biscuit and you can talk to the bird while you're over there? His name's Scooter."

Felice scampered to the corner and was soon alternating

her attention between Noodles and the bird. It might have been Trinidad's imagination, but she thought Bonnie shot her a grateful look. The plot was getting as thick as gingerbread dough.

Juliette fiddled with a stack of paper napkins, obviously eavesdropping as well.

"Look at you." Cordell grinned at Bonnie. "A mother and an innkeeper. Wow, Bon Bon. A business mogul."

She shrugged. "Not the pro sports career I'd planned, but I'm proud of it. At least one of us made it big."

Cordell grimaced. "Pro ball's a meat grinder. You win, you're the hero. You lose, everyone spits on you. If a girl shows interest, likely it's because she wants to get close to a celebrity athlete. It's the price of fame, and you're lucky to be out of it."

Cordell glanced at Juliette, who didn't even attempt to look as though she wasn't devouring every word. Instead she smiled at Cordell and tucked her hair behind her ear.

"So, uh, you'll be staying here in town?" Bonnie said.

"Yeah, until after Christmas."

"Sorry the inn was booked when you called me."

"So Locket is like some tourist mecca?"

"Sprocket," all three women said simultaneously.

"Right. Got some big plans here in town. First off, I've been trying to find you to give you this personally." He handed Bonnie a shiny white envelope from his pocket with an elaborate bow. "I hope you'll come. It's going to be a big bash on the steamboat, and it won't be right if you aren't there."

"You're the one having the party?" Bonnie said. "I thought you were here to rest and recuperate. Get away from the press."

"Surprise. I snagged a spot on the steamboat for a bash. Invited my friends and Mom, of course, but asked everyone to keep it on the down-low so we can stay out of the public eye. Might as well have fun while I'm rehabbing and taking care of business."

"What business?" Juliette sidled up.

"Business that should have been finished long ago." His voice went suddenly cold. He folded his long arms across his chest. "You know, Bon Bon, I'm real glad you got away from that skunk you married." Cordell's features hardened into angry planes. "Guy's got some nerve. Second he gets out, he saunters back into town intending to settle down like he owns the place."

Trinidad was practically leaning over the counter to catch every word.

Bonnie swallowed. "How did you know all that?"

"Have a friend at the jail who heard Gabe talk plenty about his plans to return to his hometown. He gave me a jingle and filled me in that the dweeb was getting sprung on Monday."

Monday? Hadn't that been the day Renata said the mysterious athlete had booked a party on the steamboat? Mega coincidence. Trinidad tried to catch Juliette's eyes, but she could see nothing but Cordell.

"Imagine us both rolling up in town at the same time, right?" His smile was wolfish.

"Yeah, that is a coincidence," Trinidad said, forgetting she was not supposed to be listening.

Bonnie glanced at her daughter, who was still crooning to the bird. "Gabe's, uh, had an accident. He's in the hospital," she whispered.

Cordell sniffed. "Too bad it isn't the morgue."

Bonnie gasped. "Don't say that, Cordell. You're talking about Felice's father."

"Some people don't deserve to be fathers," Cordell said, though he did moderate his volume. "My dad? He was never worth a nickel. It was my mom who got things done. Queenie Barrone never backed down from a fight. Your kid would be better off without Gabe. Crook like that." He arched a brow. "And now I heard he ran someone down and killed them."

Bonnie's cheeks went blotchy, and no words came out of her open mouth.

"It's being investigated," Juliette said. "Do you know Gabe personally, Cordell?"

"Never met the guy face-to-face, but it's a matter of time. He and I are going to have ourselves a conversation."

"About what?" Bonnie asked.

"Private stuff."

Trinidad finally remembered and brought the glass of water to Bonnie, who took a large swig. If Bonnie hadn't known that Gabe and Cordell were enemies, why was she hiding in the bathroom? There was all kinds of hidden intrigue bouncing around the Shimmy at that moment.

"Are you being protective of Bonnie? Or do you two have

history?" Juliette smiled as if she hadn't just asked a deeply personal question.

Cordell didn't seem to take offense. "We got ourselves a little history, and if he thinks all is forgiven and forgotten, he doesn't know the Barrone family."

"Please, Cordell. No threats, no matter what happened." Bonnie pointed at Felice.

He grabbed her hand and kissed the knuckle. "I know you don't like hearing about the family business, Bon Bon. Not your cup of tea so I'll respect that. Gonna take it easy and celebrate the holidays, get some business done, that's all." There was menace in his tone before he broke into a smile. "And I want to reconnect with my college sweetheart. Killing three birds with one stone."

Bonnie offered a weak smile. "Well, that's...super."

He winked at her and turned to go. "Got some phone calls to make. Nice to meet you, ladies." He turned to Juliette. "Maybe we can get some coffee sometime to go with your lid."

"That'd be great." Juliette's smile was a million watts.

Next, he stopped near Felice and scrunched down to peer into the birdcage. "You're invited to my Christmas party too, Felice. Say, what's the matter with that birdie?"

"Auntie said his feathers fell out," Felice said.

"Aww. I can relate. When I was a kid, all my hair fell out and everybody laughed at me."

Felice's eyes widened to the size of ping-pong balls. "It did?"

"Felice, Mr. Cordell needs to go now," Bonnie called.

"It's okay, bird." Cordell tapped the cage bars. "You keep

doin' your bird thing. Don't worry about the missing feathers." He stood. "You're both invited to the party too, by the way," he said to Trinidad and Juliette, but his attention was riveted on Juliette. "Hope you'll come."

She pinked. "Absolutely. We're serving the desserts."

"Well then. I'll be in for a treat."

Trinidad jumped into the flirt fest. "Thank you, Mr. Barrone."

He gave her a thumbs-up. "See you all Saturday." The bell tinkled as he pulled open the heavy door like it weighed nothing at all. "Tell Gabe I'll be seeing him around."

They watched Cordell cruise away down the sidewalk. Juliette and Trinidad turned to stare at their friend.

"Do you want to explain why you were hiding in the bathroom?" Trinidad whispered.

Bonnie stuck her index finger in her mouth and chewed the nail. Juliette reached out and pulled her hand away. "Talk, sister."

Bonnie made sure Felice was engaged in singing to the bird instead of listening in. "Cordell has a dangerous family. In college, when he had a problem, they would 'take care of it.' And he had piles of money all the time. I didn't want that kind of life. I...it's why we broke up my sophomore year."

"Okay. Past is past," Juliette said. "He's famous now, rich. He doesn't need his dangerous relatives."

"But he's threatening Gabe. That's not right."

"No," Trinidad agreed. "But you didn't know about the Cordell/Gabe grudge match until he told you. So why are you avoiding Cordell?"

"I just…don't want to go back to that part of my life. I'm a different person now."

"Seems like he is too," Juliette said dreamily.

Bonnie's phone alarm beeped. "I have a guest checking in, and I need to make sure the train car is ready. Talk to you later."

Was that a quiver in her friend's lip? Bonnie took Felice's hand and urged her to the door.

"Hey." Trinidad touched Bonnie's forearm.

Bonnie blinked. "All I want is what's best for Fee."

There seemed to be both a question and an explanation in the comment. "You're a great mother, Bonnie. Everyone knows that."

Bonnie put her hand over Trinidad's and squeezed. Her smile was hesitant. "Thanks, Trin. I know it's hard to believe, but Gabe has been a good parent too, the best he could."

It was hard to picture how Gabe had been good parental material since he'd been in jail for the past two years and married to two other women in the course of Felice's short six years on planet Earth. Trinidad decided to change the subject.

"Can I borrow Felice tomorrow maybe to try out an idea I had for a cooking class?"

"Sure, anytime." But Bonnie's tone was taut with worry, and before she could say another word, she walked out.

Trinidad accepted a nose poke from Noodles. "Something weird is going on."

"That's for sure." Juliette stared out the window, tracking Cordell's progress down the street.

"Juliette, we have to focus on business right now."

"Right. Our catering outfits should be delivered this afternoon, rush shipment and all. I'll do an inventory of the serving ware, but I'm going to need to buy some coffee to go with my lid first. Back in a minute."

Trinidad surmised Juliette's coffee mission didn't have to do with the fact that Cordell had moseyed off in that same direction. *More trouble's coming to town*, she thought until the beep of the ice cream mixer told her it was time to get back to work.

———

Even with Papa's help, Trinidad's hand ached from gluing together the gingerbread steamboats with royal icing. Her back spasmed as she hung up her apron at quitting time. "All right, furred and feathered family. Let's go home for dinner."

Papa loaded Scooter and Noodles into the Subaru. Trinidad turned off the lights and locked the Shimmy's front door when Juliette pulled up behind in her sporty green Mini Cooper and got out. "Hey, Papa."

Papa hugged her. "Come join us for dinner."

"You're always trying to feed me," Juliette said with a chuckle. "How can I resist? Would you mind if I stole Trinidad for an hour before I join you, though?"

"Steal me for what?"

"We need to go see Gabe. He's been trying to text you all day."

"I had my phone off."

"Which is why he finally left a message at the coffee shop, which Stan delivered after they closed up. He needs to tell us something."

Papa shoved his glasses up his nose. "I do not approve of any time spent with the Hooligan."

"I know," Trinidad soothed. "But I have a question to ask him anyway that needs to be face-to-face. It's important." Papa tried to argue her out of it, but she stopped him with a kiss on his cheek. "Don't worry, Papa. Gabe can't hurt me anymore. I'll be home soon. Can you get the animals back and warm up dinner?"

He acquiesced with a sigh. Grumbling under his breath, he took her keys and drove off.

Juliette and Trinidad climbed into her car.

Trinidad buckled her seat belt. "I messaged Chief Bigley about the threats to Gabe. She's looking into the Cordell connection."

Juliette nodded. "I've been sleuthing around myself. Did you know Cordell brought a brother to town with him? I heard him say so at the coffee shop."

"A large, muscular brother?"

"No doubt."

"You overheard quite a bit."

"Not overheard. I joined him for coffee." Juliette grinned. "Can I help it if I'm easy to talk to? Papa would be impressed. Cordell's driving a classic Corvette. It's his, not a rental. The plates say, IMAGOAT. That stands for…"

"Greatest of all time," Trinidad finished. "I know. The twins keep me up to speed on popular culture." She paused.

"Um, do you think you might need to be careful around Cordell if he's out to punish Gabe? Could be he had something to do with framing him for murder."

Juliette tucked her hair behind her ear. "I don't think he really meant all those threats he made."

"But Bonnie doesn't want anything to do with him. Isn't that reason enough to avoid him?"

Juliette waved her off. "Bonnie has a kid to think of and a settled life. I don't."

Trinidad decided to let the matter drop for the moment. "Why does Gabe want us to come see him?"

"Dunno. His message said it was imperative that he speak to you."

"Imperative?"

"Direct quote. I don't think he's dying or anything. I figured it was about the case. I'm going with you in the event he tries to manipulate you somehow."

"No need to worry about that. I'm tough now."

"Yeah, tough, with a marshmallowy center, which is why you give out free ice cream to anyone who looks remotely down on their luck or happens to have forgotten their wallet."

"That's humanitarian, not easily manipulated."

"Whatever you say."

Juliette parked in the hospital lot, and they took the elevator to Gabe's floor. They found him staring at the ceiling, covers drawn up to his chin. His face was still bruised, but the purple marks had begun to turn yellow and brown like the skin of an overripe banana. At least the swelling had subsided somewhat.

"Oh hey, Jules. Trina. Thanks for coming. Can I get you something?" He waved a vague hand around as if he was not, in fact, a patient in a hospital.

Trinidad did not bother to correct his nickname this time, and Juliette merely rolled her eyes.

"What's so imperative?" Juliette demanded. "Trinidad and I are busy, and we can't trot down here whenever you summon us."

Gabe shoved up his glasses, now held together with tape someone had given him. "Bonnie came to visit. She told me there's a, er, celebrity in town."

"Yeah," Juliette said. "Cordell Barrone, and he's a hunk. I love a bad boy."

Gabe flashed her a grin. "That why you married me?"

"You're not a bad boy. You're a crook. There's a difference."

He didn't seem to take offense. He plucked at the blanket, smoothed the sheet, and then fidgeted with it again. Trinidad noticed his forehead was damp with sweat though the room was cool. She folded her arms. "Gabe? Let's get to the brass tacks. What do you need to say?"

He cleared his throat. "I've been trying to think about enemies and who might have wanted to frame me for Oscar's death." He paused. "Cordell pretty much despises me."

"We got that impression. Is that why you look so scared?" Trinidad said. "You found out he's in town?"

"Scared?" he squeaked. "I'm not scared. This is how I always look."

"Pasty and trembling?" Juliette said. "Nuh-uh. Your sister

believes you're not telling her something. She encouraged us to squeeze you for every last drop of information until you're a dry, withered husk."

"That sounds like my sis."

Trinidad refocused. "I know Cordell cares for Bonnie and can't stand you for cheating on her, but I have this feeling there's more."

"Um, yeah, about that."

Trinidad and Juliette stared at him in silence.

"Remember when I told you I sort of, uh, pilfered from a lady who wanted to open a fried chicken restaurant? My… er…embezzling ruined her plans?"

"Yes." Uneasiness squeezed Trinidad's abdomen.

"While she was busy taking me to court for damages, another family member used the cherished recipe to start their own chicken chain. The lady felt she was robbed of her moment." He coughed. "By me."

Juliette pursed her lips. "I can imagine. How's it pertinent?"

His Adam's apple bobbed in his throat as he gulped. "As it turns out, the lady that I, er, wronged, was Cordell's mother, Queenie."

Trinidad and Juliette gaped.

Juliette recovered first. "Are you kidding me, Gabe? You fleeced Cordell Barrone's mother?"

"Fleeced is an unpleasant word."

Cordell's need for revenge suddenly made more sense. "Cordell knew when you were being released."

"I don't doubt it. He had contacts in jail."

Juliette shrugged. "I'm sure he didn't come all the way to Sprocket and plan an expensive party so he could rough Gabe up."

Trinidad wasn't so sure, but she figured she might as well dig into the Bonnie/Gabe mystery while the moment was ripe. "How did you meet Bonnie anyway? She introduced you to Cordell, right?"

"Bonnie and I became friends because I bought a poppy seed bagel every day at the shop where she worked part-time in college. She and Cordell were really tight back then, and she gave him my name when he was looking for an accountant for his mom. I took care of Queenie Barrone's books for almost eight years. I did a real good job at first, until I got greedy."

Greedy for money. Greedy for love. That was Gabe.

Trinidad heaved out a sigh. "Did he directly threaten you, maybe at the trial? I don't remember seeing him there."

"He was playing pro ball at the time so he didn't appear. He reached out anyway, though."

Juliette frowned. "Reached out how?"

"I got letters in prison, anonymous of course, but pretty explicit about what was going to happen to my gizzard and such when I got out. Point of information, I looked that up, and I don't think I have a gizzard per se."

Trinidad's head spun. "I can't believe you actually double-crossed Queenie Barrone."

"Sometimes I can't believe it either. I guess my goose is about to be cooked if I don't find a place to hide out until things are cleared up. I'm being released soon."

"Well, don't look at me," Juliette said. "You're not staying at my place."

"Or mine," Trinidad added. "I live in a tiny house with a dog, a grandpa, and a parrot now, thanks to whoever killed Oscar."

"Your sister," Juliette suggested. "She *has* to take you in because you're related."

"I don't want to make things awkward for her."

"Too late," Juliette said.

"Yeah, she's already in trouble because of me. Are you sure I can't stay with one of you? Bonnie said the inn is full because of the holiday rush."

"We're sure." Trinidad glanced at the clock. The hours before her first big catering gig were quickly evaporating. "Have you remembered anything about the crash? Or Harry Fortesque?"

"I've been mulling that over. Seemed like Harry was on his phone a lot. Instagram. Other than that, he was a friendly traveling companion. Even offered to chip in for gas. Nice, right?"

Nice, unless he was planning a murder. "Okay. We'll keep an eye out for Cordell if we can. Gotta go now."

Gabe chewed his lip. "Have you found anybody who might benefit from Oscar's death?"

Like perhaps Leonard? Or Papa's new friend Iris? Trinidad shook off the thoughts and marched purposefully to the door. "We're on the lookout. That's all I promised, remember? I run an ice cream shop. Your sister is the cop."

"Yeah." Juliette's smile was evil. "And you'd better keep

your eyes peeled if Cordell really is out to get you. He's six foot plus of muscle."

Gabe blanched, his swallow audible.

"That wasn't nice," Trinidad said as they took the elevator down.

"But it was fun. Did you see his face?"

And then they were both lost in a fit of giggles that took them all the way to the main floor.

"About this mysterious murder. Leonard had the best motive for wanting Oscar dead."

Trinidad agreed. The other thought that had been plaguing her tumbled out. The second person high on the list motive wise happened to be Papa's good friend. She caught Juliette's eye. "Iris could be in for a windfall from Oscar if he put her in his will. She was his only relative."

"Hmm. This is getting complicated."

Too complicated. "Where's Agatha Christie when you need her?"

Chapter Eight

THE BLAST OF COLD AIR made them hunch into their coats as they exited the building. They were crossing the walkway between the emergency room entrance and the hospital when Juliette pulled at Trinidad's sleeve. "Isn't that...?"

Harry Fortesque heaved himself out of a car at the emergency room drop-off curb. He held a cloth saturated with blood to his forehead. When he wobbled, Trinidad rushed forward to steady him.

"Harry. What happened?"

"I'll tell you what happened." Renata came around from the driver's side. Her makeup and hair were immaculate, and a rose silk blouse and matching scarf added a glow to her complexion. Her top half was incongruous with her bottom half, which was covered in ratty sweatpants with a hole in one knee. "The whizzo carpenter here conked his head on a lintel and gave himself a laceration. Probably not bad but you know human heads bleed bucketsful. It looked like a grisly murder scene..."

Harry's mouth puckered and he held up a palm. "Please," he entreated. "I can't stand the sight of blood. I'm trying to keep from losing my lunch."

Renata sighed. "Sorry, Harry. I vaguely remember from our high school days that you couldn't dissect a frog without hurling either. Let's get you inside so they can stitch you up or glue you together or whatever they do these days."

An orderly walked by, tossing an empty soda can in the recycle bin. "Hey, ma'am. Sorry, but you can't park there. It's for ambulances only."

"But I've got a wounded man here," Renata said. "He's gushing blood and everything."

Harry groaned.

"I'll park your car while you get him inside," Juliette offered.

"Thanks." Renata handed Juliette the keys and took one of Harry's elbows while Trinidad held the other. Together they guided him through the automatic doors and sat him down in the reception area to wait for a doctor. There were a number of other stricken people occupying seats as well, a cranky toddler on his mom's shoulder, a man with his leg propped up on the seat and an ice pack on his socked foot.

Renata sank down next to Harry and Trinidad. "This isn't how I was expecting to spend my evening."

"Me neither," said Harry. "I was fixing to replace that paneling since Leonard's getting antsy about the party."

"You're telling me." Renata rolled her eyes. Trinidad admired her smoky eye shadow treatment. "And if he's so determined to get things squared away, why isn't he around to take you to the hospital? No, Mr. 'I'm supposed to be resting my ankle' is off gallivanting in town."

Interesting, Trinidad thought. "Running an errand?"

"Who knows?" Renata sighed. "This is such bad timing. I really thought this date might be the breakthrough. His name's Perry and he owns a car dealership."

Trinidad put together the clues. Renata had obviously been preparing for a rendezvous. Maybe she hadn't finished dressing when Harry had his accident.

Renata fingered the tear in the knee of her sweatpants. "Perry and I met on a dating app. I swiped right." She pinked. "We were going to have a virtual date so he would only get a look at the top half of me. I figured no use in cramming myself into a skirt or high heels."

Trinidad chuckled. She and Quinn were at the comfortable stage when they didn't have to put on airs, though she did try to contain her curls and occasionally even swiped on a quick coat of lip gloss when she knew he'd be stopping by the store.

"Last time I got gussied up was my high school reunion." Renata twirled a finger in mock enthusiasm. "Go Wildcats."

Harry nodded. "You looked good. Really good."

"Were you two close in high school?"

"Not really. Me, Leonard, Harry, and a couple other people in Sprocket went to the same school. Leonard and Harry were in a shop class together once. Did you go to our thirty-year reunion, Harry?"

"Nah. Usually I skip them, but I guess I was lonely at the last one. Those things are all about people who've made it lording it over people who haven't."

"Probably, but I was hoping to make a connection with one of those people who've made it. The dating pool's shallow here in Sprocket. The reunion didn't turn up any prospects so I thought I'd give the online dating a try." She shrugged. "I'm beginning to suspect some of those four-star widowed generals aren't what they appear to be."

Harry eased his big body into a more comfortable position on the hard chair.

Juliette chimed in as she appeared from the parking lot and returned the keys. "What'd I miss?"

"Renata had an online date she's supposed to be doing but instead she came here 'cause I bashed myself." Harry slumped, still pressing the wad of fabric to his wound. "Sorry to mess things up. I could take a cab home. Can you still make your date?" he said miserably.

Renata sighed. "I canceled. I hope he doesn't think I'm blowing him off."

"You'll explain it," Harry said. "You're very believable."

Renata arched a brow. "Okay then. Believe me when I say that I'm tired of stepping over lumber, and everything needs to be shipshape by the time Crusher Barrone sets foot onto the steamboat on Saturday." She grimaced. "Oopsy. Spilled the beans. Not every day you get to rub elbows with a celebrity."

Harry laughed. "He's real tall. You can't even reach his elbows."

Renata chuckled. "Good one. I'm going to go check on the progress." She walked purposefully to the reception desk.

Harry watched her. "She's a firecracker, huh?"

His appreciative tone could not be missed. Juliette's mouth quirked as she picked up on it too. Did Harry have a romantic interest in Renata?

"Leonard should take better care of his sister," he added a moment before Renata returned.

"They're ready for you now," Renata said. "Thanks for your help, ladies."

Harry added his thanks and followed her away.

"A love connection in the making," Juliette said. "Harry's got the hots for Renata."

"She doesn't seem to share his interest."

Juliette hitched a shoulder. "Love. Whatcha gonna do?"

As they walked to the car, Trinidad considered. "Let's drive slow until we get past the main drag, okay?"

"Why?"

"Because Renata was complaining that Leonard was 'gallivanting' in town instead of helping her."

"Are your Miss Marple senses tingling?"

"Just wondered. Odd to be gallivanting with a sore ankle, and he has a motive for wanting to kill Oscar."

"And he conveniently injured his ankle the day Oscar was run down."

"I know what you're thinking, Juliette. 'One coincidence is just a coincidence, two coincidences are a clue'... If we're going to find a way to clear Gabe, we'd better find out which of these coincidences are relevant."

"Yeah, or Gabe might need to skip town before Cordell gets hold of him."

"He'll be safe with his sister watching out for him." The stiff wind teased goose bumps on Trinidad's arms.

"He can't hole up forever, and I get the feeling Cordell is prepared to stay in good old Sprocket until he concludes his business."

Shivering, Trinidad increased her pace as they hurried to the car.

———

The road that took them away from the hospital and back to Main Street was quiet, Sprocket being the kind of town that rolled up the sidewalks in the early evening. It was not yet seven, but only the Pizza Heaven had any kind of foot traffic. The exception was the Vintage Theater. The old windows were aglow and the parking lot moderately full of patrons attending the local adaptation of *It's a Wonderful Life*. The night was cold, dropping into the low thirties, and Trinidad thought she might have spotted a snow flurry or two on the windshield.

What was she doing driving around when there was Papa's warm dinner to be had and a schedule to be drawn up for the following day? Nonetheless, they motored up and down the quiet streets, looking for a vehicle that might be Leonard's.

Juliette turned up the heater. "What does Leonard drive anyway?"

Trinidad shrugged. "No idea. Miss Marple would have scanned the steamboat parking lot, but that didn't occur to me while we were there."

Juliette's stomach growled. "What's Papa cooking for us?"

"Chicken and rice. Are you hinting that dinner is rising above detecting to the top of the priority list?"

"Heck, yeah. Miss Marple had tea and snacks all the time. I skipped lunch so all I've eaten is a broken gingerbread house left over from the tasting. It was great, by the way. I love a snappy gingerbread." They drove along, passing the theater until they were almost at the Shimmy. Across the street and down half a block was the Purple Iris.

"Wait," Trinidad said, and Juliette smacked the brakes.

Parked in a side lot was a white van with "Sprocket Steamboat" stenciled in red on the door.

"Doesn't take a detective to figure out that's Leonard's vehicle." Juliette squinted. "And funnily enough, we're here at Iris's shop, aren't we?"

"We surely are. Let's watch for a minute."

They pulled into a shadowed section of the sidewalk and waited, engine idling. The shop windows were lit, and the sign still read "Open."

Juliette thumbed her phone. "The website says the shop closes at five, and it's past six now. Why would Leonard be here at this hour? Working out last-minute details for the party?"

"Would have been easier to phone or email." Trinidad's mind ran amok. Leonard might be trying to persuade Iris to sell him the land. Or threatening? Or maybe...

Juliette sucked in a breath. "Wait a minute. You don't suppose they're having a tryst or something, do you?"

Trinidad's stomach clenched. Papa was fond of Iris,

though she wasn't sure to what level. Iris couldn't be involved with Leonard. Could she? Trinidad certainly hadn't picked up on any romantic vibes at their dessert audition. Leonard sure had spoken longingly of the property Iris was sure to inherit. Another thought hit her. "Could they be in cahoots?"

"Cahoots? I don't think people use that word anymore. Someone's leaving." Juliette flicked off their headlights.

The door opened and Leonard came out, carrying a sheaf of papers rolled up with a rubber band. He clomped to the van, wrenched open the door, and heaved himself inside. It was too dark to read his expression or see anyone in the florist shop. He drove away, and a moment later the "Open" sign flipped to "Closed."

"Could you tell if he was limping?" Trinidad asked.

"He's not grace on skates. Hard to tell if he was limping or lurching. What do you think those papers were?"

"I'm not sure." Her thoughts churned. "I'll make some excuse to visit Iris tomorrow and see what I can find out."

"What reason are you going to give for that?"

Her mental to-do list clamored. "I'll think of something."

"You always do." Juliette turned on the headlights. "Time to keep our appointment with Papa's chicken and rice. Do you think there will be dessert?"

"If you're in the mood for gingerbread ice cream. We had to do something with all the prototype batches so we jammed a bunch in our freezer. It would help for someone to eat it."

"I am honored to serve," Juliette said, doffing her imaginary hat. "You know, considering Leonard was at the Purple

Iris after hours, maybe there's something to that cahoots idea after all."

If Papa's friend was involved in a murder, Trinidad intended to find out.

———

By the time Friday morning rolled around, Trinidad had her mission nailed down. On her way into town, she'd scoot to the flower shop and ask if Iris might be able to give her access to Oscar's house to borrow some supplies for Scooter. While there, she could get the lay of the land, casually mention she'd seen Leonard, and hope Iris would let something slip.

Genius, she thought, pleased with her sleuthing plans until she considered how much time it would take. The party was a little more than twenty-four hours away, and there was a ton of remaining tasks to complete. Hurrying into the kitchen, she found Papa reading the newspaper. Scooter walked up and down Noodles's back as the latter munched his kibble. Clearly, Scooter had managed his nocturnal escape again. Their mixed species companionship was growing less worrying; as long as Scooter curtailed his explorations to Noodles's mat, the nighttime poop indiscretions were easily washed away. If it were up to Noodles, the bird would probably never go back to his cage, but Trinidad's lifestyle didn't support free-range parrots. If she had more time, she'd set up a camera and find out if it was bird or beast responsible for opening the latch of Scooter's cage. She suspected Noodles was "helping" as he saw fit.

Juliette phoned while Trinidad and Papa were en route to the store with the animals. "I'll be by later with our outfits. You're going to love them."

"As long as they're comfortable."

"Fashion first, then comfort."

On that ominous note, Trinidad made a quick stop at the Shimmy to deposit Papa and her animal charges. "I've got to go to Iris's shop to ask her about Oscar's pet supplies." She felt a ping of guilt at her sneakier mission to prod Papa's friend for info.

"Ah," Papa said. "Good idea. I phoned her last night to check on her well-being. It didn't occur to me to ask her about supplies."

"Was she okay?" Trinidad prodded. "When you called her?"

"Tired from a long day. She said she had a great deal on her mind."

Like Leonard's after-hours visit? Trinidad wanted to delve deeper, to find out exactly how things stood between Papa and Iris, but she could not figure out a way to ask. She scribbled a quick to-do list on the Shimmy's whiteboard, which included a set of tasks for the twins when they arrived for their after-school shift. Since business was limited, there wasn't much foot traffic, and she and Papa were handling most of the party prep, so they'd have time to tackle an extra task.

She intended to put Carlos and Diego to work designing a flyer for the cocoa bomb workshop she'd scheduled to launch on Monday. After a practice session with Felice, she'd be all set to roll it out after the party on the steamboat. She planned to ask if Renata might let her post a flyer at the steamboat's check-in desk. Nothing to be lost by inquiring, and she'd likely garnered some goodwill helping with Harry at the hospital.

She added "Ask R. about flyers" to the list.

Rather than call Bonnie, if time allowed, she'd stop by. Maybe Bonnie might open up about what was on her mind. Another strange tempest brewing in Sprocket.

All I want is what's best for Fee. There had been such a depth of worry and sadness in that statement. But Bonnie had been doing a spectacular job in the mothering department since she and Gabe split up, so why all of a sudden had she decided marriage to her ex was the answer? Getting rehitched to Gabe could only be the short road to disaster, and Bonnie should jolly well know it.

When the whiteboard was full, Trinidad capped the pen and headed out. A brisk winter walk would be good for her, but she felt the minutes flying away like snowflakes. And wasn't that a new scattering of flurries on her windshield as she cranked up the car?

She gripped the wheel. "Go ahead, winter. Bring it on. I'm ready."

Flush with determination, she drove to the Purple Iris and walked in. The indescribable aroma of flowers, spicy mums, lush roses, and tiny baby carnations cocooned her. The interior of the shop was decorated in country vintage, with wooden wheeled carts holding potted plants and an old chicken coop displaying several prepared holiday bouquets. The whole shop was a wonderland, every corner artfully adorned. Trinidad wanted to gather the nearest armful of poinsettias and make the Shimmy just as festive. One glorious pink poinsettia specimen caught her eye immediately. It would be the perfect holiday touch at her ice cream shop.

Iris was not at her desk, a distressed potting bench with a sleek computer on the top. A ceramic iris held a selection of pencils and business cards. Everything was neat, precise, ordered, yet imaginatively arranged to the most minute detail. Trinidad could see that Iris and Papa had many traits in common.

Trinidad dinged the heavy bronze bell next to the pencils.

Iris hurried out, purple glasses halfway down her nose. She clutched a mug of coffee, startled. "Oh. Hi, Trinidad. I didn't hear you come in. I was cutting foam."

"Prepping for tomorrow?"

Iris nodded.

"Me too. A ton to do, right?"

"Yes."

Nervously, Trinidad fingered a petal of the pink poinsettia. "The party is going to be the bash of the season. I'm so excited to be catering. Leonard must be busy too." She rushed on. "I was driving by and I saw his van here last night."

"He's got all kinds of plans." Was that a tone of annoyance? Trinidad waited, but Iris did not elaborate. The silence grew between them. *Like what?* she burned to ask. *What plans?*

Iris skewered her with a look. "Not to be at all rude, Trinidad, but I'm beyond busy today. Was there something you needed?"

Trinidad trotted out her prepared story. "I wondered if there were some bird supplies at Oscar's lying around that I could have for Scooter." She reached for the poinsettia. "And I want to buy this."

Iris nodded. "Okay. I'm sorry I couldn't help with the parrot. Oscar loved that bird more than anything." She snagged a key from a hook. "Here's the key to his house. The police have released it to me. Come to find out, he deeded me the property." She didn't quite meet Trinidad's eye. "Why don't you go over and help yourself?"

"Oh, I don't know…" Trinidad started.

"I don't have time to go look for you," Iris said sharply. "If you want the supplies, you are welcome to go get them and return the key by closing since I'm having the carpets cleaned tomorrow. Okay?"

"Carpets cleaned? Are you going to move into Oscar's house?" Trinidad blurted, feeling her snooping window slowly closing.

Now Iris did look offended. "I only just heard that Oscar left me his place, and I haven't made any final decisions yet. I really need to get back to work."

This errand was not turning out at all the way Trinidad had planned. Did she have the time herself to go poking through Oscar's house? But maybe she'd see some sort of clue that might shed some light on who might have wanted him dead. Iris stood there, the key in her outstretched fingers waiting.

"I, uh, thank you. I'll pop over later and return the key and purchase the poinsettia."

"Okay. See you then. Tell Papa I said hello."

"I will. He's concerned about you with Oscar's death and all."

Iris did crack a smile then. "He's a very kind man, the kindest I've ever met."

And what did that mean? Was Iris having romantic feelings about her grandfather? Did Papa feel the same?

When Trinidad took the key, Iris vanished into her back room. End of snooping mission. What had she learned? Nothing about Leonard's visit. Nothing concrete about Iris's intentions for Oscar's property. Only a hint that Iris had fond feelings for Papa Luis.

The keys felt unusually cold in her palm as she left the Purple Iris. She knew she should go directly to Oscar's place since the rest of the day would be chock-full. It was now or never, but she felt all shivery at the prospect.

The text on her phone made her smile.

Hey, super scooper. On my way to deliver your order of hazelnuts. Got time for a coffee?

If we take it to-go, she texted back. I've got another idea that might surprise you. Meet you at the coffee shop for a quick outing?

How could I resist? Be there in fifteen.

Quinn wouldn't mind accompanying her, especially when she reassured him this sleuthing trip was all about who killed Oscar Fuentes. Though Quinn would be happy to see Gabe go down for the crime, he wouldn't want to see an innocent man convicted.

If Gabe truly *was* innocent.

Chapter Nine

QUINN USED THE WIPERS TO swoosh away the falling snow as they aimed his truck toward the hilly road. They'd just left Logan's Nut Farm to drop off Doug. He was not a fan of the unfamiliar, and he'd had to adapt to plenty of recent changes with his estranged mother landing back in his life.

"How are things going for you and Doug?"

Quinn shrugged. "Day to day. Mom's been respectful about not rushing things, but Doug takes a long time to adjust to, well, anything. Took me three months to change our cereal to the bargain brand. He'll be glad to tinker with the sorting machine for a while since she called this morning."

"Decompressing?"

"Yeah. He's been reading a book about parrots. I think he likes Scooter…from a distance."

"Noodles likes him up close and personal." She told him about the bond between bird and dog.

"Love is a splendid furred and feathered thing." He laughed as he took her hand and kissed her knuckle.

She warmed and went all fizzy and giggly inside. So silly, but she could not stop herself. Quinn was such a good man, gold through and through, unlike her first husband.

Bonnie's strange comment came back to her. *Gabe has been a good parent too, the best he could.* Her defense of Gabe was unsettling. Trinidad wasn't going to allow Quinn and Gabe to occupy her head at the same time. She breathed out, taking in the beauty of the wooded road that led to Big Egg. The twisty road allowed them to peer down into the valley below. Something in the trees caught her eye as their truck tackled the slope toward the lakes. "Hey. I see activity."

He stopped and they peered through the tangled canopy spreading out below them. "I don't see anything except the judge's house." Judge Torpine had left Sprocket after a series of tragedies came to light in the spring. The vacant home was a sad reminder of what had transpired.

"That's what I mean." She turned his chin to the right spot. "The lights are on. It's a rental now until it can be sold."

He squinted. Quinn more than likely needed glasses, which he was too vain to consider. "Oh yeah. I heard Candy was acting as the property manager to rent it out but I didn't know she'd scrounged up any tenants."

Candy Simon, the go-getting Realtor, had been trying to sell the judge's luxury home since he'd moved away, but luxury home buyers in Sprocket were sparse. She'd switched gears, hopping into the Airbnb arena. Still though, there weren't as many entertainment opportunities in Sprocket as in nearby Joseph.

"Do you mind if we take a quick detour?"

He cocked his chin at her. "So you can spy on the renters?"

"Not spy exactly. Just curious is all."

Quinn was silent a moment. "And we are interested why?"

She smoothed her palm over her knee. "Well, you know, because…"

"Because Gabe has put the idea in your head that someone else is responsible for killing Oscar and you're determined to keep tabs on any and all visitors to our fine village?"

He had both hands on the wheel now, and there was a strained quality to his voice over the idling engine.

"Quinn, I am asking questions on Gabe's behalf. That doesn't mean he's taking up space in my life again."

"I think it does."

She exhaled. "Like it or not, Gabe is Felice's father, and he's marrying Bonnie."

He rolled his eyes. "Why in tarnation would she marry that guy again?"

"Juliette and I have been trying to figure that out, but so far, it's a mystery. For some reason, Bonnie wants them to be a family again, his character aside. If there's something I can do to keep Gabe out of jail, I need to do it. For them."

"Even if he deserves to be in jail?" Quinn snapped. "What about that, Trinidad? If Gabe ran a man down even accidentally, he should be arrested for manslaughter. That's justice. He shouldn't get a pass because he's a father." He sighed. "But deep down, you don't think he did it, do you?"

Did she? She hesitated. "There are strange things about the case. Harry says he got out of the car well before the crash. Odd. There were tire tracks indicating Gabe's car stopped and someone got out and back in before it veered into the creek. Scooter survived, which tells me Oscar fell on his back, so Scooter must have wriggled out, but when Stan and I saw Oscar, he was on his stomach. He had to have been repositioned."

"Wouldn't need to turn him over to check a pulse on the wrist or neck. Why roll him over?"

She considered. Quinn had a permanent worn spot in the back pocket of all his jeans. "Wallet," she said, straightening. "Someone turned him over and pulled out his wallet."

"To rob him?"

"I don't know. I'll ask." She whipped out her phone and dialed the police station. The desk clerk put her through to Chang. She put it on speaker so Quinn could hear.

"Hello, Trinidad," Chang said warily. "What can I do for you?"

"Quick question. I wondered if Oscar's wallet was found with his body."

"Oh, well, you know, I'm not supposed to discuss the case with anyone *even* if there are bribes involved."

"Have you been bribed?"

He sighed again. "Chief offered to babysit the kids if I'd give her an update, and man, you have no idea how tempting that offer was. Anyway, I can't tell you any particulars, but I guess it won't hurt since it's in the report, which I told the chief when she asked. Yes, his wallet was found next to him with forty-three dollars inside. Theft clearly wasn't the motive. Credit card and ATM intact there as well as ID."

"Hmm," she said. "And robbery would be impractical anyway. Why would someone target a pedestrian on their way up a hiking trail? Not likely they'd be carrying much money."

"That's what I thought. I considered maybe it was a cyberstalker. I mean, Oscar had a following for his bird photos and such, but there have been no threatening comments to his posts."

"Why kill a bird-watcher?"

"I get stuck on that part too. The theory that makes the most sense is that Gabe ran Oscar down accidentally. Maybe he fell asleep at the wheel, and then after he checked the body, he panicked and drove into the creek. Harry said he was driving like a fiend, which was why he got out and decided to walk."

"But Harry…"

"Is also a suspect, I know. I'm not a rookie, am I?" Chang sounded peevish. Perhaps the pressure of handling the case was getting to the exhausted father of four. "And why was Gabe driving that circuitous route in the first place? Not a real nature lover and he could care less about bird-watching."

"My thoughts too."

"It's all under investigation, which is a fancy way of saying I've inherited a case that sucks up all my time and makes me come in early and stay late and miss meals. My wife always said I should have gone into her father's shoe repair business, and I'm beginning to agree with her. Oh, hey. I gotta go. Mrs. Mavis just brought in her famous pecan coffee cake. I can smell it through the door, and if I don't get a piece now, it'll be gone. Talk to you later."

She said goodbye.

"I can't see Oscar having a cyberstalker," Quinn said dubiously.

"Makes about as much sense as a theft."

"He posted bird pictures. Not like his page was a hotbed of intrigue."

"Look." Trinidad pointed as a car pulled up to the rental house. It was a sleek Mercedes. A man got out, tall, broad shouldered, a tattoo encircling his neck. He wore wrap-around sunglasses.

"He looks just like…"

"Cordell," Trinidad said through her teeth. "Must be his brother."

"Every bit as big as Cordell. I read something about his brother Reg managing his career."

Did he manage Cordell's revenge plots too? Trinidad watched as Reg opened the front door and called to someone inside. A female voice answered, and Trinidad caught a quick glimpse of a short woman in black, her hair pinned into an ornate knot on the back of her head. The door closed with a bang.

Trinidad sniffed the air. Then sniffed again.

The aroma made her mouth water.

"That smells so good. French fries?" Quinn said.

"No." Trinidad's gut tightened. "It's fried chicken. I think I know who the woman inside is."

Quinn's eyebrows shot up. "Uh-oh. That's not…"

"Cordell's mother, Queenie," she said. "She hates Gabe for stealing from her, and she blames him for the end of her fried chicken empire dreams. Now she's here in Sprocket."

A smile spread over Quinn's face. "This is about to get real interesting."

———————

Trinidad put thoughts of Queenie out of her mind as she unlocked the door of Oscar's cottage. She was feeling slightly sick from the twisting, turning road they'd taken, or maybe from clapping eyes on Cordell's kin. The front of the structure was landscaped with neat clusters of shrubs that collected the flakes of snow in icy stencils. The yard pitched down in a rocky slope that eventually butted into a sandy crescent, the shore of Big Egg. They took a moment to admire the view, the air crisp and cold. On the far shore, the Sprocket Steamboat blossomed white against the blue water. There were no other structures visible to infringe on the picturesque scene.

"I can see how this land would be valuable for Leonard," Quinn said. "Perfect deepwater spot for another dock and the only section of shore big enough to accommodate the steamboat. He really could build his empire, as Renata puts it."

Unless Oscar refused to sell? "I get the sense Renata thinks her brother is a couple of scoops short of a sundae."

"They probably say that about all visionaries."

People might even say that about Trinidad. She eased the door open and they entered. A planked floor extended into a cozy family room with a worn armchair that gave her a pang when she pictured Oscar sitting there. On the table next to it was a perch where she imagined Scooter admiring the view or preening on Oscar's shoulder as they watched TV together. There was a canister of peanuts nearby, in their shells for Scooter, and a can of the honey-roasted variety that she presumed was for Oscar. Bird magazines were piled into a tidy stack on the floor next to the recliner.

"It's weird being here, isn't it?" She blinked back tears.

Quinn nodded and pulled her in for a squeeze. "Sure is. Like we're violating Oscar's privacy, even though he's no longer with us."

She was grateful he hadn't said "dead." Quinn was sensitive and she loved him for it.

"Iris said she thought there might be parrot treats in the pantry cupboard." They entered the modern kitchen, complete with a trash compactor and wine chiller. On the table was a spiral-bound notebook and two mechanical pencils. She began opening cupboards.

"Here's the one with the bird supplies." Quinn pulled out a box of colorful toys and a pile of newspapers as well as a bag dated and labeled "Freeze-dried fruit and veg."

"Looks like carrots, peas, banana chips, and corn. Oscar sure took good care of Scooter. Bird eats better than me and Doug."

"He was organized too. I can barely remember to give Noodles his monthly flea medicine." She wandered to the neat bulletin board in a small nook above the tile counter. Tacked there was a photo of Iris standing next to a sour-looking man in a brown sweater. "Must be her deceased husband."

Quinn looked over her shoulder. "Neither of them are brimming with joy."

"I understand it wasn't a happy marriage. Oscar introduced them. Iris said he tried to make it up to her by helping
her get a florist business started in Sprocket after she was
widowed."

Quinn rested his chin on Trinidad's shoulder. "Um, not
to be a gossip or anything, but I've seen Papa chatting with
Iris a few times."

She turned quickly. "You have? Where?"

"Once in town. Once at the greenhouse. He showed her
around. She was impressed with his vanilla production."

She chewed her lip. "Did they seem...you know, fond of
each other to you?"

"Your grandpa is fond of everyone except Gabe."

"Yes, but...I mean..."

"Romantically fond?"

She nodded.

"I dunno. Would that be a bad thing if they were?"

Would it? No, she wanted to say. Papa had been widowed for thirty years. Why shouldn't he find a lovely plant
aficionado to share some time with? But the other half of her
brain shouted the biggest objection she could think of. "Iris
benefitted greatly when Oscar died."

Quinn frowned. "Just because she inherited this piece of
land doesn't mean she was involved in killing him for it."

"Right. Iris is probably a perfectly nice woman. Of course,
she doesn't like birds. And Leonard was visiting her after
hours. And she's definitely ruthlessly committed to seeing
her shop succeed."

"So are you," he teased. "If I didn't come in for ice cream

sometimes, I might never see you." He patted his stomach. "Gonna put on a spare tire just trying to see my girl."

She laughed. Quinn had a way of making her worries melt away like ice cream on a sizzling summer day.

"Maybe we could build a place like this someday."

We? Her heart thunked. "I'd be happy with a home where it wasn't small enough to start the coffee machine from the master bathroom." *Or anyplace you are*, she wanted to add.

"Are those our nuts?" He disappointed her by moving away and picking up a canister of hazelnuts. "Humph. Not from our farm. Imagine living in Sprocket and not buying hazelnuts from Logan's."

She couldn't conceive of it any more than a tourist buying ice cream from the grocery story instead of the Shimmy. Unfurling a paper bag, she loaded up some of the supplies for Scooter. Her gaze drifted back to the photo and then to the neatly printed paper underneath. She read off the list. "December 1 common goldeneye. December 8 snow buntings. December 15 tree sparrows. I recognize some of these species names. Juliette said she saw Oscar's Instagram post about the yellow-breasted chat the day he was killed. This must be a record of the birds he'd posted on his page and when."

"Always on a Wednesday at the same time." Quinn shook his head. "Like clockwork."

"Yeah," she said thoughtfully. "Like clockwork."

"What's on your mind?"

"Do you find it funny that Gabe woke up from the accident wondering about a yellow-breasted chat?"

"I wouldn't be surprised at anything oddball that came out of Gabe's mouth, but yeah, that's mighty strange since that was the bird Oscar posted the day before he was murdered."

"Juliette showed me the post. He told his followers he was hoping to spot a chat. Could that be an indication that Gabe wasn't responsible? The killer might have been targeting Oscar. He knew where he'd be and when thanks to the social media posts."

Quinn looked at the dates and names. "Not just him. Leonard and Stan usually went with him. He called them the 'three birditos' in his hashtags. Anyone would know those guys did their bird-watching thing every Wednesday, rain or shine."

Trinidad mulled it over. "All right, so maybe someone was trying to kill Leonard or Stan and got Oscar instead." She hesitated. "But Leonard backed out due to a sprained ankle, and Stan had to help at the coffee shop."

A wall clock chimed ten thirty. "I've got to hurry back or we won't be ready for the party tomorrow. I forgot to tell you. I'll be there." He grinned.

"Really? That's fantastic. How'd you wrangle an invite?"

"Leonard was at the Full of Beans lamenting how to get a bunch of chairs from the storage closets on the upper decks to the dining room. I have a strong back and a big mouth. I offered to help," Quinn said.

"For free?"

"Course not. I work for every last nickel, but this time I bartered."

She raised a questioning eyebrow.

"You know how Doug's really curious about machinery."

"For sure." He'd sat on a quiet chair at the Shimmy many times watching Papa with the shake machine.

"He's dying to know about the paddle wheel on the Sprocket Steamboat, and Leonard is going to fire it up at the party. In exchange for the labor, Doug's getting a private viewing of the paddle wheel in action, and we're allowed to stay for the treats because he needs us to help with the tear-down too."

"Brilliant," Trinidad said.

"I'm to make myself scarce around the guests, but I'll be there to see you in action for your first ever catering gig."

She hugged him. "That makes me feel like a million bucks, as my dad used to say."

"You are worth a million bucks."

"Wish my bank account reflected that," she said with a sigh. "Gotta run."

"No rest for the weary." He scooped up the bags.

She spied a stack of newspapers in the recycle bin. Yep, she'd definitely require those to keep Scooter's cage clean. As she scooped up an armful, they slid in all directions, and she saw a Post-it note stuck crookedly to the remains of a legal envelope. It must have gotten mixed in with the other recycled papers. A message was scrawled on the sticky note.

All set on will amendment. Spoke to Iris and mailed her a copy as well. There was a date scrawled, Friday of the previous week.

No signature.

She stared at the note until Quinn joined her. "Will amendment?"

Trinidad nodded. "Probably naming Iris as a beneficiary or executor."

"Makes sense, I guess. He didn't have any children, so why not give his estate to Iris?"

"That's not what's bothering me. When we took Scooter to Iris, she said she didn't know how Oscar's estate was being disbursed. She said she'd only just found out when I talked to her before we came here."

"You think she lied?"

"I suspected because she said he'd talked to her about being Scooter's guardian. Now I know for certain she lied. She knew Oscar changed his will and she'd inherit."

As she looked back once more, perusing the bird schedule that Oscar had kept so meticulously, the pang hit her again. By all appearances, Oscar had been a simple man with a passion to share with the world and his own beloved pet.

She imagined the car plowing into him, how he might have tried to wrap his arms around Scooter to shield him. How he might have felt in the last moments of his life as the car that struck him drove away and left him to die alone. And now she knew for sure that his one and only relative, Iris, was a liar. What might she have done to hurry along her windfall?

If only you could tell us what you saw that day, Scooter, she mused as they left Oscar's place behind.

Chapter Ten

IRIS WAS BUSY WITH A customer when Trinidad returned the key, so she quietly slid it onto the counter and slunk away. The pink poinsettia would have to wait. She wasn't sure her morning mission had accomplished anything except to further her confusion. At least it cemented in her mind the fact that Oscar's land was indeed a plum for Iris or Leonard if he could convince her to sell.

At the Shimmy, Noodles clambered up on his arthritic legs and pulled open the door for her when he saw her coming. "Thank you, sweetie." She gave him an ear rub. He used her proximity to poke his nose into the bag of bird supplies. "Treats for the beaked, but how about a Chilly Dog for the canine?" She quickly fixed him a dog-safe mixture and presented it to him in a bowl. He gently grasped the bowl in his teeth and settled back on his mat next to Scooter. He didn't eat, merely wagged his tail in anticipation until she sprinkled some of the freeze-dried veggies through the bars of Scooter's cage. With his friend treated as well, Noodles set to work on his Chilly Dog. Trinidad gazed at her darling pet. If there ever was a model for how to love thy neighbor, it was Noodles.

Papa was deep in concentration as he used a piping bag to construct his fleet of gingerbread steamboats. "One hundred, to be safe."

"They look marvelous, Papa. You even got the paddle wheel just right."

He bowed. "Thank you. Iris said they were amazingly true to life."

"Oh. Did she stop by?"

"We had a quick café together since there was no one in the shop. She is troubled by some big decisions, she said." He added a swirl of frosting to the stern of the nearest boat.

"What big decisions?"

"What to do with Oscar's property, I gather, since the lawyer explained she has inherited it."

Trinidad didn't mention Iris had known full well about her inheritance.

Papa added a flourish to the stern. "Should she sell? Live there? Far from town but with much nicer amenities than her room above the shop."

"Sell to whom?"

He shoved his glasses up with the back of his hand. "She said there were several people who might be interested."

Several? "Did she mention names?"

"No," Papa said. "Just several."

Trinidad pondered that development as she prepared the base for the ice creams and started in on the last of the basketball cocoa bombs. Business was sluggish. Cold air gusted in through the door along with every patron to remind her that winter had truly arrived like an unwanted party guest. She'd installed a space heater in the animal corner so Noodles and Scooter would be toasty.

They worked on party preparations until six p.m. when Juliette breezed in carrying a box. "I'm here to transform you into a professional caterer."

Trinidad arched her brow. "That sounds painful."

Juliette pulled out plastic-wrapped garments. "Here you go. Black slacks for you, a white shirt with a black vest, and matching aprons. Oh, and the thing that makes it all come together." She held up a shiny pink bow tie.

"Beautiful, but awfully formal." When was the last time she'd been out of jeans and T-shirts? "Is yours the same?"

"It's a fancy event, Trinidad. We gotta look the part. And yes, mine is the same except for one thing." Juliette held a short black skirt up to her waist and grinned.

Trinidad folded her arms. "Are you by chance trying to catch the attention of a certain basketball star?"

"Me?" Juliette batted innocent eyelashes. "Now why would you say a thing like that?"

"Bonnie said he's dangerous, remember?"

Her smile was devilish. "That was before he went to the pros. Ancient history. Now he's merely a hunky athlete with dreamy chocolate eyes."

"And a strong desire to hurt Gabe."

"Everyone has that desire at one point or another." She took back the garments. "I'll give them a wash and iron. And by the way, Bonnie asked me to bring Felice over for the cocoa bomb trial. I'm going to get her now. We can whip up a test batch of those or whatever it is you're planning, but we'll stop and get a pizza because I'm starved. Be back soon."

"Perfect. And thank you, Juliette."

She bustled out. Trinidad worried as she worked on chopping the peppermints for the frozen hot cocoa ice cream topping. Juliette was intelligent, beautiful, and loyal, but her taste in men was suspect. Cordell Barrone wasn't kidding around about his hatred of Gabe. Why else would he threaten him in prison and happen to know the moment Gabe was released? But if he'd orchestrated the murder to frame Gabe, it was an extremely elaborate plan. He'd have to know that the birders would be on the mountain that day.

She stopped, knife frozen in the air... Which he easily could have discerned from Oscar's regular birding posts.

Still, Cordell would have to know the time Gabe would be departing for Sprocket to arrange for Harry to intercept him. And how could he be certain Gabe would stop for coffee at the diner on his way? A troubling thought hit her. Perhaps Harry had been following Gabe? He'd trailed him to his mother's and tracked him to the diner, pretending their meeting was a chance encounter.

Likely Gabe would stop at the diner, since he was fresh out of prison and Upper Sprocket was an eight-hour drive from their mother's place with few other businesses along the way. He would have to make a pit stop. Further, Gabe's addiction to coffee was not a secret either. Her mind pin-balled back to Cordell. If Cordell had hired a hit man, wouldn't it have been simpler just to have Harry murder Gabe instead of frame him?

But a frame job would mean the cops wouldn't be looking for a murderer for hire.

The one thing she could not wrestle with was the choice of Oscar as a victim. Cordell would have to have no regard for human life if he'd randomly picked an innocent old man to die in order to frame Gabe. No one could be that horrible, could they?

The peppermints coated her knife with sticky bits as she chopped. One sharp candy shard poked her finger.

The question was...exactly how bad was basketball's bad boy?

———

Trinidad massaged her aching lower back. Except for the last-minute details left for the following morning, everything was ready for the steamboat. Papa had gone home for the day and taken the reluctant Noodles.

Trinidad consoled Scooter through the bars of his cage. "You'll be fine here tonight by yourself, I promise. We'll be back bright and early tomorrow." She decided on a trial separation because lugging the cage home every night was a pain and it exposed Scooter to a chill. Would Oscar rather have had Scooter risk a chill or be left alone at night? She sighed. When had she become a bird guardian? Maybe Stan would come through and take Scooter to the Full of Beans.

She'd be buying a lot more coffee if that happened.

Trinidad plugged in the beat-up radio she'd snagged at the thrift store and found a classical music station.

"There, see? Some nice background ambiance instead of a quiet shop."

Scooter fluffed his downy gray chest. She thought he looked downcast.

"You're projecting," she grumbled to herself.

Chief Bigley strolled in, wiping her feet on the mat. She wore jeans and a sleek down jacket. "Starting to snow." She surveyed the counter lined with boxes of basketball cocoa bombs and gingerbread steamboats.

"Hi, Chief," Trinidad said. "Off duty today?"

"For the next week, as a matter of fact. Figured it was a good time since Chang is holding down the fort on the Gabe investigation."

"So you're getting in some R and R?" Trinidad said dubiously. "And you decided you needed some ice cream? I thought you were the yogurt and granola type."

"I am." Bigley jammed her hands into her pockets. "You busted me. I'm here to compare notes with you about Gabe's situation."

Trinidad shared the bird schedule she'd found at Oscar's house and the sticky note. She held it up in a plastic bag. "Thought you'd want to give it to Chang."

"Hmm. We've already contacted the lawyer but he was away doing some ice fishing so we didn't get the details. Looks like Iris lied in her police statement too. Claimed she was unaware she'd been named Oscar's heir. I'll get Chang to dig deeper."

"I still don't see how Gabe got roped into the whole thing. He didn't even know Oscar."

She gestured the chief into a chair at a pearly pink table and shared her suspicion of Cordell.

"Risky for a pro sports star to murder an innocent guy just to frame Gabe."

"What do you think happened in that car?"

The chief drummed her fingers on the table. "It's a working theory, but imagine Harry Fortesque is in the passenger seat of Gabe's car. He knows from Oscar's Instagram that he will be there. As they approach Twisted Pine Overlook, Harry slams Gabe's head into the window or hits him from behind or whatever and takes over the wheel. He drives the car into Oscar. Gets out to check the body, looks at the wallet. Returns to the car, continues on past the trees and sends it into the creek, hoping to kill Gabe and pin the whole thing on him."

"Were Harry's prints on the steering wheel?"

"The car is a hot mess of prints since my mom loans it out to everyone in her neighborhood. Nothing definitive so far."

"But it's the *why* that I can't understand. *Why* would Harry kill Oscar? Are they connected?"

"The only connection I can find is that Harry, Leonard, and Renata all went to Wildcat High together, but so did half of this town. All three maintain they never interacted much in school. Harry was into 4-H and Leonard was a jock. There was only one shop class they both took at the same time. Renata was into the student government. They had a biology class together I think, but it was a big school, so more than forty kids in that particular class. After graduation, they seemed to have no interaction except possibly at the last reunion. Renata looked on a Wildcat High School bulletin board and found Harry's business card. He has a DUI arrest from years back but nothing else of note. He's drifted from job to job, not much in the way of carpentry. He's billing himself as sort of a handyman, which is why Renata hired him."

"Not a very good one."

Bigley's gaze sharpened. "What do you mean?"

"His hands are soft, not the hands of a workman. And he is somewhat klutzy. He had to go to the ER for a head wound."

"Interesting." Bigley thought it over. "Then there's the Cordell angle."

Trinidad watched a sprinkle of snow coat her front window. "Chief, aren't you risking your career with all this snooping when you're supposed to steer clear of the investigation?"

"He's my brother."

"Not to be rude, but he's also a train wreck."

Bigley shook her head. "Yeah, but you don't get to pick and choose your siblings. Friends, you get a choice. Gabe's my brother, and I don't believe he ran down Oscar in cold blood and drove off, accident or not. I'm going to prove that one way or another."

"Where's Gabe now?"

"At Bonnie's. He thought it was bad for my career for him to stay with me."

"I thought there was no room at Bonnie's."

"She's found a corner, I guess. Not happy about it with Cordell sniffing around, but they've got a wedding to plan and all." Her eyes narrowed. "About that. I've seen Gabe in love plenty of times. He turns into one of those cartoon characters with hearts in their eyes. This time…" She pointed to her own irises. "No hearts."

Trinidad perked up. "You think they're not in love?"

"I think Gabe's not in love and Bonnie's about as excited for this wedding as a colonoscopy. You?"

Trinidad hesitated, worried about being disloyal. "I agree with your assessment, but what could that possibly have to do with what happened to Gabe and Oscar?"

"Nothing outwardly, but it was the reason Gabe came to town, he told me. Otherwise he could have stayed with our mother. Bonnie and Gabe aren't telling us something, and I want to know what it is."

"You and me both. Will Gabe be arrested, do you think?"

"Hinges on the crime scene analysis and such, but I wouldn't be surprised if that's the outcome."

"Maybe he'll get lucky and they'll find Harry's prints on the wheel."

"My brother isn't the lucky type," Bigley said gloomily.

Felice and Juliette pushed in. A cloud of pizza scent made Trinidad's mouth water.

"Hey, gals. Thanks for helping me out, Fee. You're my guinea pig for these kid-friendly cocoa bombs."

Felice laughed. "It'll be fun to be a guinea pig." She hung up her coat and hurried over to see Scooter.

"That's the spirit." Trinidad glanced at the chief. "Would you like to stay and be a guinea pig too?"

Bigley hesitated. "Sure. Why not?"

Surprising, Trinidad thought as she fetched some paper plates and napkins. When the pizza was eaten, she handed out aprons to Juliette, Felice, and the chief. "Do you want to take off your cute hat, Fee?"

"No thank you," Felice said.

Felice was sure attached to her knit cap. While Juliette changed the shop sign to "Closed," Trinidad covered a table with butcher paper and Felice sprayed the mini muffin tins with oil. "I figured out a way people can make the bombs even if they don't have fancy silicone molds."

Juliette nodded. "Power to the people."

Chief Bigley helped Felice tie her apron, looping it twice around the child's narrow waist. "Maybe you can make some of these to give out at school for your birthday."

Felice lined up the muffin tins. "I have school at home. Mommy teaches me."

"Oh. Do you like it that way?" the chief asked.

"Yeah. The kids weren't very nice at school when I went."

Not nice? And that was *before* her father was accused of murder. Trinidad handed everyone a bowl of ganache. "Are you ready to stir?" They set to work, a sweet aroma filling the space.

"I asked Renata and she said you can bring all the flyers you want." Juliette helped Felice spoon the brown goo into the tiny tins. "She said Leonard doesn't like people handing out stuff, but she's in charge of the lobby and he should stick to his side of the boat."

"Excellent," Trinidad said. "I figure six kids should be enough to make a class worthwhile. If we get more, all the better."

Juliette caught a blob of chocolate before it dripped off the spoon. "Cordell had a few empty seats here and there, so Renata said he's being magnanimous and asked Mayor Hardwick to distribute twenty tickets to whomever she liked. Isn't that sweet? I love a man who isn't afraid to be generous."

Trinidad still wasn't at all sure that Cordell was the person Juliette imagined him to be. She reheated the chocolate when it solidified too much to work with. *Note to self, have a second batch on the double boiler to keep at the ready.*

"It's nice that your mom is getting married," Bigley said to Felice.

"Uh-huh."

"Did you know your dad was coming to town?"

"Yep. Mommy told me last week."

Trinidad shot Bigley a sharp look. Was that why the chief had stayed? To pump Felice for info? She inserted herself. "Here, Fee. Fill that compartment a little more, okay? You too, Chief. Yours is flimsy." *Like your excuse for being here.*

She had to admit, it was interesting to know that Bonnie had been aware for a week that Gabe was traveling to Sprocket and she hadn't mentioned it. Cordell knew, Bonnie, and who else?

After the muffin cups, Trinidad showed Felice how to spread white chocolate tinted red on a pan and make curls after it dried. "These are going to be the top of the bombs to make them pretty."

While the chocolate was still soft, she supplied an assortment of holiday sprinkles and flaked peppermint. "Now for the fun part."

Felice applied some pretty Christmas sprinkles as well as the chocolate curls for the right festive touch. While they set, Trinidad warmed up the milk. "Ready to pop them out?"

Felice and Juliette gently prized the hardened chocolate shapes from the molds.

"All right. Here's a mug for everyone. Drop your cocoa bomb in it, and get ready for the big moment. Use two if you want it extra chocolatey."

Felice watched in wonder as Trinidad poured the hot milk over her cocoa bomb, the white milk shimmering into brown bliss. "Maybe Mom and my daddy can have these at the wedding."

"If they want them, they'll have them," Trinidad said a little too loudly.

"I didn't even know Gabe and your mommy were getting married until a few days ago," the chief said. "And I thought I knew everything that happened in Sprocket."

"Daddy said they have to do it quick."

The chief handed Felice a spoon. "Do what?"

"Get married."

"Why quick?" Bigley said before Trinidad could waylay the conversation.

Felice sipped, giving herself a chocolate mustache. "To keep the secret."

"What secret?" Juliette and Bigley asked at the same time.

Fee was still staring into her cup, watching the sprinkles

swirl as she stirred. "I don't know what the secret is, but Mommy said they were running out of time."

She took another swallow of the rich beverage. "Being a guinea pig is great," she said, smiling.

Trinidad smiled back but she knew all three grown-ups were thinking the same thing.

Running out of time for what?

Chapter Eleven

"AROOOOOOOOOO," NOODLES YODELED SHORTLY AFTER ten o'clock.

"Noo," Trinidad called from the loft after she pulled off the earmuffs she'd been using to drown out the canine complaints. "I've gotta get some sleep. Please stop."

"It's no use," Papa said from below. "The pup is pining for his parrot."

The strangeness of that statement… "But…" she started, then stopped. There was no use explaining to Papa or the dog why it was a bad idea to lug the bird back and forth from the Shimmy each day. Heaving out a breath, she pulled on clothes and clomped down the ladder.

Papa was in his pajamas and robe, sitting in the small chair, reading his worn Bible with the aid of a book light. She wished she could be content with a mere five hours of sleep. They were on the cusp of their biggest ice cream endeavor ever, a make-or-break moment, and she could not catch a wink with Noodles lamenting.

"I have a suggestion," Papa said. "I will arrange for a travel cage from Telly. Much easier to transport and keep the bird from getting chilly."

"A travel cage sounds like a good short-term solution until we find a permanent home for Scooter, but for tonight, I can't listen to this racket until dawn. I'm going to go fetch the bird."

He closed the book. "I'll go with you."

Noodles was already up and wagging hopefully. She wanted to scold him, but honestly, that silvered muzzle and the apologetic lick he supplied dried up her complaints. She exhaled and scratched him under the chin. "All right. Let's go get your friend and maybe we can all salvage a few hours of shut-eye."

They climbed in the Subaru and drove south to Main. The businesses were dark, pools of meager light from the streetlamps catching the sparkling tinsel wreaths affixed to front windows. A trickle of snow was enough to make her turn on the wipers to clear the glass. Again she felt the thrill of panic. Winter. What if her shop failed?

Then you've failed.

And that was the crux of it. The Shimmy was a representation of how she'd reinvented her life and herself. It was the dream that filled the spot left by a ruined marriage and wrecked self-confidence.

If it dies, you'll find a new dream.

But the notion was so huge and overwhelming it left her too exhausted to think about.

At the Shimmy, the animal reunion was noisy and

adorable. Scooter greeted Noodles with an excited flap of his wings and a cooing sound. "Wowee!" he chortled, and Noodles replied with a yip. No language barrier here. She felt badly for separating the two friends. But honestly, didn't she have a business to run? A party to cater? How had she come to run an animal rescue operation?

Covering his cage to prevent a draft, she carried Scooter while Papa held the door and locked up behind them.

The warbling and coos filled the back seat as they drove. Noodles licked the bars by way of encouragement. At the intersection with Little Bit Road, she noticed a Corvette making a turn up the road.

She caught the "imagoat" license plate. Cigarette smoke drifted from the open window.

Trinidad slowed. "That's Cordell."

The car sped up, and without thinking it through, she turned after him.

Papa shot her a look. "We are in pursuit?"

"There's only one reason he's on this road."

To prove her point, Cordell stepped up his pace. Trinidad did the same, causing Papa to grab the side door handle. "Is this wise, Trina?"

Wise or not, she had to try and prevent whatever Cordell was planning. "Call Bonnie, Papa. Tell her to warn Gabe."

Papa dialed. "No answer."

She clamped her jaws together and stayed on Cordell's tail all the way up to the Station where he surprised her by stopping, engine idling, until he turned and drove in their direction. Palms clammy, she rolled down the window.

Cordell peered at her. His brother Reg looked around his shoulder, cigarette between his fingers. Was that a baseball bat across Reg's lap?

Gabe, please don't show yourself right now.

"Hi," she babbled. "I saw you driving. Wanted to make sure you got to your destination okay. It's a twisty road."

Cordell's eyes narrowed. "Does every visitor to Sprocket get a safety patrol?"

"Oh no. Just the special ones. You're a friend of Bonnie's. I called her, by the way, to let her know you were headed up here. She's busy right now, um, with wedding planning, so she said you should come back later."

His lids slitted. "Thanks."

Papa called through Trinidad's window. "A beautiful vehicle."

"Yeah, she's a gem." Cordell looked closer at Papa. "Didn't I see you out in a sweet Chevy yesterday?"

Papa beamed. "A Bel Air."

"Nothing better than an evening ride in a fine car, am I right?"

"Indeed you are."

She craned her neck. "I see you've got a bat there. Looking to practice? Did you know there's a batting cage in Joseph? It's about twenty minutes from here, but it's probably closed right now, at this late hour, when people usually aren't driving around."

Reg blew out a plume of smoke and leaned his thick wrist on the bat. "We don't need much practice."

Her nerves were hopping like rabbits. "Uh-huh. Well, if you change your mind…"

Cordell shook his head. "Nah. We're here to see the sights. Probably drive around some more. Heard Lingerlonger Road has some pretty extreme views."

"Lingerlonger is not completely safe at night if you're not familiar with the area. Lots of twists and hairpin turns. Mostly dark. Very dangerous, like I said."

He grinned. "I'm all in for a little danger. How about you, Reg?"

His brother nodded, face stone-cold serious.

Trinidad swallowed. Might as well be direct. "Mr. Barrone, you wouldn't happen to be driving up here with a baseball bat to inflict bodily harm on Gabe Bigley, would you?"

Cordell's face now matched his brother's. "Why not? He deserves it."

"He surely does," Papa piped up.

"Papa," she said, aghast.

Papa was unfazed. "Of course, vengeance is the Lord's and it would not be right to wish the Hooligan harm, but in terms of deserving, one has to admit…" Papa shrugged.

Cordell laughed. "I'm with you, sir. What Gabe deserves is a whole lot different from a cushy jail sentence and a return to his hometown." Cordell jerked his chin at Papa. "He cheated on Bonnie, Juliette, and your granddaughter. He stole from my mother too, you know. Took advantage of a senior citizen."

Papa tsk-tsked. "I am not surprised. This man…" He waved a disgusted hand.

"Not helping, Papa," Trinidad murmured. Scooter whistled.

Cordell looked in the back seat. "You got a bird back there?"

"Yes. He belonged to Oscar Fuentes." She tried to read his expression. Blank at first.

"The guy Gabe killed?"

"Allegedly," Trinidad said.

"Nothin' alleged about it when the car you're driving runs someone over. Too bad he didn't wreck his own wheels and off himself instead of an innocent guy." Cordell's mouth was a hard line.

Had that been the plan? Cordell hired Harry to kill Gabe but Oscar got in the way? "Did you know Oscar?"

"Never met him."

What about Harry? She was about to ask but Cordell thrust his chin at them.

"All right then. You folks have a good evening, huh?" He drove out of the parking lot and back down the road.

She let him pass and phoned the Station again. This time, Bonnie answered.

"So you think he was coming to threaten Gabe?" Bonnie said.

"Kind of late to pop by and visit his old college friend or see the sights."

She exhaled. "Cordell's never been worried about propriety. I'll warn Gabe. He's sleeping on an air mattress in the dining car since I don't have any empty rooms."

Bonnie's tension was palpable. "Bonnie…"

"I have to run, Trinidad. Thanks for the info."

Bonnie's dismissal stung. What secret was too big to

share with her and Juliette? She thought about Felice's remark earlier that evening.

Running out of time…

She felt the same. Instinct told her Cordell wasn't going to delay his quest to exact his own version of family justice. The party was looming ever closer. And the list of suspects was not growing any shorter: Leonard, Iris, Cordell, Harry, or some partnerships within that list.

Time seemed to be ticking away with more and more urgency.

Why did she have the feeling that something was about to explode?

—————

Trinidad hadn't realized how time had flown by until Juliette showed up at the Shimmy at 11:00. She was dressed in a chic sweatsuit, their catering garb on hangers draped over her shoulder.

Trinidad explained the nighttime errand and her encounter with Cordell.

Juliette huffed. "Since we didn't hear any sirens, I presume Cordell didn't get his hands on Gabe. No harm, no foul."

"You're taking this whole threat to Gabe pretty lightly. What happened to Miss Marple, ready to clear Gabe's name?"

"Miss Marple is still on the case, but she doesn't think Cordell had anything to do with Oscar's death." Juliette laughed. "And this Miss Marple happens to like Cordell. He's got a sensitive side that he tries to hide."

At the moment, Trinidad couldn't think of anything concrete to change Juliette's view of Cordell. Scooter was installed back in his shop cage, Noodles curled on his adjacent mat. She'd enlisted Papa to transport the animals home after Trinidad and Juliette left for the steamboat.

"Can you watch the shop for a minute? I want to ask Stan if he's made a decision about taking in Scooter at the Full of Beans."

"Noodles might die of unrequited love."

They looked over at the two companions, and Noodles wagged his tail as if he knew he was being discussed. Guilt squeezed her heart but she steeled her nerves. *You don't run an animal shelter.*

"I promise I'll take you every day to visit, Noo." She pulled off her apron. "Before I talk to Stan, I'm going to go by the Purple Iris and snag that poinsettia if Iris is in her shop. This place needs more Christmas cheer. I'll be back before the ice creams are finished churning."

"Promises, promises, but if you see Cordell at the coffee shop, tell him to stop over because I have a question to ask him."

"What question?"

"I dunno, but I'll think of something," Juliette said with a grin.

"How does Bonnie feel about you pursuing her college boyfriend?"

"Bonnie's made it clear she's going to hitch up with Gabe

again, so Cordell is on the market. She doesn't want him back anyway. It's Christmas time and Cordell's on vacation. What better timing to find the woman you can't live without?"

Resisting an eye roll, Trinidad pulled on her jacket and hustled across the street to the florist shop.

Pushing in, she found it empty. Sad too was the fact that there were no more pink poinsettia plants on the counter.

"Nuts," she muttered before spotting one in the alcove Iris had decorated to look like an elaborate woodland fairy garden. The niche was screened from the rest of the store by a cluster of white branches decorated with twinkle lights, and there, tucked into a nook, was a lush pink poinsettia. As she reached for her prize, she heard the back door open.

"Mr. Pinkerton," Iris said.

Trinidad froze.

"Call me Leonard."

She was about ready to step forth with her intended purchase when she caught Iris's distressed tone.

"Mr. Pinkerton," Iris repeated sharply. "I'm providing a service per our contract. I do not want to discuss selling my land to you, and I don't appreciate your cornering me in my shop."

Trinidad sucked in a silent breath.

"So it's *your* land now?" Leonard snapped. "You decided to keep it?"

"I haven't decided anything. I only just found out he'd deeded it to me."

Trinidad clung to her poinsettia basket, torn between

propriety, embarrassment, and burning curiosity. Through the glimmering branches, she saw Iris walk behind her counter, Leonard opposite, leaning on his hairy forearms. Was he favoring one ankle, or had the injury been faked? She couldn't tell.

"I'm only asking that you consider selling it to me," Leonard said. "I'll give you a fair price. I need that land."

"You made yourself clear on that point already."

"And I was Oscar's friend for years." Leonard leaned forward another inch.

"You made that clear too," Iris snapped. "Meaning that I am not entitled to the land but you are?"

"I didn't exactly say that, but yeah, when you put it that way... He'd talked about letting me buy it until your marriage busted up and he felt sorry for you." He paused. A sly tone crept into his voice. "That was a whole thing, right? What happened with you and the hubby?"

It was so quiet Trinidad was sure they could hear her shallow breaths.

Iris's face went brick hard. "Why don't you say what you mean, Mr. Pinkerton?"

"You know full well what I mean. Your husband was accused, but you were in on it, right? That's why the cops questioned you too. Heck of a thing, taking advantage of people's grief."

Trinidad saw Iris grow a few inches, stiffening as if she'd been slapped. "I had nothing to do with it. I didn't know he was using the information to rob people."

Rob people?

"Fortunately, he died before he went to trial, I heard. But still the scandal. That type of thing could ruin a person's business."

Robbery, scandal, death. She could hardly keep up.

"So you're threatening me?" Iris's voice quavered. "If I don't sell you the land, you'll smear my reputation in this town?"

"No threats." He shrugged. "Think about it. That's all."

"I won't be able to provide the flowers for your event tonight, Mr. Pinkerton. Find yourself another florist."

Leonard laughed. "Oh, I don't think so. If you welch on my event, I'll make sure everyone in Sprocket knows and your business will dry up in two shakes. Small towns don't forgive and they don't forget. See you for the party." He shuffled by, and Trinidad drew as far back into the foliage as she could, wondering how she was going to get out of the shop.

Should she crawl sheepishly from her lair and pretend like she hadn't overheard? But that would be ludicrous. Boldly step forth and admit she'd eavesdropped the entire dreadful conversation? Her problem was solved when Iris, lips pressed in an outraged line, whirled around and returned to the back room.

With a shaky breath, Trinidad put down the poinsettia and hurried out the door, wondering as she went.

What had actually happened between Iris and her husband?

And was Leonard really prepared to blackmail her into handing over Oscar's property?

There was one person who knew both Oscar and Leonard well. It was time to get herself a coffee pronto. Maybe even a double.

———————

Cordell was not patronizing the Full of Beans as Juliette had hoped when Trinidad entered, but inside she found a lovely photo of Oscar and Scooter on an easel next to a vase of white roses. It gave her a pang to see the two of them together. Murder or manslaughter had separated two loving creatures and ended the life of a sweet man. Was he killed because of his land? She was still digesting what she'd over-heard at the florist shop. Stan startled her by appearing at her elbow.

"Hello, Trinidad. That is a lovely photo, don't you think?"

"Yes, it is."

He sighed. "Since the…death, Leonard and I haven't made any more plans for bird-watching. It simply doesn't feel right without Oscar. I feel such guilt at having stood him up in view of what happened."

And Leonard had too. "I'm so sorry, Stan."

"Maybe I could have seen the car, pushed him out of the way."

"Don't blame yourself. Please. You might have been hurt too."

He nodded, absently wiping a nearby table free of invis-ible dust.

She looked around to be sure that nobody else was

listening in. The only patron was the Realtor Candy Simon, deep in a cell phone conversation at the corner table.

"Stan, did Oscar tell you what happened with Iris and her husband before she moved here?"

He looked surprised. "Well, um, yes. I don't like to gossip, though."

"I know." She lowered her voice. "But I think maybe Leonard might be using whatever happened to pressure Iris into selling him Oscar's land."

The disgust was evident on Stan's principled face. "I am shocked that Leonard would do that, yet I know he was pining for that property. Even tried to work out a deal with Oscar to lease it, but Oscar was a quiet man who didn't want crowds or tourists, and he didn't need the money Leonard offered. It became an awkward subject that we avoided during our birding adventures."

"And the Iris situation? Oscar must have shared with you both if Leonard was aware."

Stan coughed delicately. "Iris was married to Oscar's friend Albert. He felt bad that he'd introduced them because Albert was somewhat of a louse. He burned through all her savings and then turned to other ways to make money."

"What other ways?"

"Breaking into people's homes while they were attending a loved one's funeral. Terrible really. He completed a half dozen such thefts by the time he was arrested."

"And the police thought Iris might be involved too?"

He folded his cleaning cloth. "She had a part-time job at a florist shop delivering funeral arrangements among other things, so it was logical to assume she'd fed him the information, but she maintained he'd acted entirely on his own and Oscar believed her. Albert died of diabetic complications when he was under house arrest and awaiting trial."

She had to ask. "Did the police think she might have done something to cause his death?"

"That I don't know. She was not charged with any crime, as I said. After he was put to rest, Iris had to sell everything to pay legal costs and settle the debts he'd left her with. Oscar encouraged her to come to Sprocket and gave her money to start her shop."

Interesting. Oscar's death had certainly given Iris a leg up in the world. Might she have hired Harry to kill her cousin, and Gabe had gotten accidentally roped into the mess? Trinidad made a mental note to ask Bigley or Chang if they'd sniffed out any connections between Iris and Harry.

"By the way," Stan said, "I've spoken to Meg. She has agreed that we could take Scooter into the shop."

Trinidad's heart leapt and fell all in the same moment. "You don't look too happy about it."

"Ah. Part of the grieving, I expect. Scooter was Oscar's baby, and it will be a daily reminder."

She knew Noodles would experience his share of grief at losing Scooter too. It made her stomach go squirmy.

"Meg requested we wait a week to give Bob the cat a few days to adjust to being at our condo. Will that work for you?"

"Yes, Stan, thank you."

Feeling like a gossip herself, she texted the chief about Iris and her past in case she wasn't already privy. Papa would not approve, most likely, but if Iris had done what Leonard implied, Trinidad didn't want her grandfather nursing any fond feelings toward the woman.

But for now, she had to turn her attention to the Christmas party. Leonard might be a blackmailer, but until she knew for sure, he was simply the man signing her first catering paycheck.

Business owners on the brink could not be choosy about where they got their payment, she thought grimly as she hustled through the ice-cold air back to the warmth of her shop. Still, she felt wrong about it. Blackmailing Iris was one thing, but had Leonard had a part in Oscar's death?

Chapter Twelve

DECKED OUT IN THEIR SPIFFY catering duds, Trinidad and Juliette boarded the steamboat promptly at 2:00.

Renata was dressed for the occasion in black slacks and sweater with a red sequined trim and a scarf threaded with silver. "Welcome, dessert ladies. The tables are all set except for one that Quinn and Doug are lugging down from the third floor." Her phone pinged, and she glanced at the screen. "Leonard is asking where his dress pants are. Like I'm his wife instead of his sister. Maybe I should be on dating apps trying to fix him up instead of me."

That'd be a trick, Trinidad thought, considering the man was married to his steamboat. Not to mention the fact that he appeared to be the kind of guy who'd threaten to smear a woman's reputation to get what he wanted.

Trinidad wheeled the cart into the steamboat's tidy kitchen and set the gallons of gingerbread ice cream on the counter. If her timing was right, the rock-hard ice cream would be at scoopable temperature just in time for them to fill one hundred of the crystal dishes for Papa's Gingerbread Hill desserts and top them with the boats. She'd practiced with a small batch and a timer. All she needed was some teen muscle. With Juliette's help, they would dispense the frozen hot chocolate ice cream right at the buffet where she'd already set the supply and plenty of extra scoopers.

The hours passed in a blur of activity.

At four o'clock, the twins hurried in. "I am completely stoked that we are going to see the best basketball player of all time," Carlos said.

"He's not better than…" Diego started, but Trinidad forestalled the argument by handing them both aprons.

"You can argue later while you're scooping. For now, please carry the hot cocoa bombs to the tables and come right back."

They tied on the aprons, and she noted they'd followed directions by wearing black slacks and the shirts Juliette had ordered for them. The fancy dress orders hadn't extended as far as their feet, which were shod in bulky athletic shoes. Oh well. She didn't figure a pro athlete would make too much fuss about the boys wearing those. She and Juliette tagged along behind, pushing a rattling cart chock-full of teeny glass dessert plates and bowls.

The dining room was scented with pine from the fresh sprigs nestled in between fat white and red roses. Each table was covered with a shimmering silver tablecloth and a scattering of red glass ornaments to enhance the floral displays in the center. Easier on the budget, Trinidad thought, to cater a dessert-only party rather than a full dinner. Maybe Cordell wasn't such an extravagant spender after all.

She nodded to Iris, who was primping the flowers, snipping with a pair of small scissors from her pocket.

Trinidad waved. "All set?"

Iris didn't smile. "Yes. Mr. Pinkerton requested I stay on-site and collect the flowers and vases after the event. I'd rather not stick around but…" But like Trinidad, this was Iris's shot at establishing her business. Iris pulled a stack of business cards from her pocket. "Figured I'd put these somewhere."

"I'll set them up with my flyers at the check-in desk if you'd like."

Iris shrugged and handed them over. "Okay." She frowned as Quinn and Doug rolled in another table. "What's that for?"

Quinn shrugged. "Last-minute guest additions, I think Leonard said."

Iris grimaced. "I guess I'm not done with setup then." She stalked away.

Quinn and Doug erected the table before Quinn hurried over and kissed Trinidad. "For luck. Not that you need it. You look snappy." He straightened her bow tie.

"At least I'm wearing comfortable pants. Practical."

"Practical and fantastic," he whispered in her ear.

Juliette put out bowls of crushed peppermint and twirled. "I was aiming more for chic than practical with my skirt. How did I do?" Juliette didn't wait for Quinn's answer. "Let the games begin. I hear the guests arriving."

Renata ran into the dining room, heels clacking, and tossed a cloth to Trinidad. "Can you get this on that extra table quick? I hear Cordell's mother is a stickler for detail, and she's headed up the gangplank right now."

Trinidad poufed out the tablecloth while Iris hustled to provide another centerpiece. Herding the twins, Trinidad raced back to the kitchen to be sure they had enough additional bowls for the Gingerbread Hill desserts.

Diego scoffed. "You don't have to worry. I figured on a ten percent overage and ten extras to be on the ultrasafe side. We're good."

She let out a breath, pulled on rubber gloves, and slid a skewer into the ice cream. Slightly pliable. Progressing perfectly.

"Whaaa…?" she heard Diego say. Turning, she found Cordell and his brother Reg standing in the kitchen with a diminutive woman between them. She had a chic black hairdo, the feathery streak over her forehead dyed platinum. She wore a pantsuit in an elegant gray that matched her low heels. Her perfectly lipsticked mouth was set in a polite smile, but her black eyes were cold.

Diego stared at Cordell. "Are you…I mean…can I…?"

"Cordell the Crusher Barrone," Carlos breathed, immediately grabbing his cell phone for a photo.

Trinidad hastily stepped in front of them. "Hello, Cordell, Mrs. Barrone."

He smiled, resplendent in a supple leather jacket over what looked to be a silk shirt in the same creamy color as his pants. "Hey, all. This is my mother, Queenie. She wanted to see the kitchen."

Again the lipsticked smile. "I never eat anywhere unless

I see the kitchen first." Her voice was surprisingly strong for a woman no bigger than a minute. Then again, she was the head of a ferocious household, Trinidad knew.

Trinidad beamed her most welcoming smile at Queenie. "Happy to have you visit. The ice cream is still a bit hard, but would you like a taste?"

"No thank you," Queenie said. "I don't eat anything with milk."

The lactose-free guest. "No problem." Trinidad explained all about the gingerbread ice cream.

"I may try it later," Queenie said. "I brought my own dessert in case I don't care for what you're serving."

Reg held up a small cooler. "Dairy-free ice cream made by our cousin Shaya. She runs the best restaurant in San Francisco."

"It's all right if you like pretentious food. I was in the restaurant business myself actually." Queenie's face took on a glittering hardness. "But my plans were ruined."

Ruined by a certain crooked accountant. Did Queenie know that Trinidad was a former spouse of the man who'd stolen from her? Her throat went dry.

Carlos and Diego stood sputtering like two boiling teakettles while Reg led Queenie around to look inside the refrigerator and freezer. Trinidad was relieved she'd done a thorough cleaning before they'd moved in any supplies. Still, her breath hitched as Queenie poked her aquiline nose into every nook and cranny. Cordell approached the boys.

"You want a picture, don't you?"

"Well, if it's not too much trouble..." Diego started.

"Yes," Carlos said.

Cordell stood behind the boys, towering over them as Trinidad took the photo.

"Okay. Gonna get upstairs and meet my guests." Cordell winked. "Catch you at the dessert table."

Her normally verbose teen helpers were completely tongue-tied as Cordell rejoined his mother. Queenie didn't say a word, taking Reg's arm and gliding away.

Diego blinked. "Did we really just have an up close and personal with Cordell Barrone?"

And his mother? Trinidad thought. She figured they must have passed inspection because Queenie hadn't headed straight for the exit. Trinidad checked her watch. "It's four thirty, boys. Half hour until blast off."

They were both still dazed.

She handed them each a scoop and set a timer on Diego's cell phone. Juliette texted her.

Guests are arriving. You won't believe what Cordell's mom is like.

Oh yes, I would. Trinidad headed for the dining room. The chatter of voices greeted her as she crossed through the lobby. She'd not gotten to the threshold when she heard a groan.

Harry stood in a corner opposite the hostess check-in desk, holding Renata's wrist, but he was taking pains to keep his face turned from her.

"Don't worry. It'll be okay. I'll get help." He opened one

squinched-up eye. "Trinidad, Renata needs help." Still holding her hand, he lurched a step backward, knocking over a poinsettia in a decorative basket.

Renata yanked away. "It's a small cut, you big oaf."

"Are you okay?" Trinidad hurried over. "What happened?"

"Just a slit on my finger. All I need is a Band-Aid, and this guy is acting like a tourniquet is in order."

"Blood's a serious thing." Harry breathed hard out his nostrils and didn't look at Renata. "It's so…you know… leaky." His wide face paled.

Renata shoved him into a chair. "For goodness' sake, how do you do your job? A tiny drip of blood…"

Harry groaned. "Don't say drip. Please."

Renata heaved out a breath. "I don't have time to prop up a queasy carpenter. Trinidad, can you grab me a bandage from behind the desk? I don't want blood on my clothes."

Trinidad fetched one, unwrapped it, and fastened it over Renata's cut.

"Thanks. Crisis averted. I want to be sure that the extra table is set." Renata yanked a look at Harry. "You aren't going to pass out or anything, are you?"

Harry leaned his head against the varnished wood behind him. "No, ma'am." He dared a look at her and smiled. "But it's real nice of you to worry about me."

"Goofball," Renata muttered under her breath as she scooted by.

Trinidad wanted to follow Renata into the dining room but she wasn't totally sure Harry wouldn't topple over like a kid's block tower. "I'll get you a glass of water."

"Nah. I'm all right. Deep breaths will do the trick." He wiped a hand over his sweaty face. "Do you think she likes me?"

"Renata?"

"Yeah. She sounds annoyed with me and everything, but maybe deep down, right? I sure had the hots for her in high school." He rested his thick forearms on his thighs. "She went with Jeremy to the prom even though I could have told her she was his third choice." He paused. "So do you? Think she likes me?"

"I couldn't say. I've got to, um, go see if the milk is hot." If he was fit enough to entertain a love match, he probably wasn't going to faint.

"You know, 'cause I'll be leaving town soon in case I get some sort of encouragement from her to stay."

Don't hold your breath. But if the number one suspect on her list was leaving town…she might never get the chance to ask her questions. "Harry, before I go, did Gabe tell you anything about why he was taking the long way into Sprocket?"

"Dunno. Figured he wanted to do some bird-watching or something. That's what I told the cops."

"But Gabe doesn't know a thing about birds." She paused. "Do you?"

"Me?" He looked uncomfortable. "Naw, not really about the wild kind. I follow some people on Instagram, though, but I'd never get into bird-watching. I told you about my parakeet. His name was…"

"Pecky, yes, I remember. But bird-watching didn't take Gabe out of his way." She paused. "Unless you suggested the route for another reason."

He cocked his head. "Now why would I do that exactly?"

She felt a frisson of fear as he stood, dwarfing her. "I don't know, Harry."

He took a step forward, and she eased back.

"I told the cops what happened. I don't know why Gabe wanted to drive that way or why he'd run over a poor old guy, but he did and that's the truth."

Quinn strolled in, took one look at the two of them, and made it to her side in a flash. "How's it going, Harry?" There was steel in his green eyes.

"All right." Back to his relaxed self. "Did you find a home for that funny bird, Trinidad?"

"Uh, yes, I think I did." *Well, a coffee shop actually but who would quibble over that?*

"Nice to know," Harry said. "I'd better go see about unsticking that window Leonard asked me about."

He left, and Quinn slung an arm around her. "I don't like that guy, especially when he's standing too close to you."

She shivered. "I might have been prodding too much about the accident and he felt irritated."

"Or threatened." Quinn kissed her temple.

She wished she could stay there, nestled into the crook of his arm, but she was mindful of the steady stream of guests trickling in.

"I have to make myself scarce," Quinn said. "But I'll have eyes on you."

She accepted another kiss before he scuttled off, eager to get back into the noisy hum of the party. On her way, she took a moment to set the overturned poinsettia basket upright, shoving back in the ribbon and glass ornament Iris had no doubt inserted with care. In the dining room, Queenie was installed at the table, surrounded by a throng of people all wishing Cordell well and slapping him on the back.

Trinidad tidied a stack of napkins on the dessert table, and Juliette started laying out the bowls in neat rows.

"Well, hello," Trinidad said as Bonnie and Felice approached. They wore similar colors, both in pink, but Bonnie was in a pantsuit and Felice in an adorable holiday dress. She wore a different hat this time, complete with sparkling ribbon and a silk poinsettia.

"Hi, Auntie," Felice said. "Where's Noodles and Scooter?"

"They didn't get invited."

Felice frowned. "I woulda invited them."

Bonnie kept her hand on Felice's shoulder, rubbing nervously. "I know, honey, but it looks pretty fancy in here. Let's take a walk outside and see the lake."

But Cordell had already spotted her and loped over.

"Bon Bon." He bent to kiss her. "And Felice. You both look gorgeous. Come on over. I want you to meet some people, and then I'm going to give a toast and get the desserts going."

Bonnie shot them a desperate look, but there was nothing to be done. Juliette watched while Trinidad opened up the ice cream, straightened the pitchers of hot milk, and texted the boys to start scooping.

Juliette handed her a scoop and took one for herself. "Bonnie looks like she'd rather be anywhere but here."

Queenie was outright staring at Bonnie and Felice, posture perfect in her seat. Bonnie shifted from one large foot to the other as she stood awkwardly next to him.

Cordell finally rapped his knife on his water glass. "Thank you everyone for coming. It's a treat to be here in Sprocket to celebrate Christmas with you all. So let's pack down some desserts, huh?"

Not eloquent but effective. The twins rolled in the bowls of Gingerbread Hills with perfect aplomb as the guests oohed and aahed. They were a mixture of people Trinidad had never met and locals she suspected Mayor Hardwick had been instructed to invite to round out the guest list. En masse, they began to filter through the buffet. Trinidad was madly scooping up hot chocolate ice cream when Cordell sidled up next to her and spoke in her ear.

"I got a surprise for everyone at the end of the evening. Got extra cocoa bombs in case people get cold?"

Cold? "Are we going outside?"

He grinned. "Not telling."

"Okay, well sure." Trinidad immediately dispatched the twins to put on another pot of milk to simmer. They scurried off to complete the mission. Thank goodness she'd brought extra bombs. She waved Renata over as she worked her smiling way from table to table.

"Cordell has planned a surprise, and the guests will be going outside."

Renata blinked. "He has? What kind of surprise?"

"I have no idea, but he asked me to prep extra cocoa bombs in case people get cold."

"Huh." Her brows drew together. "It's one thing after the next, isn't it? I wonder if he filled Leonard in, but you'd think my brother would have told me."

Leonard was close to the elaborate staircase, nodding intently, sandwiched between the mayor and a guest. Trinidad wondered about the topic of conversation.

Trinidad and Juliette scooped frozen hot chocolate ice cream for the next forty-five minutes. They dispensed their bounty to everyone from Mayor Hardwick to the pizza lady Cordell had apparently ordered from multiple times during his stay. The guests were chatty, high spirited, breaking into boisterous jokes with Cordell. Queenie sat regally, smiling at those who came to her table. Trinidad noticed even the ambitious mayor took a moment to perch at Queenie's side.

"She never misses a chance to meet an important visitor, does she?" Juliette said.

"No, she doesn't," Trinidad agreed.

When the bulk of the people had moved from the frozen hot chocolate station down toward the Gingerbread Hills, she called the twins into action to bus the tables. Cordell hardly had time to finish his last spoonful before the boys were hovering around snatching up plates and balled napkins. She noted Diego sliding a phone from his pocket, and she hastily moved behind him. "We'll take it from here." She maneuvered him and his brother toward the lobby. "Please go make sure the extra milk is hot, and I'll text you when we're ready."

"Aww man," Diego said. "Can't I get one lousy photo?"

"You got your one lousy photo already."

"But I mean one with him like actually eating and talking?"

"It's called a candid shot," Carlos put in.

"It's called stalking," Trinidad corrected. "This is his party, and he didn't invite the paparazzi. Go on. Scoot."

Grumbling, they ambled down the hallway toward the galley. She waited to make sure they weren't circling around to regroup. On her return trip, something out the window caught her attention, a quick shadow of a familiar dark head. She blinked. Her eyes were tired, that was all. She moved close enough that her nose almost touched the glass.

"No. It couldn't be." She jogged out on deck where the cold air made her eyes tear up. The deck was silent from stern to bow, lit only by liquid pools from the ornate fixtures. There was no one there. She shook her head to clear it. Too much stress. Not enough sleep. There was no way she could have seen whom she'd imagined.

Gabe Bigley could not possibly be aboard the Sprocket Steamboat.

That would be a death wish, and even Gabe wasn't that nutty.

Still, her stomach did an uneasy flip as she returned to her duties.

"Where'd you go?" Juliette pulled on a clean pair of gloves.

"I thought I saw something out on the deck."

"Was it a what or a who?"

"Never mind." Trinidad scanned to make sure the room was readied for the cocoa bomb delivery.

Quinn and Doug had volunteered their services to

replace the banished twins. Juliette and Trinidad cleared the tables, and Doug, wearing rubber gloves, arranged the mugs in neat rows that Trinidad carried tray by tray to the guests.

When she put a mug in front of Queenie, the woman shook her head. "No thank you."

"I've got almond milk to offer you."

"I mean I don't care for anything else."

Trinidad noted Queenie hadn't touched any of their desserts. *Oh well. Can't please everyone.* When the mugs were distributed, Juliette dispensed the cocoa bombs with silver tongs, and Trinidad readied the pitchers of hot milk for the tables.

Bonnie offered one of her trademark smiles as Trinidad stopped at their table. Felice looked tiny in the chair next to her, especially with Leonard occupying the spot on her other side next to his sister. Trinidad wanted to ask Bonnie if Gabe was holing up at the Station, but she didn't want to ruin the moment.

"You didn't want to sit with Cordell, Bonnie?" Trinidad said.

"No. He asked but we're fine here."

Leonard rubbed at his chin irritably. "Would rather have had some dinner than all this froufrou sugary stuff." He caught sight of Iris standing at the window and beckoned her over. "Sit down, why don't you?"

Her mouth tightened into a thin line. "I'd rather not."

"The guests feel awkward when someone is hovering like that. Makes 'em think you're ready for them to go so you can clean up."

Which was probably exactly how Iris was feeling.

After a momentary hesitation, she slid into a seat. Harry appeared a few seconds later. "Hey, mind if I sit down? Looks like there's an empty spot." He didn't wait for an answer but assumed the chair next to Renata, gazing at her with puppy dog eyes. Trinidad wondered why Harry the carpenter was making himself at home at the party. Was he still sleeping on the boat? From Leonard's hard look, she figured he was wondering why Harry was there too.

Renata didn't seem to care one way or the other.

She pointed her bandaged finger to the glossy cocoa bomb on the tray. Since they'd been the last to the buffet line, they were not yet finished with the other offerings. Trinidad delivered a tray of cocoa bombs. "I'll deliver the milk so you can enjoy them when you're done with dessert."

"They look fantastic. Almost too pretty to eat." Renata laughed. "Almost, but not quite."

"Does the milk go first or the bomb?" Bonnie asked.

"You can do it either way, Mommy, but it works best to put the bomb in first. Auntie Trinidad showed me when we made 'em," Felice said. "This is gonna be fun."

Flourishing the tongs, Trinidad plopped a basketball hot cocoa bomb into each mug. "Don't pour the milk until you're ready."

"Everyone," Cordell boomed, standing at his table. "We should bomb the place together."

Awkward phrasing, she thought, scurrying to the next table. Once everyone had their bomb in the mug minus Queenie, the hot milk pitchers began to circulate, and there were exclamations from the guests as the delicate outer shells melted into chocolatey perfection. Food and entertainment rolled into one.

Nailed it, she thought with a huge swell of pride.

"They love them." Juliette grabbed her wrist. "We're a smash."

"Yes, we are." Trinidad's throat was thick with emotion. Quinn winked at her as he hefted a platter of dirty dishes to take to the galley. Doug, still wearing the gloves, gave her a thumbs-up, an unexpected display of feeling. She felt like pumping a victorious fist in the air. Instead she graciously accepted compliments with all the suavity of a seasoned catering professional.

The next half hour was a blur of bustling, bombs, and bussing of tables. From the corner of her eye, she noticed Felice hoisting the hot milk with her mother's help. She'd almost forgotten about imagining she'd seen Gabe on the deck. A draft bathed her face. Reg had wrestled open two of the old wooden windows to allow some cooling in the overheated room. *Luscious*, she thought as the winter breeze soothed her overheated cheeks.

She looked for Leonard to see what his reaction would be to his precious heat escaping into the night, but she did not spot him around the guests who'd started to mill around the room, many sipping from their mugs. She was checking the clock when there was an earsplitting crack.

The crack was followed by a scream that trailed off into a gurgling splash.

Chapter Thirteen

JULIETTE PUT DOWN A MUG with a clank. "Did you hear that?"

For a moment, Trinidad could not place the sound, but Quinn bounded out of the dining room, through the lobby, and onto the deck with Doug on his heels. Heart thundering, she put down her tray and ran after him.

That scream…the crack…almost like wood giving way…the splash. There could be only one explanation that fit. She was vaguely aware of other people jogging along behind her, but all she could think about was the way the scream had been swallowed up by an ominous gurgle. Someone had fallen into the lake. Who?

Puffing from the exertion, she skidded onto the deck, which was slick with tiny snowflakes. The lamps hardly dented the darkness. As her eyes adjusted, she saw a few neatly placed chairs. A long splinter of wood lay across one, but no sign of the screamer.

Frantically she scanned the slippery wood. Finding no

one there, she pressed herself to the railing and squinted over the side into the tarry depths. Quinn and Doug ran toward her from the other direction, coming to a halt at her side. Quinn's eyes shone wide in the darkness. "I can't see anyone. You?"

She shook her head, desperate to find out. If someone was in the water, they could be drowning even as she sat helplessly by. The lake water was frigid. Hypothermia wouldn't be too far off.

"There's a guy down there," a guest shouted.

Trinidad's head snapped back and forth. "Down where?"

"There." Doug's voice was so quiet probably only Quinn and Trinidad could have heard. He pointed urgently.

Trinidad strained to see. A blur of an arm, or was it a leg, broke the surface of the water and then vanished again. Before she could decide who it was or how to help, Quinn stripped off his coat, handed it to Doug, and dove in.

No! she wanted to scream. What if he hurt himself? Her precious Quinn? Goose bumps raced along her spine.

"Good grief." Juliette clutched Trinidad's elbow. "This is nuts. I called the police. Can you see whoever it is?"

The railing pressed into her stomach as she strained to see. One minute turned into two. Splashing and shouting echoed from the water. She finally battled back her stupor and ran to the life preserver attached to the wall of the boat. Doug helped her tug it free.

"Quinn!" She tossed it in.

Harry appeared at her shoulder, breathing hard. "Wait. Who is that down there?"

"I don't know."

He huffed out a breath. "I'd jump in and all, but I don't know how to swim."

There was more splashing, and she'd almost decided to jump in herself and help when Quinn swam into the pale circle of light, towing a familiar bedraggled man along with him.

Her brain simply would not believe what she was seeing.

Bonnie gripped Juliette by the shoulder, her long fingers like a vise. "Is that…?"

"Gabe," Trinidad confirmed.

"But…I mean, why?" Bonnie craned her neck upward. "Where did he fall from?"

Trinidad had been so caught up in the who she hadn't considered the where. She too peered upward into the gloom. The higher decks were also dim thanks to the insufficient lighting. Nonetheless, two levels above them on the Texas deck, three faces stared down at her.

Leonard's, bald head gleaming like a second moon against the dark sky.

Iris, expressionless, hands gripping the railing.

And Cordell, arms folded, watching with a look of calm on his face.

Or was it satisfaction?

———

A couple of sturdy guests hauled Gabe and Quinn from the water. They were both hustled inside, and Gabe was deposited on a chair in the lobby. Renata hustled up, carrying two striped towels.

"I cannot believe it." She draped one towel around Gabe's shoulders and handed another to the dripping Quinn. "What just happened? Why can't one single thing go to plan around here?"

Gabe shivered, wiping his forehead with a corner of the towel. "Describes the entire last decade of my life."

Trinidad hurried to Quinn's side. "Are you okay?"

"Fine." He swiped at his dripping chin. "Aquaman here doesn't weigh much."

"You." The word was fired like a cannonball, snagging the attention of the gathering spectators. Queenie elbowed her way past Harry and planted herself in front of Gabe. Cordell edged in behind her. "I was hoping you'd died in prison."

Cordell wrapped a long arm around his mother's spindly shoulders. "Me too, but he didn't. Never even served his full sentence."

"I, uh, hello, Queenie," Gabe said.

"That's Mrs. Barrone to you, wise guy," Cordell snarled.

Leonard pushed forward past Iris, who was watching the proceedings. He glowered down at Gabe. "Wait one red second. You aren't a party guest, are you? What are you doing on my boat?"

Renata shook her head, hand on her hip. "Nope, he's definitely not on the list."

"A stowaway." Carlos was recording the goings-on with his cell phone. When had the twins emerged from the galley? Probably when they heard the commotion like everyone else.

Diego shook his head. "I don't think the term stowaway applies. That describes someone making a journey without paying. This steamboat isn't actually going anywhere tonight, so I think party crasher would be a more appropriate term than stowaway." Diego ducked to avoid his brother's shoulder punch.

"Who cares, geek?"

"That's enough recording," Trinidad said. "Please put your phone away."

Carlos heaved out an aggravated breath but complied.

"Police are on their way," Juliette reported. Bonnie was next to her, gripping Felice's hand. The child wasn't tall enough to see over the people gathered in front of her.

"The party crasher was about to explain why he snuck aboard my boat." Leonard glowered. "And it better be good."

Gabe blinked. Water ran from his clothes onto the carpet. Renata brought more towels to put under his chair.

"I thought I'd kinda wander in," Gabe said, "you know, under the radar, and hang out for a while to, uh, apologize to one of your guests if I had the chance. I figured she'd probably use the ladies' room in the lobby at some point so if I kept watch on it from the deck, I could intercept."

Trinidad couldn't believe what she was hearing. Surely, Gabe hadn't been attempting to right his list of wrongs with such a foolish act. Trinidad could only watch the train wreck unfold.

"Apologize?" Leonard folded his arms across his belly. "To whom?"

Gabe squirmed. "Mrs. Barrone."

"Oh, Gabe." Bonnie let loose an enormous sigh. "You didn't."

"Me?" Queenie snorted. "You owe me a lot more than an apology, you worthless sack of skin. I spent thousands in court and missed out on a once-in-a-lifetime location for my second restaurant because of you. It was the perfect spot and you ruined my chance to get it. You thought waltzing into my son's party and saying you're sorry was going to make things go away?"

"No, but I thought it might make Cordell less inclined to want to kill me."

"It doesn't," Cordell said.

"Umm, along those lines." Trinidad cleared her throat. "How exactly did you fall into the water, Gabe?"

"I was keeping watch through the dining room window on the main deck, but I heard someone coming so I went up to the next level, but the footsteps continued so I kept going."

Leonard glowered. "Texas deck's off-limits. Didn't you see the sign?"

"Uh, yeah. I did. But I was only going to stay there until the coast was clear, so to speak."

Cordell loomed impossibly tall in the crowded space. "And you got some nerve crashing my party. The world's your oyster, isn't it?"

"No, I..." Gabe gulped. Bonnie scooted Felice close to Trinidad, pushed forward, and took Gabe's wet hand. He shot her a grateful look, but her expression was more stoic than sympathetic, Trinidad thought.

"No harm done, right? Just a broken railing?" Bonnie said.

"A broken railing that needs to be paid for." Leonard stabbed an index finger at Gabe. "By you, buddy boy. Now I gotta keep that ridiculous excuse for a carpenter on for another day."

Felice tipped her face to Trinidad. "Is Daddy in trouble?"

Trinidad patted Felice's shoulder. "Everything will work out, honey."

"How did you fall, Gabe?" Quinn's jaw was clamped tight with cold. "Can you explain that at least?"

"Like I said, I heard someone following me up the stairs so I kept going up. On the third deck, I ducked into the first open room I came to. It was dark, and while I was searching for a light switch, someone inside the room shoved me backward with such force it sent me flying out the door and crashing through the railing. It's a good thing I got propelled far out over the water or I might have broken my neck on the lower decks."

"I'd have paid money to see that," Queenie said. It was obvious where Cordell inherited his vindictive streak. Trinidad hoped Felice didn't understand the remark.

Leonard cocked an ear. "Cops are arriving. They'll straighten all this out."

"I'm sure the police are going to want to hear from everyone within arm's length of the accident." Trinidad cleared her throat. "Gabe has explained why he was on the third floor, but..." She hoped she wasn't going to lose her party payment. "Cordell, Leonard, and Iris, you were all up there too."

Leonard snorted. "Aside from the fact that it's my boat..."

"Our boat," Renata corrected.

Leonard did not seem to notice. "I can go anywhere I darn well please. I was fetching a new light bulb for the ladies' room. The one above the sink was burned out, and that's where we keep them in a storage closet on the third deck. I had to take it slow because my ankle is still wonky. I'd no more than cleared the top step when I heard the wood break and saw that guy going right through it. That's all I know."

Iris found her voice and held out a cardboard box. "The party was winding down so I figured I'd get a jump on the packing up. Leonard asked me to store my materials on the Texas deck, even though it was completely inconvenient."

"We got a dumbwaiter," Leonard said. "And there's no place on the main deck to pile up boxes. The second floor was refinished today so you can't walk on it. Sorry it was an inconvenience to you." His tone dripped with sarcasm.

Iris glared at him. "Anyway, I started up the stairs when I also heard a crash and shout."

Juliette had somehow managed to sidle next to Cordell, who slipped his arm around her. Trinidad focused on Iris. "Did you pass Leonard on the stairs?"

"No, but I was focused on my feet because the steps were slippery with ice."

Trinidad fixed her attention on Cordell. "Mr. Barrone, why would you be up on the third deck? I mean, with all your party guests downstairs enjoying the festivities?"

"Didn't know we had a Sherlock aboard. Are you wondering if I pushed Gabe over?" Cordell's smile was sly, the arm he had around Juliette loose and casual. "I would have loved to, but that's not how it happened. I wanted to be sure the surprise I'd planned was ready to go. Fireworks, launched from a guy I hired to row out into the middle of the lake. Red and green ones for Christmas. Phone reception around here is hit or miss so I didn't hear back when I texted him. Didn't want to trot everyone outside for nothing. Visibility isn't great from the lobby level. I figured I'd climb to the third deck and see if the boat guy was stationed in the water." He stared. "And who do I see sneaking up the stairs but this loser?" He cocked a chin at Gabe. "There was no way I was going to let him crash my party so I followed him. Got to the third floor and I was trying to figure out which room he'd hidden away inside when he came flying out of the stateroom and tumbled over the railing. I didn't push him. But if I'd had the opportunity, I would have." He shot a look at Bonnie. "Sorry, Bon Bon. Gotta tell it like it is." His gaze found Felice and quickly darted away.

Gabe sighed. "It was a dumb idea to come. I thought I could tell Queenie I was sorry and I'd pay her back over time, a payment plan or something, and Cordell wouldn't want to hurt me anymore. We could all get on with our lives."

"Wrong," Cordell said. "I still want to hurt you."

The explanations were whirling like a stand mixer. Three plausible stories to explain why Leonard, Iris, and Cordell were upstairs. There was also a shadowy staircase on the far end of the deck so someone else could have easily snuck away. More suspects?

And here was yet another near-death experience for Gabe. Had it been a plan to kill him? Unlikely. It would have had to be a spontaneous act since no one had known Gabe intended to crash the party.

Cordell certainly had a motive to hurt Gabe. He'd made no effort to disguise that fact. Another sinister thought wormed its way in. Was it possible that she was scooping from the wrong flavor entirely? Was Iris the target and the timing had been off? Did Leonard hate her that much for scoring him out of Oscar's place that he'd try to kill her when she went upstairs for the supplies?

Then again, perhaps Iris wasn't the quiet violet she appeared to be. Maybe she'd set up a trap to kill Leonard and keep him from slandering her name all over town. She could have tampered with the light bulb, knowing Leonard would need to fetch more from upstairs where she'd probably seen the supply of extras.

"Auntie." Felice tugged at her hand.

"Yes, sweetie?"

"Can I go back to the table? I didn't finish my cocoa yet."

She stroked Felice on the top of her pink hat. "Of course." She caught Doug's eye. He was standing well away from the group, monitoring his brother's condition in his silent way. She led Felice over. "Doug, would you mind walking Felice back to the dining room? She wants to finish her cocoa."

He nodded and held out his arm for her to take, since he eschewed skin-to-skin contact. Felice was accustomed to Doug's wishes and happily took his sleeve, chatting as they departed. At least she wouldn't hear any more threats against her father.

Trinidad's head ached and she heaved a relieved sigh

when Officer Chang arrived. She did a double take as Cynthia Bigley trotted up the gangplank after him.

Bigley caught Trinidad's startled glance. "I was at the station working on some paperwork."

"You mean trying to bribe me with caramel cheesecake," Chang said.

Bigley held up a finger. "Which you resisted like a champ, for the public record. You didn't tell me one blasted thing, and that cheesecake took me three hours to put together."

"I enjoyed the cheesecake very much." Chang hooked his thumbs over his utility belt. "I am a professional first and foremost." He raised his voice. "Chief Bigley is here to help take statements. That's it."

Trinidad saw Bigley exhale slowly for composure. She was not used to being bossed by her second-in-command. Or by anyone, for that matter. "Yes, sir. It's your case."

Chang waded through the crowd, and the two officers began to separate people into smaller groups and jot down notes and phone numbers.

"What about my fireworks?" Trinidad heard Cordell say. "They're supposed to go off at ten, and I want my guests to get their money's worth."

Bigley shrugged. "Seems like they've gotten plenty of excitement already."

Queenie glared from the shelter of Reg's arm. "Gabe's sister shouldn't be messing around in this case."

"Don't worry. I'm here as a scribe." Bigley wiggled an imaginary pencil. "And I won't be handling my brother's statement."

Queenie shook her head. "Not good enough. Why don't you call in other cops?"

Bigley stood taller, her posture that of a bull daring another one to charge. "This is a small town, ma'am. We have a total of three cops. If you want Officer Chang to call in reinforcements, you can plan on staying on this boat for another couple of hours at least. If not..." She shrugged. "Then I'm the scribe."

Bigley turned her back on Queenie and strode off to interview Leonard.

Trinidad admired Bigley's gumption.

She figured her own personal details and contact info had to be on file after she'd been involved in no less than two murder investigations since she'd hit town the year before, so she escorted the twins back to the dining room to begin the mop-up effort.

Leonard and his light bulbs, she thought as she passed the ladies' room. Hesitating on the threshold, she looked around to see if anyone was watching before she slipped inside long enough to flick on the light with her elbow. True enough, one of the two bulbs had failed, leaving the tiny room half in gloom. Leonard had been telling the truth about the bulb being out. Then again, he might have screwed in a dud bulb to give himself an alibi. Had both lights been working earlier? She hadn't had any time to visit the powder room so she had no idea.

Arriving in the dining room, she grabbed a tray and began to gather up the mugs and discarded plates. She went to the table Bonnie and Felice had occupied. Felice was sipping.

Doug sat one chair away. The unused mugs were pulled together in an untidy grouping.

"Real good, Auntie. Everyone loved them. I gathered up the mugs and poured in more milk in case people come back, but it wasn't too hot anymore." Felice's chocolate milk mustache made Trinidad laugh.

"A future caterer. I'm sure everyone is done." Especially since Felice had collected them in such a way that they were all mixed up. Yet she noticed two of the mugs held intact bombs, bobbing in the cooled milk Felice had added. "I guess not everybody enjoyed theirs." She continued to accumulate dirty dishes, placing them in the plastic tubs that the twins shuttled back and forth to the galley.

Bigley used a cleared table in the corner to interview the witnesses. She crooked a finger to Trinidad, who hurried over.

Bigley consulted her notes. "I asked Leonard how he knew the light bulb was out in the ladies' room. He says Renata told him, and Renata said she heard it from Harry, who heard a guest mention it but he can't remember which one."

"Clear as mud?"

"Just about."

"Does it seem odd to you that Harry would take note of a guest's remark about the light bulb? And then conscientiously report it to Renata?"

Bigley frowned. "Everything about Harry seems odd to me. Why is he staying aboard the boat in the first place? I asked Leonard that question, and he said he's not going to pay for anyone to stay in a hotel when they can sleep on a cot for free. We checked the railing, and as far as we can discern, it pulled away when Gabe hit it. Was it tampered with or did it fail naturally? We can't tell since there's been some wind action, and the pieces that hit the water are long gone."

"Who's the culprit?"

"And who's the intended victim? And what does this have to do with Oscar's death if anything? We need a motive."

Trinidad's gaze traveled across the lake toward the slice of land where Oscar and Scooter had lived.

Bigley stretched her long legs. "I know what you're thinking. If Leonard or Iris wanted Oscar dead, they might also be inclined to want each other out of the way."

"And maybe one of them hired Harry to do it. Who would you put your money on?"

"Leonard. He knew Harry at least somewhat."

Trinidad cocked her head as another idea hit. "Do you think Leonard and Renata might be conniving together?"

Bigley laughed, startling Trinidad.

"Sorry," Bigley said. "You don't hear the word 'conniving' too often in law enforcement." Her smile faded into a thoughtful frown. "That did cross my mind. They'd both benefit if Leonard bought the land and expanded his business."

Queenie arrived, escorted by Reg. "You asked to speak with me, Officer Bigley?"

"Chief Bigley, and yes." She gestured Queenie into a chair. "We'll be done soon," she said to Reg. Reluctantly, he stalked off.

Feeling the same reluctance, Trinidad did too. The mundane work of cleaning up after a party felt strange after the earlier excitement. The guests were buzzing with interest and wild speculation that she tried to overhear as much as she could, finding reasons to roll her cart through the lobby more than was strictly necessary. On her last trip, Quinn got to his feet as Chang dismissed him.

"Did you come to any conclusions?"

Quinn shook his head. "Only that I need a hot shower. I've been cleared to go. Sorry I didn't help with the cleanup."

"We had plenty of worker bees."

"Great. I'm sure Doug will be okay getting a rain check on the paddle wheel operation."

They were almost back to Doug and Felice's table when Trinidad stopped so abruptly Quinn plowed into her from behind, leaving a wet splotch from his soggy T-shirt on her back.

"What?"

"The cocoa bombs."

"Uh-huh."

"Felice was having fun and refilled all the mugs from her table, but the milk was too cool. Two of the bombs were still intact when I bussed the table."

"Uh-huh."

"Meaning the people sitting at those spots didn't pour in the milk while it was hot."

"Uh-huh."

"Maybe because they weren't there?"

Quinn frowned. "Oh, I see. You're thinking they might

have slipped away from the table for a nefarious reason instead of participating in the group bombing? Who was sitting there?"

"Bonnie and Felice, Leonard, Iris, Renata, and Harry. But Felice moved all the mugs around so I don't know whose was whose."

"What would have caused them to leave the table, these mystery people?"

"Someone could have slipped away to tamper with the light bulb so Leonard would go upstairs and get clobbered."

Quinn frowned. "Implicating Renata, Harry, or Iris. Another possibility is Iris might have slipped upstairs to kill Leonard. Maybe she was working with Harry, who tampered with the bulb. Is there any connection between the two?"

"I don't know. Or what about Renata and Leonard working together to attack Iris? With her out of the way, they might have a shot at buying the land."

"That's the problem with motives," Quinn said. "You start guessing and they get more and more outlandish. I mean, I can't stand Gabe either. I could have seen him climbing up there and decided to teach him a lesson to get him out of your life once and for all."

She cocked her chin. "You're not that kind of guy, Quinn."

"No, but I'd do anything for you, Trinidad, and I don't want him around you."

She took a calming breath. "I told you before. I am through with Gabe. There is nothing between us anymore. I'm not some sheep-eyed pushover."

"I didn't say you were."

"But when you say you need to keep him away from me, as if I can't make good decisions for myself, that's what you're implying."

"This has nothing to do with you."

"It has everything to do with me." *With us.* She felt the twin tugs of fondness and irritation.

"I don't want to make you feel that way. I'm…worried is all." He reached for her and her angst melted away.

She longed to fold herself into that soggy embrace, but she had a job to do. Instead she kissed his cold cheek. "You go home and get into some dry clothes. I've got more cleanup to do."

"I'll stay."

"You're finished up with your interview, and I don't want you getting pneumonia or something. Go on home." She pushed him along toward Doug.

"All right. But I want you to text me when you get back to the tiny house."

"Will do. Now scoot. The party had a rough end but I am still going to finish strong and collect my paycheck. Plus I'm supposed to serve extra hot cocoa bombs to interested guests after the fireworks, so there will be a second wave of cleanup."

Trinidad, Juliette, and the twins scurried around in cleanup mode while most of the remaining guests meandered out onto the deck to catch Cordell's surprise. Bonnie helped Felice out of her seat. "Might as well go see the fireworks, though I feel like we've already witnessed them."

Trinidad looked around. "Where's Gabe?"

"Officer Chang packed him into a taxi and sent him back to the train cars."

Trinidad shivered. "Well, at least we know Cordell and his posse are still on the steamboat so he won't risk any more personal injury tonight."

Bonnie looked over Felice's head and mouthed "need to talk to you soon."

"Sure thing," Trinidad mouthed back. Finally.

Bonnie nodded and walked Felice out of the dining room.

"Do you think she's ready to come clean?" Juliette loaded the last set of dirty dishes into a tub. "She asked me to come see her too."

"We'll see. Too many secrets already in Sprocket, but at least we've gotten the party mostly squared away."

The boom of fireworks made Trinidad jump. She was glad Quinn and Doug were well away since they were both sensitive to explosions. Noodles went bananas about fireworks too so she hoped the sound would not carry to the tiny house.

Iris set a heavy box down on a bare table. Her face was sheened with sweat, cheeks pink. "That's the last of it." She checked her watch. "I should have been out of here hours ago. Next time I'm writing the hours in the contract. Where's Mr. Pinkerton? I'd like my payment."

"You and me both."

They found Renata flung in a chair in the lobby, arms crossed. She waved them off when they inquired about payment. "I don't have the checkbook. My brother is up schmoozing with the guests, trying to convince them they all had a wonderful time, falling bodies aside. You either need to wait until he's done or come back tomorrow for your payment." Renata's hair was mussed and she'd rubbed some of her mascara into a smudge. "I can't even believe what happened here tonight."

Iris looked gloomy. "Imagine the Yelp reviews. I hope people mention the nice flower arrangements at least."

"And the desserts."

"Way to abandon a sinking ship, so to speak," Renata said. "It's going to be hard for the business to recover from someone catapulting over the side mid party."

Trinidad knew she should feel contrite, but the fact that her feet were aching and she wouldn't be picking up her check that night made her cranky.

Iris appeared to be cranky too.

"With everything that's been going on in this boat, the last thing I want to do is come back here tomorrow." Iris tucked her chin and stared stonily at the patterned carpet. "Who knows what will happen next?"

An explosion boomed through the air and made all three of them jump. Red and green light reflected through the window, painting them in a sickly glow.

Next? Trinidad didn't even want to think about it.

Chapter Fourteen

TRINIDAD'S SHIRT FELT ITCHY AND her bow tie was starting to come loose when she finally arrived at the tiny house after eleven. Quinn leapt from his seat next to Doug and hugged her. "I figured Papa would be up late so it'd be okay for us to come over and wait for you."

She hugged him, grateful. "What a day. Are you suffering any ill effects from your dive?"

"Still got water in my ears, but that's about it."

Doug laughed as Noodles hustled over with a bottle of water in his mouth. The dog would often pick up on words and translate them into a need for help. "Thank you, sweetie." She took it from him. "How's your birdy buddy?"

Scooter scuttled back and forth on his perch, whistling. "He does seem pretty happy here," she said reluctantly.

Papa handed her a bowl of rice and beans and kissed her cheek. "I'm working on teaching him some Spanish."

"Really? After all those years with Oscar, he only said two phrases."

Papa shrugged. "Perhaps he is a native Spanish speaker like me. We share a mother tongue." Papa bent to the cage. *"Más vale pájaro en mano que cien volando."* Scooter chortled in reply.

"What's that mean?" Quinn asked.

"A bird in hand is worth more than one hundred flying," Trinidad said with a laugh. "Basically, it means work with what you've got." She squeezed Papa around the shoulders before he urged her into a chair to eat. "Maybe you should start with something easier like hello or how are you?"

Papa grinned. "He is an advanced student, I have no doubt."

"Wowee," Scooter said.

Papa laughed. "A work in progress anyway."

"Aren't we all," Quinn said. "Tell us about the rest of the event while you eat."

She reviewed their mop-up efforts and the fact that she wouldn't get paid until the following day and Bonnie's urgent need to see her.

Papa frowned. "This Bonnie situation. I still cannot fathom why she would remarry the Hooligan."

"You and me both," Quinn said. "I mean that blockhead really thought he could trespass on the steamboat and charm his way into Queenie's good graces? From the look she and Cordell gave him, he was lucky all he got was a dunking."

Trinidad resisted the urge to shovel in the rice and beans, though her stomach was doing a jig. Noodles cocked his head and trotted to the door. They all watched as he pulled down the lever and opened it.

"Are we having a visitor?" Her words died away and she

forgot she was hungry at the sight of Gabe, duffel bag in hand on her teeny doorstep, knuckles raised to knock.

Papa marched up to prevent his entry. "What are you doing here?"

Gabe sighed. "Hello, Mr. Jones. Sorry to bother you."

"It is late. We are not receiving visitors." Papa reached out to close the door on him.

"I'm desperate."

Papa hesitated, but only for a moment. "You reap what you sow, young man." Then he began to fire off a Spanish tirade until Trinidad stepped up.

"Come in for a minute. I want to ask you a question." She ignored the glares from Quinn and Papa as she scooted aside so Gabe could plant himself on the sofa while she resumed her seat at the table. "When you stepped into that room on the third deck and you got shoved over the balcony, what did the hand feel like that pushed you?"

Gabe blinked. "Felt like a hand."

She smacked her fork down. "I know that, but were the fingers delicate? Long? Strong? Manly? What?"

"Are you trying to get at if it was a woman or a man? Cynthia asked the same thing."

"Well?"

His brows drew together in a bumpy furrow. Eyes closed, he breathed in and out before he opened them again. "Actually..."

She leaned forward. Noodles whined. Scooter chirped.

"I don't know. Only thing I can tell you is the person was strong."

She blew out a breath. Leonard, Iris, Harry, even Renata were all hearty and hale. "Tall or short?"

"Hands hit me about here," Gabe said, pointing to his clavicles, "so I suppose it could be average height or taller."

Which described all three people who had peered down from the upper deck. "Have you remembered anything else from the car accident?"

He brightened. "As a matter of fact, I told Cynthia that I think I know why I woke up with birds on my mind."

Her breath hitched. "Why?"

"Because Harry was looking at bird pictures on his phone as we drove into Sprocket."

"Bird pictures? Like on the web or Instagram?" Her mind raced. If Harry had been following Oscar's faithfully posted photos, he'd know exactly where and when Oscar would turn up.

"I don't know. My eyes were on the road. The last thing I recall is him looking off into the trees and saying something about a yellow-breasted chat, and then my memory goes on the fritz."

"Maybe because he conked you on the head just then," Quinn said.

"To frame me for killing Oscar?"

Quinn folded his arms. "How should she know? She's not your assigned detective."

"Right." Gabe looked at Trinidad beseechingly. "You've been great to me, better than I deserve. It's a matter of time before the examination of the car is complete and I'm arrested since all evidence points to yours truly. Cynthia won't say as much, but I can see the writing on the wall." He pulled in a breath. "But until that time, here I am, which is why I hate to ask you…"

Trinidad pushed her food away, sensing the penny was about to drop. "Ask me what?"

"Well, I can't stay with Cynthia. It's too inappropriate since she's already skating on thin ice, and with Cordell and Queenie being even more upset with me right now, I don't want to draw any danger to either of them at the Station so…"

Quinn's jaw went tight. "So what? Please tell me you didn't have the gall to come and ask to stay here."

Papa blinked. "Surely not."

Gabe offered an apologetic smile. "I'm afraid that's exactly why I came."

Trinidad's mind boggled. Gabe had brass, that was for sure. "I'm sorry, but you can't stay here."

"*Sí.*" Papa nodded vigorously.

"I won't be any trouble…" Gabe started.

Trinidad pushed her bowl away. "I have two adults, a dog, and a parrot taking up all the square footage in this tiny house, and that's quite enough. Not to mention the fact that you're not my favorite person."

"Nor mine," Papa said.

Quinn was about to add to the pile when Gabe started talking again. "I know. Totally understand, but Bonnie and I are going to get married next week, the day after Christmas if I'm not in the slammer. Nice, huh? Once we're married, I'm pretty sure Cordell won't storm the property to kill me. Anyway, I don't have the money to rent a hotel room until the wedding, and I need to stay close until the DA decides whether or not to charge me with manslaughter." He chewed his lip. "Unless Cynthia—he looked at Trinidad—"or anyone else can come up with a way to clear me."

"You can't stay here," Trinidad repeated.

"Right. Okay. I figured as much. I wondered if I could maybe sleep in your car? I could hop out when you need to go to work. Or maybe I could help out in the shop. You have a cot and a bathroom there, right?"

"Yes, but…"

"I always wanted to know how to make ice cream." He brimmed with that boyish enthusiasm that erased the lines of fatigue.

"No way, Gabe." Quinn stood. Doug got to his feet, looking uncertain. "You don't get to do that. Waltz into town, upset everyone's lives, and play on the sympathy of a good woman. I won't allow it."

Papa beamed at Quinn. "*Sí. Exactamente.*"

This good woman can take care of herself. The thought got all tangled up in her mouth and refused to come out. She did not need these two men, as much as she loved them, speaking for her. With emotions running high, it was best to deal with the number one problem.

Trinidad tried to think of someone, anyone who might be willing to take in Gabe Bigley, but considering the town generally believed he'd killed a beloved local, it would be nearly impossible. But she couldn't let the man freeze to death on a Sprocket sidewalk, could she? Gabe was right.

There was a cot in the back room of the shop and a teeny utilitarian bathroom. Then she peeked at Quinn. He was so upset that Gabe had roped her in to investigating for him. She didn't want to introduce any further tension, but it was her decision at the end of the day.

"I..." she started.

"You can stay with me." Quinn glowered at Gabe. Doug mirrored Trinidad's astonishment.

"He can?" Trinidad said.

"I can?" Gabe squeaked.

Papa shoved the glasses up his nose. "This man?" He pointed to Gabe. "You are inviting this man to stay in your home?"

"Not my home, the farm office. We'll throw a sleeping bag down and there's a toilet. Even a small black-and-white TV. It won't be comfortable, but you won't freeze to death. And you have to help do some chores. And this isn't permanent, mind you, only until the wedding or you get arrested, whichever comes first."

Gabe nodded. "Absolutely. Thank you."

"Yeah, yeah. Don't thank me. I'm only doing this because I don't want you around Trinidad." Quinn grabbed his jacket and yanked open the door. "Get in my truck."

Gabe waved and trotted outside. Doug gave him a generous head start before he did the same. Trinidad followed Quinn onto the porch and caught his sleeve.

"You didn't have to do that."

"You were about to say he could sleep in the shop, weren't you?"

Her face warmed. "Yes. I can't let him freeze to death."

Quinn's mouth tightened and then he sighed. "I'll endure the Hooligan so you don't have to."

She smiled and felt her throat thicken with unexpected tears. "You're a good man."

"No, I'm a jealous, angry man, but I love a good woman." He kissed her again and turned her back to the house. "Go on inside. Cold out here."

Dazed from the kiss, she complied. *I love a good woman.* Noodles closed the door for them, and Papa turned the bolt.

A good woman...but he didn't seem to know how strong a woman she was quite yet.

"Imagine Quinn taking on the Hooligan to protect you. That is chivalry," Papa said. After a pause, he added, "That is love."

Her face glowed as she helped Noodles settle onto his mat and covered Scooter's cage, though it would be only a few moments before the dog freed his friend to come and join him on their cozy mat. Love. Chivalry. And trust? Did she and Quinn have enough of that?

Quinn had freed her from a cage too. After Gabe, she'd thought she'd never trust herself again, but she'd learned how. No matter what happened between her and Quinn, she would never be crawling back behind those jail bars again. That was what Quinn didn't understand. She wouldn't let Gabe freeze, and she'd do her best to dig up support for his case, but the woman she'd become had found her own identity, and she wasn't giving it up for anyone.

"Papa?"

He dried the last dish and put it away. "Yes, Trina?"

"I, uh, I wondered...about Iris. And you."

He blinked, took off his glasses, polished them, and put them back on. "What did you wonder?"

"If you were, you know, fond of each other."

Papa's brow furrowed and then he smiled.

Her pulse thrummed. "It'd be okay and all." *If she isn't involved in a crime, that is.* "As long as she made you happy."

Papa's gaze was soft. "Trina, when I married your grandmother, God put all the pieces in my heart together just right. They are still just right, even though a few are cracked now. There are no empty spaces that need filling. I am not lonely, Trina, because she's here." He pointed to his chest. "She'll always be, like you will, like my son is."

Her vision blurred with tears and she delivered herself into a warm, garlic-scented hug.

"I love you, Papa."

"And I love you, my darling girl."

Trinidad the scooper sleuther kissed her Papa Luis, climbed up the ladder, and burrowed beneath the blankets. Tonight, she had no empty spaces in her heart either.

The next day, Trinidad walked up the icy gangplank. Iris's purple van was already parked in the lot. An early bird, that Iris. Morning snow had coated the railings in fleecy sleeves, and Christmas lights still glowed on the sun deck of the steamboat. Only seven days until Christmas, and she had done precisely zero holiday shopping. At least the Shimmy was closed on Sundays during the winter so she had the rest of the day to snag some presents. Her gift list wasn't too long: Bonnie, Juliette, Felice, Quinn and Doug, Papa. She knew what she'd do for Quinn and his brother. A half gallon of her finest, custard style vanilla ice cream, ceramic bowls with their names painted on them that she'd already commissioned, and a new ice cream scooper since he'd told her they used a bent serving spoon to dish up their treats at home. A warm fizz bubbled in her soul thinking of Quinn and how much she'd come to love him. It was replaced by a worrying thought.

Gabe was sleeping on the floor in Quinn's office. That could not possibly turn out well. The fuse was already sputtering down. If only she could find a piece of evidence to help clear her ex. But that would mean fastening the blame on another suspect. Iris? Renata? Leonard? Harry? Cordell? The police could place none of them in the vicinity when Oscar was killed except Harry. And at the boat incident, it was Iris, Leonard, and Cordell staring down from the balcony. Perhaps there was no connection at all between the two events.

Her head began to throb as she made her way into the lobby. Renata was eating a bowl of ice cream though it was barely eight a.m., toying with her green neck scarf as she examined a stack of papers.

"Don't judge me for my food choices. You left extras in the freezer and I needed something after last night."

Trinidad raised her palms. "No judgment from me. I'm just a lady looking for her paycheck."

"That I can do. Leonard handed over the checkbook this morning."

Iris walked in. "Uh, not my business and all, I'm only here

for my check too, but your brother and the carpenter guy are about to deck each other, no pun intended. I was thinking maybe you could write our checks real quick while those two duke it out?"

But Renata was already zipping from behind the counter and beelining for the exit doors, muttering something about her life being a circus.

Iris sighed. "All I want is a crummy paycheck."

Trinidad could hear the shouting as she raced behind Renata. Iris fell in behind and the three of them burst onto the main deck. Leonard and Harry stood facing each other like two bulls pawing the ground.

Leonard was shorter, coming only to Harry's nose, but his purpled face left no doubt about his mood.

"I never should have hired you," Leonard shouted.

"And I never should have taken the job," Harry hollered back. "You haven't appreciated one single thing I've fixed on this boat."

"That's because you haven't fixed anything."

"I refinished the second deck, didn't I?"

"And it's still not dry. And don't think I didn't notice the big footprint you left."

Harry stabbed a finger at him. "That's your trouble, buddy. You only notice the things that go wrong. You don't even appreciate your own sister."

Renata stepped close. "Come on now, fellas. This isn't the time for all this macho posturing."

Leonard did not even look at her. "I'm not posturing. He's done a crappy job. I never should have hired him.

Attending the same high school doesn't count as a qualification. Why did I let you talk me into it?"

Harry slapped a hand on his thigh. "See? Blaming your sister."

Renata spoke through gritted teeth. "Leonard, you were only too happy to hire Harry when you saw how cheap he worked, weren't you? You get what you pay for, as I'm constantly telling you."

"Skinflint," Harry said, seemingly unaware he'd been insulted.

Leonard folded his arms across his thick belly. "I haven't even gotten near what I paid for, plus he's been sleeping on my boat and mooching food and crashing Cordell's dessert party, which was completely inappropriate."

"I heard the music." Harry sniffed. "Did you want me to stay in that crummy cabin like some sort of troll?"

"Not like a troll, like the hired help, which you are," Leonard thundered.

Harry winced. "Man. That's low. Fine, I'll leave, if that's what you both want." His gaze slid to Renata, a gleam of hopefulness there.

Renata remained silent, glaring at her brother.

"Yes," Leonard snapped. "That's exactly what I want, and this is my boat, but you're going to fix that paneling in the cocktail lounge first. I paid you five hundred bucks for materials and labor. You can fix it or pay back the cash before you go."

Harry's brows drew into a line like two angry caterpillars staring each other down. "I'm emotional right now and I'm in no condition to be using a nail gun. I'll be back to fix the paneling and get off this rusty tub of a boat by sundown." He spun on his heel and marched away, muttering to himself.

"There's no rust on this boat except what's between your ears," Leonard shouted at his departing back. "And don't think you'll get any references from me."

Harry stomped down the gangplank, turning only once as if he might say something else but thought better of it.

Renata heaved out a massive breath. "Well, that was a disaster."

Trinidad figured it would be on Renata's shoulders to find a replacement carpenter if the paneling wasn't repaired.

Leonard groaned. "Gonna have to have the deck refinished again. That klutz messed it all up."

"Why don't you do it yourself?" Renata pointed a finger at him. "And before you start complaining about your sore ankle or your weak back..."

"I was going to say I don't have time. A captain has more important matters to attend to." He shot a look at Trinidad and Iris. "Renata can write your checks."

As he ambled away, Renata shouted after him. "It doesn't take much of a captain to sail in circles. All you know how to do is turn left."

Her words rang in the air. There was no indication if Leonard heard her or not.

"Come on, ladies," Renata said, shoulders slumped. They trailed her in silence back to the front desk where she referred to her computer.

"Thank you, Renata. I'm sorry everything's been complicated but the party was a success, right?" Trinidad might as well remind her of the big picture, especially if there were going to be more parties to host that might need her dessert services.

"I guess." Her ice cream had melted into a puddle of brown goo. A sad waste of Papa's gingerbread ice cream. "I don't know how it all went wrong. Harry seemed like he could take care of things. I spoke to him on the phone after I saw his ad. He turns out to be a terrible carpenter with some weird crush on me."

Hmm. So Renata *had* been aware of Harry's affection to some degree. "Did he show much interest in high school?"

Renata considered, tapping the pen to her chin. A dreamy smile played over her lips. "I was pretty popular, so I got lots of attention." She shrugged. "Maybe he was honestly interested. Who knows?"

"Do you think Harry could have had something to do with Oscar's death?"

Renata stopped, pen in hand. "He's a worthless carpenter, but that doesn't make him a murderer. The police haven't arrested him."

"Then again, they haven't arrested Gabe yet either," Iris said. "Why would either of them kill my cousin?"

"I don't know, but Harry was in the car before the accident," Trinidad said.

Renata finished writing two checks and tore them carefully out of the book. "This is all way out of my sphere."

Trinidad figured she wouldn't have too many more opportunities to fish for what Renata knew so she pressed on. "Isn't it possible Harry agreed to come work for the steamboat to give himself a reason to be in Sprocket?"

"Two questions," Iris said. "First, why would he want to kill Oscar, and second, why would he stick around afterward?"

"As to the first question…" Trinidad shifted uncomfortably. "Oscar's land is a prize."

Iris's lip twitched. "If we're following that logic, I have more motive than Harry. Oh wait. You are thinking maybe I hired him to kill my cousin?"

"I wasn't saying…"

Renata smacked the pen down. "Or maybe my brother hired him? Is that what you're implying since he's interested in the land too?"

Now both women were glaring at Trinidad. "Uh, well, I mean, there could have been other people who might have wanted Oscar dead." Even though she couldn't pull up one other name at that moment.

"I didn't hire Harry," Iris said coldly.

"And I didn't either," Renata added. "Well, not to kill Oscar anyway, and my brother is a complete jerk, but I can't see him arranging to have people bumped off, especially not one of his few friends."

Iris stowed the check in her pocket. "Point two. If your theory is correct and Harry killed Oscar, why would he stick around, working on the steamboat? Wouldn't a hired killer do the job and take off?"

"I, uh, dunno." Trinidad felt like a child dressed up in grown-up clothes.

Renata slapped the ledger closed. "Look, I have a bunch of work to do. Thanks for everything."

And don't let the door hit you in the bum on the way out…

Check in hand, Trinidad had the sinking feeling she wouldn't be asked to cater again on the steamboat. Implying the owner planned someone's murder wasn't putting her in anyone's good graces.

Swift move, Trinidad.

She tried to walk briskly back to the food truck, but Iris caught up with her as she readied her keys to unlock the door.

"I have to know," Iris said. "What about me makes you suspect I arranged my cousin's death?"

"I wouldn't use the word 'suspect' particularly." Trinidad's face flamed hot. "I was only trying to sort out motives. You, um, said you didn't know about Oscar's will, but a note I found at Oscar's place from the lawyer indicated otherwise."

Iris scoffed. "I don't even want to know how you found that out. So I lied. You must have an inkling of why."

Trinidad shook her head.

"You know about my deceased husband, right?"

"Well, yes, but..."

"How did you hear about it?"

Trinidad frantically tried to think of an explanation that didn't involve her skulking in Iris's florist shop behind the foliage during her argument with Leonard.

"Oh, I can't quite remember."

"Uh-huh. Leonard has probably already started spreading it all over town. My husband had no moral compass, kind of like Leonard. He was selfish, irresponsible, and happy to manipulate whomever he needed to. I did not know he was using the funeral information on my delivery paperwork to plan robberies all across town. Can you imagine how humiliating it is to have everyone know your husband was stealing from people?"

"I don't have to imagine it. I lived it."

Iris blinked. "Oh yes. I suppose you did."

"I do understand what it feels like to be betrayed by your spouse."

"At least no one believed you'd aided and abetted Gabe. Most people probably even felt sorry for you." Iris paused a moment. "I lost everything. The house, savings, it all went to the lawyers. Then he died. What was I left with? A mountain of debt that I'll be paying off for years, suspicion from the police, and people in my town who will never believe my innocence. I was happy when my husband died, to be perfectly frank." Iris didn't flinch saying the words. Her silver hair flashed in the brilliant light. "I didn't hasten his death, but I'm not sorry it happened. I'd be lying if I said I was. I didn't fess up about the will because I knew what everyone would think and I'd be seen as a criminal all over again."

Trinidad saw resolve written in the lines of Iris's face. No matter what Iris claimed, it was possible that she'd arranged for Oscar to die to inherit his property, to help erase the debt she'd racked up from her husband's nefarious pursuits.

"And I've decided I'm not going to sell the property to Leonard no matter what. Even if he smears my name all over town. He's not getting what he wants." Iris pursed her lips. "I can see your wheels turning about that accident on the steamboat last night, so let me set you straight. No, I did not hide upstairs hoping to hurt Leonard or toss him overboard, though I cannot say he wouldn't deserve it. I'm a florist. My business is my passion. I want to stick to flowers and be left alone."

With that, she left Trinidad standing there, enveloped in cold.

"And I want to stick to *my* business and scoop ice cream," Trinidad muttered as she climbed aboard the food truck, figuring she should leave the sleuthing to Miss Marple, who seemed to have plenty of resources and no business to run.

But Gabe might be days away from going back to jail. And something told her more bad outcomes were on the horizon if she didn't figure things out in a hurry, or at least help Chief Bigley crack the case. How? How was she supposed to do that? She didn't have the slightest clue.

Chapter Fifteen

DETERMINED TO MAKE GOOD USE of her precious time off and clear her mind with shopping therapy, Trinidad journeyed into nearby Joseph where she spent a few hours acquiring Christmas gifts. Hats and mittens for Bonnie, Juliette, and Felice, a rare set of Mario Lanza cassette tapes at a thrift store for Papa, and a new stuffed toy to replace Noodles's raggedy beaver. For Scooter, she found a little hanging toy with a silver bell at the bottom, and the bank provided a crisp fifty-dollar bill for each twin. Money was king where the teens were concerned. She pulled out her precious check for the party payment, anticipating the thrill of actually putting money into her account instead of adding to the stream of withdrawals.

Her mouth dropped open. The check was made out to Iris. In the aftermath of Harry and Leonard's altercation, the checks had gotten switched. *So much for the savvy small business owner, Trin.* Iris undoubtedly had Trinidad's. With a groan, she shoved it in her pocket and dialed the florist shop. No answer and she did not have Iris's cell number. Her deflated funds would have to wait for an infusion.

As she drove back to Sprocket, she worked on a mental to-do list, at the top of which was churning the ice cream for Doug and Quinn. Uneasy visions of Gabe on Quinn's office floor surfaced. The police would be finished processing Gabe's car for evidence at some point. Was his arrest imminent? And why hadn't she heard any details about the post-Christmas Bonnie-Gabe wedding? She resolved to have the anticipated talk with Bonnie when she brought Felice for the hot cocoa bomb class the next night. As for Gabe, she hoped Quinn hadn't snapped and crammed him into the nut sorting machine.

She picked up Noodles at the tiny house, prying him away from Scooter. "We'll be back soon, I promise, but you need your exercise too, old boy." With Noodles bundled in his winter coat, they drove to the gazebo at the park near Messabout Creek and strolled the snowy grounds before they returned to town. Of course the florist shop was locked up tight, windows dark, as was the small apartment upstairs. No sign of Iris anywhere. Enjoying her Sunday off.

There was nothing further to be done but to return to the Shimmy. Noodles enjoyed a biscuit from the weekly supply Papa baked up for him, and Trinidad cooked the custard base for the vanilla ice cream. The vanilla essence scraped from the cured orchid pods Papa had grown in his greenhouse tickled her nose. The soothing sweet aroma helped her put aside the uncomfortable encounter at the steamboat and her concern about Gabe and Quinn. After the glossy mixture cooled and did time in the churner, she scooped the delicious slurry into decorative Christmas containers that she figured Quinn and Doug might find useful and stowed them in the walk-in freezer to ripen. The perfect Christmas gift, made with love. She found herself smiling.

"Hungry?" she asked Noodles.

The dog wagged his tail.

"How about we treat ourselves to a slice of pizza for a snack?" Pizza Heaven had followed her lead when she'd created the Chilly Dog by offering its own canine-safe pizza to the delight of locals and visitors. The pet-friendly establishment sported plenty of doggie bowls, and furry friends were welcome to dine in. She led Noodles to the shop and they placed their order, waiting at a small table by the front window that looked out across the street at a corner of the stately Vintage Theater where she was told the annual "Spruce Up Sprocket" Christmas tree distribution would take place. The shop owners were instructed to ornament their trees using a theme, and she and Juliette had enjoyed picking out the perfect decor. Such a lovely season, she thought. If only there wasn't Oscar's death and Gabe's impending arrest to mar the festivities.

As they savored the warmth of the fragrant shop, Trinidad recalled that only four days prior, she had found Oscar lying dead at the overlook. Poor Oscar. Poor Scooter. Though she forced herself to try, she could not believe that Gabe had done the terrible deed and then tried to flee the scene. But if not Gabe...

Harry. Had to be. Her thoughts kept circling back to

him. He'd knocked Gabe out, taken the wheel, run Oscar over, and afterward crashed the car into the creek, hoping to kill Gabe. So his interest in Scooter was born out of guilt? Did that make sense? She stroked Noodles and decided it did. Animals were easier to love than people, for sure. They supplied unconditional adoration, didn't argue or point out a person's shortcomings, and were content with the simplest of things. Maybe Harry had killed Oscar and become remorseful at making Scooter an orphan. Could birds be orphaned, or was that strictly a people thing? Diego would probably know.

The motive was still problematic. Had Harry been hired or acted on his own? Maybe he had the hots for Renata for years and decided to kill Leonard for the way he treated his sister but accidentally got Oscar. That made zero sense since they'd seemingly had no connection in the decades between high school and the present. Then again, they could have been in a relationship and made sure not to advertise it in Sprocket. Who would be the wiser if Renata and Harry had a secret liaison?

When her name was called, Trinidad fetched her slice of gooey pepperoni and the pup pizza, which consisted of a small crust decorated with cooked slices of sweet potato and a sprinkle of ground beef. No spices, onions, or garlic in this dog-friendly snack.

While Noodles swabbed the whole thing with his tongue before starting to chew, she ate her own portion to the last crumb. Shored up by the power of pizza, they exited the store, collected her bag from the Shimmy, and climbed into her car. Quinn and Doug were regular guests for Sunday dinner. She wondered with a shudder if Gabe would be tagging along. This would be an interesting gathering. Quinn and Gabe did not belong in the same room together, she thought, motoring off down the road. She was about to tootle on past the corner of Main and Fruitvale when she saw the bustle of activity at Chubby's Pub. Chubby himself, a painfully thin man with a lengthy beard that he kept fastidiously braided, was gesticulating from the doorway.

What in the world…? Harry Fortesque faced Chubby, his expression clearly outraged even from a distance. Cordell and his brother Reg watched the encounter from their small sidewalk table, beverages untouched in front of them.

On instinct, she pulled to the curb. Chubby's had the world's best scratch-made hummus and soft pita after all, so maybe she'd bring them for a special Sunday dinner treat. It was as good an excuse as any to indulge her burning curiosity. She half opened the window for Noodles, who shoved his head out to take in the tumult before she exited the car.

"Get lost," Chubby said to Harry. "We don't hand out free drinks in this town, and anyway, I told you you'd had enough."

"I haven't." Harry swayed on his feet. "Not nearly enough."

Chubby thundered in a voice belying his size, "When I say it's enough, it's enough."

Trinidad watched in fascination as Harry unfurled to his full height, his lips rubbery from too much alcohol. "I do not agree," he said stiffly.

Senses tingling, she edged closer.

"Give it a rest, buddy," Cordell said from his seat. He was dressed for the elements in a jacket, expensive-looking jeans, and leather boots. "You're making a racket, and me and my brother here are trying to have a planning session. Small towns are supposed to be quiet."

Harry ignored Cordell and continued to try and make his case with Chubby.

Trinidad wiggled her fingers at Cordell and Reg.

Cordell arched his brow. "Well, if it isn't the ice cream lady. Checking on my safety again? You're a local. What's going on in this town? Always drama. Can't a man sit and enjoy a beverage without interruption?"

Trinidad's idea of a winter beverage tended more toward hot cocoa loaded down with marshmallows. "Sprocket is busier than you might think. I thought you'd be on your way out of town now that the party's done."

"Nuh-uh." He eyed the argument between Harry and Chubby and rolled his shoulders, which had to be twice the width of her own. The winter sun highlighted a neck tattoo she hadn't noticed before, the depiction of a dagger that pointed menacingly toward his ear. "I got another couple days here at least. Maybe I'll even stay for Christmas. Taking Mama to the airport today, though. She says this town doesn't agree with her."

Probably no place agreed with Mama Queenie. "Sprocket isn't for everybody."

Harry's volume was rising. "Nothing…" he slurred. "Nothing goes right for me."

Trinidad hoped that might be the beginning of a

confession. She suddenly remembered a phrase she'd heard somewhere during her formative years. *Mad drunkenness exposes every secret.* Was she going to be privy to Harry's deepest secret if she stayed a few moments longer? She eased a step closer, but Cordell distracted her with a question.

"You don't happen to know where Gabe is holing up these days?"

"No. You aren't still looking to rough him up, are you?" Irritation overrode her discretion. "This isn't the Wild West, duels at dawn and such, Mr. Barrone."

"Debt's got to be paid." Cordell's charming smile vanished. Reg nodded in silent agreement.

Were these two for real? They were actually going to stay in Sprocket until they got their opportunity to beat Gabe up like two bullies hanging around after school for their victim? Chubby had retrieved a push broom and was now using it to prod Harry away from his establishment. "Go, you big ox."

"I will not be swept away like grass clippings." Harry's spittle flew. "It's disrespectful."

With a grunt, Cordell got to his feet. "All right, I've had enough. Shut your pie hole, man. You aren't gonna find the answer to the problem in the bottom of a glass. The bartender says you're done, you're done." He took hold of Harry's arm.

Harry tried to jerk loose, but Cordell's strength was unmatchable. He forced Harry farther down the sidewalk toward his own car with the personalized plates Juliette had admired.

Chubby waved an appreciative hand and took his push broom back inside.

"Where are you headed?" Cordell said to Harry. "Out of town? I'll give you a lift to the bus station or something if it will get you to shut up."

"Fixing some paneling…booted out like an old turnip." Harry snuffled. "Never shoulda come…"

Cordell frowned. "What?"

Trinidad explained. "He's been staying in a room on the steamboat, so he probably has things there still. He's supposed to finish a paneling project before he leaves."

Cordell nodded. "I wouldn't recommend the use of power tools while inebriated. All right. We'll take you back to the dock." He looked at Trinidad. "Unless you want to drive him?"

She was tempted. What kind of answers might she get in Harry's compromised state? But good reason won out. Not the greatest idea to haul a drunken person around town, especially someone twice her size. "No, I don't." She paused. "That's kind of you. Since you don't know him, really, do you?" *Or did he?*

Cordell shook his head. "Nope." He grinned. "But I hear he told the cops that Gabe was a crazy driver. Adding another shovelful of dirt on Gabe's coffin before he gets buried back in jail is worth a ride from me."

Cordell's venom repelled her. But hadn't she carried around an enormous load of resentment against her ex as well? Juliette certainly seemed to find reasons to like Cordell, his ferocious streak aside.

Reg opened the rear door as Cordell shoved Harry forward. He twisted, falling on his back across the supple leather. "If you throw up in my ride, I'm dumping you on the side of the road and leaving you to the vultures."

As Harry wriggled farther onto the back seat, his phone fell to the floor. She scooped it up, seeing a glimpse of a text message for an instant before it vanished.

...need to talk.

She didn't get to see the sender before Harry snatched the phone and fixed a bleary eye on her. "You're the bird lady."

"Er, yes. I have Scooter, Oscar's parrot."

"If you didn't find him an owner, I can give him a good home, I promise. All the seeds he wants. And peanuts. And a little parrot hammock. And a sweater, 'cause he's missing all them feathers."

"Uh, well, I've already found a new home for him."

"That's good. He really deserves one. Wouldn't want to live with me anyway after what I've done."

She leaned closer, heart pounding. "What, Harry?"

"Things I've done wrong," he wailed. "So, so wrong."

Her nerves prickled. Her inner Miss Marple urged her on. "Get it off your chest and you'll feel better."

He closed his eyes. "I will?"

"Absolutely. I'm listening, Harry. Did you kill Oscar?"

Harry opened his mouth to answer, then he sighed, flopped back against the leather, and began to snore. She blew out a breath and slammed the door to find Cordell grinning at her.

"This detecting stuff is a pain, am I right?" He laughed. "Harry's not the answer. Gabe's gonna go back to jail where he belongs, and there's nothing you can do about it. You're better off rid of him anyway."

Reg joined in the chuckling.

Ignoring them both, she tromped back to her car and got in. Gunning the engine, she drove away. She was almost back to the tiny house when she realized she'd forgotten all about the hummus and pita.

Papa made up for it by offering her a slice of freshly baked bread and butter while they waited for their dinner guests to arrive. Noodles checked on Scooter, leaving the canine-avian canoodling only long enough to open the door for Quinn and Doug. Trinidad greeted them and scanned to see if Gabe was following up the step. He wasn't, but Chief Bigley was. She carried a pie that looked to be of the apple variety, which Trinidad knew she must have purchased at the gas station. Sprocket was probably the only town in which a person could buy a freshly baked pie and fuel their car at the same time.

"Your grandfather invited me when I called to chat with you, Trinidad."

"Good, because I've had a day, let me tell you." While they settled at the table, she whispered to Quinn. "How's the houseguest situation?"

Bigley rolled her eyes, overhearing the remark. "Yeah, Gabe told me you invited him to sleep in your office. Real big of you, considering."

Quinn waved away the comment. "It wasn't altruistic. I don't want him around Trinidad." He sighed. "I told him he wasn't invited to dinner, but he was afraid to be left alone so I parked him in Papa's greenhouse. We brought him a baloney and cheese sandwich, and it's warm in there," he said defensively to the chief.

"I understand." She rubbed her brow as if trying to smooth out the worry lines. "Unless something changes, I would expect Gabe to be charged in the next week."

That made them all go quiet.

"In my mind, Harry was behind it, but I haven't learned anything concrete to pin it on him, and Gabe's confession and the fact that he was apparently driving…" She looked morose. "The guys at the lab haven't found Harry's fingerprints on the steering wheel so…"

"Well, I can tell you one thing I've learned," Quinn said. "Your brother's got secrets."

All eyes fastened on Quinn.

"Explain," Bigley said.

"I was in the office late last night, looking for a phone number, and he was babbling away in his sleep."

Trinidad remembered suddenly that Gabe used to talk in his sleep on a regular basis. At times, he'd even sing. "What did he say, exactly?"

"Mostly I couldn't understand, but there was one phrase that I got loud and clear. He said, 'No one will ever know.'"

Bigley didn't ask anything further, simply got up and marched out the door toward the greenhouse. Without a word, Papa, Quinn, Doug, and Trinidad left the steaming pot of chili and followed suit.

They found Gabe sitting on a plastic crate, eating his

baloney sandwich. He jumped when they all filed in. "Oh hey. How's it going?"

Bigley's hands went to her hips. "Spill it. You said, 'No one will ever know,' in your sleep. I want you to explain to me what that means right now."

The greenhouse lights painted his skin in a sickly cast. "I, uh, oh gee. Did I talk in my sleep again? I was probably dreaming or something. Too much late-night television. Remember how Mom was always busting me for sneaking into the family room to watch horror movies after everyone went to bed?"

Cynthia ignored his remark. "When you lie, one side of your mouth droops."

That would have been helpful to know, Trinidad grumbled silently.

He fingered his chin with the hand that wasn't holding the sandwich. Finally he answered. "I can't tell you."

"Why not?"

"I just can't."

"That's not an answer."

He shrugged and licked a spot of mayo from his thumb. "Sorry, sis. I really am."

The chief's hands twitched as though she wanted to throttle him. "You don't seem to get it, do you? You're going to jail very soon for manslaughter and hit-and-run. Did you hear me? Back…to…jail, where you'll live in a cell again with other individuals who don't care about your stamp collection and don't want to discuss architecture with you. Jaaaaaiiilllllll," the chief intoned. "And there's nothing I can do to get you out of this mess because you're lying to me."

Gabe winced. "Well...I'd tell you if I could."

"You can. You've got two working lips and a tongue." She snagged his lower lip in a pinch. "So start talking. What's the secret about?"

"Nnnnhhhhsmmmm," he mumbled through her pinch.

She let go. "Try again."

"Sis, I am grateful for everything you've done for me." His eyes found Trinidad's. "And you too, Trina. And..." He looked at Quinn and got a hostile glare in exchange. "Well anyway, I don't want to go back to jail, especially for killing a man I didn't even know. I'm an embezzler, not a violent criminal." He regrouped. "Anyway, this...matter about which I was sleep talking doesn't pertain to the Oscar situation."

"I should be the judge of that, Gabe. I'm the cop, remember?"

"It's not related, I can assure you."

The chief continued her attempt to bully her brother without success. "Have you told Bonnie about the secret?"

Gabe shoved an enormous bite into his mouth. "Not talking," he said around the mass of food.

Tension hummed around the chief like overloaded electrical wires.

"Gabe." She bent over so she was staring right into his face. "What's left of my patience is all but gone. Tell me what you know."

He shrugged. "I'm sorry, sis, really and truly I am. I can't."

The moment stretched out in steamy silence until the chief shook her head. "I am beginning to sympathize with Cordell and his desire to pummel you."

Gabe didn't answer, continuing to chew.

The greenhouse humidity added a sense of heaviness to the air as they trickled out into the jarring cold.

Gabe wasn't talking, that much was clear. Part of Trinidad actually admired his grit. Whatever it was, he was willing to face dire consequences rather than reveal it.

Bigley stopped Trinidad on the porch step. "If Bonnie knows something, you have to get her to tell you."

"I can ask, but if she won't talk…"

"You have to make her talk."

Now it was Trinidad's turn to fist a hand on her hip. "Like you made Gabe talk back there?"

Bigley sighed and bowed her head. "You know we're running out of time."

"Yes." Each day that passed, Trinidad expected to see Chang clapping Gabe in handcuffs and escorting him off to be booked. "I'll see Bonnie tomorrow at the cocoa bomb class, and I'll try to get some answers."

"Try hard."

"I will," Trinidad promised. They returned to the house and ate the chili and bread, but the conversation was subdued and the chief left before the pie was served.

The text from Iris came after the dishes were done and the guests departed.

Got your message. Sorry the checks were mixed up. Working at Oscar's tomorrow to box up some things. Can you meet me at his place in the a.m. to exchange?

Trinidad agreed to drive to Oscar's at 7:00 the next morning.

Later, as she told Scooter good night, the bird pushed his head against the bars. Obligingly she scratched him with her fingertip. He nestled close, eyes closed in pleasure. Was he sad in his wee bird heart that Oscar was not there anymore?

Noodles sat at her feet, waiting for them to go through the ritual. She'd tuck him in. Noodles would wait until she climbed the ladder before releasing Scooter and snuggling close with his pal all night. A bird and his buddy, the best of friends. Her throat thickened and she realized she could never break up this duo. It would break both their little hearts and hers too.

She sighed as she considered all the ramifications of adding a parrot to her zany life. Though she didn't know the first thing about parrots, she'd learn, like she was doing every day.

It was settled. Scooter would not be delivered to Stan's coffee shop, nor would she be handing him over to Harry.

How could she, when she felt deep down in her bones that Harry Fortesque was a killer.

———

Trinidad figured she'd snag the check from Iris and then pick up the animal brigade and go into the Shimmy. It would be a late night, since the cocoa bomb class would commence at 5:00 with Felice and three other participants who had signed up. Four people wasn't a robust turnout, but maybe with some word-of-mouth action, the numbers would increase and she could stage a few more throughout the winter. Juliette would be present to help the youngsters create their masterpieces.

The snow from the previous night had melted away, but the skies were thick with iron-gray clouds that promised more, according to Quinn's unofficial weather forecast. She was glad she'd made sure her tires were newish and the wiper blades had been replaced. There wasn't another soul along this lonely road, and she figured maybe it explained why Iris had decided to keep the property. The quiet location seemed to suit her personality, a stick to herself kind of person, except where Papa was concerned. Papa thought Iris was a wounded bird who simply needed some kindness.

Trinidad wasn't so certain.

She cracked the window to catch the sound of the lake slapping gently against the shore. Through the trees, she snagged glimpses of the Sprocket Steamboat, her decks gleaming with moisture or ice. The charm of the vessel was completely at odds with all the boiling emotions she'd encountered aboard. Queenie with her hatred of Gabe. The angry faces of Iris, Cordell, and Leonard peering down over the railing. Later Harry and Leonard shouting at each other while Renata looked helplessly on.

Had Harry fixed the paneling and packed up his things? Trinidad had left instructions with Papa not to let him in if he happened to sober up, change his mind, and report to the tiny house looking for Scooter. Harry was not to be trusted. Certainly not with Noodles's best friend.

The cold nipped her cheeks as she got out, crunching through the light layer of snow on the long circular drive. Iris answered the door. A red bandana covered her hair. She wore a roll of packing tape like a bracelet. "I'm glad you came. I found more bird things Oscar would want you to have for Scooter."

Trinidad followed her into the living room. There were boxes neatly stacked, ranging in size from shoeboxes to cartons. The furniture remained in place and it did not appear that anything had been touched yet in the kitchen. Iris picked up the check from the counter and exchanged it with Trinidad's.

"Have you decided what to do with the property?"

Iris brushed a cobweb from her hair. "I thought I had until I spent some time here. I can understand why Oscar liked it. Quiet and peaceful. In the summer, I'm sure you could catch a great breeze from off the water." She glanced out the picture windows toward the lake. "Oscar actually offered to let me stay here when I first came to Sprocket. I refused, of course. It was awkward. He had a lot of guilt about what Albert did to me, since he introduced us and everything." She shrugged. "He tried to help me as best he could. Not everyone would have done that."

Iris's introspection was a change from the all-business woman Trinidad had heretofore known. Maybe going through Oscar's belongings had mellowed her. "It's a lovely home, that's for sure."

Iris looked at Trinidad. "What would you do? Sell it or keep it?"

"Me?" It surprised her that Iris would ask. Or care. "Considering I'm living in a tiny house with two animals and my grandfather, I probably would keep it. Of course, everybody's desires are different. I intend to stay in Sprocket a good long while. I understand this property's worth quite a bit. You could give up your business and live comfortably, maybe, if you didn't want to stay here."

Iris's eyes narrowed. "Would you? Give up the Shimmy?"

"No. I don't have children so the Shimmy is my baby."

Iris nodded. "I feel that way about my shop too. For me, it's so much more than a business. It's everything."

Trinidad understood. More than a business. More like a heartbeat, the proof that she was an overcomer, an independent woman who could survive and thrive, no matter what life lobbed at her. She and Iris had faced similar obstacles, betraying husbands, financial ruin, second chances.

They might even become friends, business allies... Unless Iris was not the person she seemed to be.

"That box there under the window has some bird food and a heater that clips to the side of the cage. Might be handy since Scooter's got some missing feathers." Iris unfurled a length of tape and busied herself sealing a box. "Are you keeping it?"

"It?"

"The bird."

"Yes, I've decided to add him to the gang, even though Harry offered to take Scooter with him."

Iris looked up from her taping. "Harry? The carpenter? Why would he?"

"Good question, especially since he's leaving town."

Iris opened her mouth to say something, then closed it and began picking at her roll of tape.

Trinidad fetched the box neatly marked "bird" and hefted it. "Thanks for passing these things along." A glint of something bobbing in the lake about ten feet from shore caught her attention. She peered into the glittering water and gasped. Dropping the box with a thud, she pressed close to the glass, feeling the cold through the thin pane that grazed her forehead. "Oh no."

Iris put down her tape. "What's wrong?"

Trinidad gulped. "Look."

Iris moved to her side and stared out at the waters of Big Egg. Trinidad pointed.

"What is that?" Iris said. "A boat?"

"Not a boat," Trinidad said, stomach heaving. "A body."

Chapter Sixteen

THEY RAN OUTSIDE, DOWN THE short flagstone path that led to the edge of the water. A body floated facedown a foot or so underneath the surface, bobbing gently in the waves.

"Is that...?" Iris whispered.

"Yes," Trinidad whispered back, though she didn't know why. "It's Harry Fortesque."

"What's he doing here?"

Nothing, she wanted to say. *He's dead.*

Though he was floating facedown, his big, blocky body and catcher's mitt hands made identification unquestionable. His position and the languid quality of his limbs also made it clear that he was lifeless. The heels of his sneakers danced to the surface and then vanished below again in a macabre jig.

Iris's voice was still hushed. "Should we fish him out?"

"I don't think so. I'll call Chief...I mean, Officer Chang directly and we'll wait until he arrives." Trinidad phoned the station with shaking fingers, surprised when the chief answered the call.

"I'm covering the desk because I don't have enough to keep me busy and the receptionist is out with a sore throat. What can I do for you?"

"Well, Chief, I'm sorry to tell you there's a dead body in Big Egg."

The chief didn't miss a beat. "Anybody I know?"

Trinidad filled her in. She heard the jingle of car keys.

"I'll...I mean, Chang and I will be there in fifteen. You and Iris don't touch anything, especially the body."

"Yes, ma'am." Trinidad disconnected. Together she and Iris went outside and stared at the corpse, unable to look away.

Iris shivered. "How do you suppose he...you know, got that way?"

Trinidad too was chilled to the bone. "He couldn't swim and he'd been drinking yesterday. Maybe he fell overboard when he went back to the steamboat to get his things after Leonard fired him."

"Or maybe he dove in himself. Suicide?"

She thought about his despair at Chubby's and her heart contracted. Had Harry been miserable enough to take his own life and she hadn't even been willing to give him a lift back to the steamboat? But Cordell and Reg had. That fact would need investigating.

Iris went inside and brought out two musty wool blankets to wrap around them. Trinidad supposed they could wait inside just as well, but it didn't seem right to leave Harry floating there alone. Iris must have felt the same because she stayed too, her teeth chattering like castanets.

Trinidad's thoughts spun adrift. How had Harry Fortesque gone from belligerent drunk to dead in the water in the space of twenty-four hours? Accident? Suicide? Or murder?

Her mind tackled the first two options. She pictured Harry staggering aboard in search of his things or determined to repair the paneling before he left town. Balance compromised, he'd pitched over the railing and into the water. Maybe he'd struck his head? But Leonard slept aboard the steamboat in the captain's quarters, while Renata had an apartment in Joseph. Had he heard Harry thrashing around? A splash? The hapless carpenter was as graceful as a rhino in the Macy's crystal department, so if he'd been conscious, he'd have made a ruckus. Wouldn't Leonard have come to investigate?

Iris pulled the blanket tight around her chest. "I don't think I'll ever be able to look out that picture window again without remembering this."

Trinidad swallowed some bile, watching the ripples break around Harry's body and continue until they lost themselves against the shore inches from where they stood. She frowned. "But if he fell off the steamboat…"

"Or jumped."

"Or jumped," she conceded, "how did he wash up clear across the lake?"

"Probably the wind or the current."

She remembered Stan saying visitors to Sprocket would lose their boats every so often if they weren't secured well to the dock. Her gaze traveled across the mile expanse of water to the steamboat, tiny in the distance. Could a body have floated all the way from the boat and come to roost near Iris's property? She peered closer at Harry.

"Do you have binoculars, by any chance?"

"Oscar had no less than six pairs. A by-product of bird-watching." Iris walked inside, returning to offer a pair to Trinidad while she took the other. They trained them on the ghastly site.

Trinidad almost wavered as Harry's outstretched limbs came into focus, white and ghostly. But this was what detectives did, didn't they? Miss Marple would not have let queasiness stand in her way. Trinidad gripped the binoculars again. "Do you see that? Sticking out from the left shoe?"

Iris focused the lenses. "What is that?"

"Looks like a nail." Trinidad tried to zoom in but the constant bobbing made it tricky. When the water stilled for a moment, she saw more clearly a flat nailhead protruding near the ankle through the vinyl of the shoe. "How did that get there?"

"Leonard said he was a terrible carpenter, so I guess that's fodder for the mill."

Time passed in excruciating slow motion until Chang and Bigley arrived in the same squad car. Trinidad and Iris were only too happy to huddle near the step while Chang and Bigley photographed Harry's body from a zillion different angles.

Using a long pole, they dragged the corpse onto the shore and took another slew of pictures. Trinidad couldn't stop herself. She studied the still form, water oozing out as if relinquishing its claim.

Bigley and Chang joined them and asked preliminary questions before dismissing Iris. "Why don't you go get warmed up, Ms. Fuentes?" Chang said. "Maybe fix yourself a hot drink?" His tone was hopeful.

"I'll make us all coffee." She disappeared into the house.

"That really is a nail in his shoe then?" Trinidad asked.

Chang nodded. "Yes. Looks like a framing nail. Probably went deep enough to hit bone. Those nail guns, man..." He shook his head. "My brother put one clear through his hand one time when we were building a porch on the house. Orthopedist had to yank it out with a pair of pliers."

"We sent an officer..." Bigley started, but Chang cleared his throat and continued.

"*I* dispatched Officer Todd to the steamboat. Leonard was asleep until Todd roused him. He said he'd been at a late-night movie in Joseph and didn't hear or notice anything unusual when he returned. Renata answered her cell and said she'd been at her apartment all night. We'll check out both of their alibis, of course."

"Odd about the jacket," Trinidad mused.

Chang typed a note into his phone. "The jacket?"

"If he was using the nail gun to repair the paneling like he'd been paid to do before he left town, he wouldn't have been wearing a jacket like that, most likely. The added bulk would have made it harder for him to maneuver."

Chang kept nodding. "Unless he shot himself in the ankle while he was preparing to do the work or something. He could have staggered and fallen overboard."

"I guess that might have happened." Trinidad shoved her

frozen hands in her pockets to warm them. "He was terrified of blood. Almost fainted when he banged his head. As soon as that nail went into his ankle, he was probably down for the count."

"And tumbled overboard." Chang jotted another note.

Bigley shook her head. "Not likely he'd have washed up clear across the lake."

Trinidad perked up. "You don't think Harry could have floated across the lake by himself?"

"No. His jacket could've provided buoyancy for a while, but it would have filled with water eventually and sunk him long before he reached the opposite shore unless…" Her gaze drifted across Big Egg. "There's a rowboat moored at the dock near the steamboat. We'll give that a thorough going-over." Bigley held up a palm at Chang's frown. "When Officer Chang gives the order."

Trinidad's thoughts scudded like the waves. What if this wasn't an accident? Had someone used the rowboat to transport Harry to the middle of the lake and then dumped him in? His jacket had kept him afloat long enough for them to spot him? Was someone worried that he would awaken and shout for help? That he'd fight for his life? Or was her imagination running rampant?

She told them of her encounter with Harry at Chubby's. "Cordell and his brother Reg were there. They gave Harry a ride back to the boat last night."

"Very altruistic for that pair," Bigley said.

Chang added to his list. "This whole case just grew a new head."

"I'll talk to Cordell and Reg." Bigley spoke quickly. "If that's okay with you, Chang."

"I guess so." He shrugged. "At least we know Gabe's not involved in *this* death." He grinned. "First thing I did before we came here was call Quinn since Gabe's sleeping on the floor at his place. Quinn said Gabe was there all night with no access to a vehicle. Your baby bro wouldn't have had enough time to walk clear to the dock, kill Harry, and walk back."

"Not to mention he had no motive to kill Harry," Bigley snapped.

"Didn't have one to run Oscar down either," Chang shot back. "And the guy seems to turn up whenever there's a problem."

A depressing cloud infiltrated Trinidad's thoughts. Super Sleuth Trinidad Jones had been certain that Harry, not Gabe, was the one behind the wheel when Oscar was killed. Now her number one suspect was dead. *Way to go, Trinidad.* It looked like Gabe was going to jail now for sure.

─────────

A solid two hours later, Trinidad reported to the shop where she found Juliette and Papa manning the helm. Noodles left his post near Scooter's cage to give Trinidad a gentle going-over, as if he could sense a residue from the horrible situation she'd experienced.

Juliette and Papa sat down with her in the empty shop and she told them the full story, fleshing out the quick text she'd sent earlier.

"But if Harry framed Gabe and now he's been murdered..." Juliette said.

"Then who hired him?" Papa asked.

"Exactly." Trinidad slumped. "I feel like we're back to square one." She was surprised to see Leonard pull up to the curb across the street in his van, headed into the Full of Beans. With Harry out of the picture as her number one suspect, Leonard had risen on the list. "I feel the need for coffee all of a sudden."

"Me too."

Juliette and Trinidad hurried into the cozy shop as Leonard heaved himself from the counter where he'd placed an order and into a chair.

"I'll get us some coffees," Juliette said, "while you find a table."

"Make mine a peppermint hot chocolate instead." Trinidad meandered along, pretending to consider the available seating choices, stopping near Leonard's table. "Hello, Mr. Pinkerton. How are you doing?"

His eyes were puffed. "You heard what happened?"

She decided not to reveal that she and Iris had discovered the body. "Yes. I know Harry's dead."

"I'm not sure what to think. I mean, that idiot carpenter is out of my life, but man. Did you hear he drowned?"

"Yes. Terrible."

"Only a guy like that could shoot himself in the foot with a nail gun and fall overboard."

"Is that what happened?"

"That's what I gathered from the cops. It's bad for business, you know? At the Christmas party, there was this fight.

And now people will hear that Harry fell overboard. Sheesh. Guy can't get a break for love nor money. What am I gonna do for some positive publicity?"

Juliette arrived with their drinks on a tray and handed Leonard the coffee he'd ordered. "I figured I'd bring it over since you had a bad night." She slid into a chair as easily as if she'd been invited, crossing one leg over the other and sipping.

Much more awkwardly, Trinidad sat as well.

Juliette took a sip. "Did you hear him fall overboard?"

Darned if Trinidad hadn't been trying to figure out how to ask that very question.

"Nah. I was in Joseph watching a movie."

"Which one?" Juliette was all guileless wide eyes.

Leonard rattled off a name Trinidad hadn't heard of.

"Oh, I saw that," Juliette said. "Were you surprised by the ending?"

"Me? Uh, no."

"Really? Why not?"

A stain of color worked its way up Leonard's cheeks. "Actually, I fell asleep. I don't know how it ended."

Fell asleep? That'd be a handy alibi. Buy a ticket to the show, stay for a few minutes, then sneak out. Who'd know?

Juliette tapped the lid of her coffee. "It happens. So what was it like when you got back to the boat? I mean, that must have been so weird. Did you realize what had happened?"

He lifted a meaty shoulder. "I didn't realize anything. I unlocked the door and headed up to bed. Didn't even turn on the lights. Could have been a massacre in the dining room and I wouldn't have known."

"Did Harry have a key to let himself onto the boat?"

Leonard huffed out a puff of air. "Yes, which was an error on my part, but he needed access to various storage areas so it was easier to give him a master than keep unlocking stuff myself. I suppose that key is in the bottom of the lake now."

Leonard seemed more upset about his missing key than Harry's death.

"Odd, right?" There was a crafty gleam in Leonard's eyes. "Finding the body near Iris's property?"

"You don't think she had something to do with it?" Juliette looked incredulous.

He shrugged. "Woman like that? Who knows? Her husband died under mysterious circumstances, you know."

Trinidad was trying to figure out what to ask next when Renata pushed open the door. Her hair was neatly fixed and she wore a pair of dark jeans and a sleek winter coat complete with a patterned scarf, but her eyes were red and swollen. She took in the three of them sitting there and walked up, clutching her bag.

"You've heard."

Juliette and Trinidad nodded.

Leonard slugged some coffee. "More bad publicity."

"Is that all you can think about, Leonard? Your precious boat?" Renata hit the *t* at the end of the word hard.

He shrugged. "You're too soft. Why should I act sad about a guy I didn't even like?"

She pressed her lips into a tight line. "Common decency maybe?"

"What do you think happened, Renata?" Trinidad said.

"Happened?" Renata cocked her head. "I think he fell overboard. He can't...I mean, couldn't swim, you know." But her eyes scanned her brother's face for a brief moment. A tell, the police officers whom Trinidad had encountered in her stenography work would have said. What was contained in that briefest of glances?

"We need to book something on the boat," Leonard said. "To make people forget this last unpleasantness."

Renata gathered her purse closer. "You can book it yourself."

"Okay." Leonard was oblivious to her seething tone. "I have an idea. I'll fill you in on the details if it pans out."

Renata marched out of the store without even ordering a coffee.

Juliette and Trinidad left Leonard to his musings and walked back to the Shimmy. "How did that whole encounter seem to you?"

Juliette smoothed her wind-tossed hair. "Strained. And Leonard is clueless."

"There was one moment when I wondered..." Trinidad trailed off.

"Wondered what?"

"Renata is a lot more emotional about Harry's death than Leonard. There was a second that made me think. What if Renata suspects her brother killed Harry?"

Juliette's eyes rounded. "Makes perfect sense. Leonard had reasons to kill Oscar, and maybe he hired Harry to do it. Things went sour and..." She snapped her fingers. "Leonard got rid of his hit man."

"Mm-hmm. He conveniently hurt his ankle the day Oscar was killed. And last night, he was at a movie that he can't remember. Coincidence?"

Juliette grinned. "That's another coincidence. Are you going to talk to Bigley about it?"

"Yes, but I've got to do something first. Two things, actually. I need to tell Stan I'm keeping Scooter."

"You are?" Juliette clasped her hands. "I'm so glad. I didn't want to say anything to influence you since I certainly wasn't volunteering to take him, but your dog has totally bonded with that bird."

"Yes, that's for sure. What's one more added to the gang?"

Juliette smiled. "You're the best, Trinidad."

"And you'll be the person I ask to bird sit if Papa and I go out of town."

"You got it. So what's the second thing you need to do?"

"Deposit Leonard's check. If it turns out he did kill Harry, I want to make sure the money clears the bank first."

Juliette laughed and squeezed her around the shoulders. "Money before murder?"

"Milkshakes before mysteries," Trinidad said, but inside her stomach was tight. Another body and a long way from nabbing the killer.

━━━━━━━━━

The snow did begin to fall as Trinidad flipped the sign to "Closed" and headed to the Vintage Theater to pick up her Christmas tree. The icy sidewalk outside the Vintage

Theater seeped right up through her sneakers. She hoped Mayor Hardwick did not make too big a production about the annual Christmas tree distribution. With five days until Christmas and a body added to the charming scenery, they could use all the holiday cheer they could muster. The tradition in town was for all the owners along Main to display their four-foot spruce trees, lighting them at precisely 5:00 o'clock each evening.

Cheerful carols belted out of a speaker set up inside the theater. The mood was upbeat, though she could see from the sideways looks she was getting that word had spread about her finding Harry in the lake. If she wasn't careful, she was going to get a Jessica Fletcher *Murder, She Wrote* reputation. Bad enough Juliette kept urging her to express her inner sleuth, she didn't want Sprocket to be the next Cabot Cove homicide capital. At the moment, the only person she wanted to be was a humble ice cream shop owner. Then again, the milling Sprocketerians might be chattering about her felonious ex Gabe's horrifying return to town. She pulled her fuzzy hat farther down over her brow and turned up the collar of her coat.

Since it was her first Christmas in Sprocket, Quinn had advised her to line up early for the "Spruce Up" event if she didn't want to stand on the sidewalk too long making small talk with the locals. Small talk was another thing she wasn't interested in.

Mayor Hardwick stood on a box and began to fire off the rules. "You'll decorate your tree with appropriate thematic decorations and display it on the curb outside your shop until December 30th, at which point the truck will come around and collect them for recycling. And by appropriate, I mean normal stuff, not teeth." She directed that remark to Dr. Ramone, the town dentist.

"They were artificial teeth," he called back. "And you're lucky I'm not a proctologist."

Hardwick ignored the remark and kept on with her list. Trinidad waved to Iris, who was several spots back in line. Her tree would no doubt look amazing, festooned in the finest flowers and ribbons. Iris didn't exactly smile, but Trinidad thought she looked a few degrees warmer. Perhaps discovering Harry's body had formed a rickety bridge between them. She was finding it harder and harder to believe Iris could have had anything to do with Oscar's death. Or Harry's.

Quinn jogged up, breath puffing white. "Whew. Had to change out a tire. Almost missed the sprucing up." He planted a kiss on her temple. "Doug's helping Juliette and Bonnie get set up for your bombing class."

"We really need to come up with a better name."

He nodded, distracted. "You're second in line. Sweet. Gabe came too, unfortunately, but I'm not going to let that get me down."

She'd momentarily allowed herself to forget Gabe's whereabouts. Gabe was the burnt-out bulb on her holiday string, but she resolved not to let it squash her spirit either. The first person in line whom she'd thought was gas station owner Mr. Mavis turned out to be Leonard. He pushed back his knit cap.

"Oh, hello, Mr. Pinkerton."

"Good that you're here. I got a business question to ask you." He didn't waste any time on niceties. "Do you make cakes?"

"Me? Well, no…"

Quinn nudged her. "What about those amazing ice cream cakes you told me about?"

She covered her puzzlement when she saw his eyebrows telegraphing her a message. "Oh, those. I, uh, yes, I make ice cream cakes. Decorated and everything."

Leonard perked up. "So you can make it look fancy? Like with frilly stuff and all?"

She had not actually constructed an ice cream cake before, but who was she to turn up her nose at a moneymaking gig? "Absolutely." Her excitement was pinpricked at the sudden thought that the man standing before her asking for ice cream cakes might be a murderer. Before she could backpedal, Mayor Hardwick finished her remarks.

"Leonard, you're first," the mayor snapped. "Pay attention and come get your tree. There are fifteen people in line behind you turning into popsicles while you jibber-jabber."

"Talk to you in a minute. Gotta load this tree and buy some lights before the hardware store closes." Leonard snagged a tree and hauled it off toward his van.

Trinidad waited until Leonard was out of earshot. "I wasn't aware the Shimmy offered up ice cream cakes, Quinn."

He grinned, pulled on a pair of leather work gloves, and grabbed the next tree. "See how I'm helping you expand the business?"

She followed him, inhaling a wash of pine scent. "But what if Leonard's a murderer?"

Quinn shot her a startled look through the branches. "You think he shoved Harry overboard?"

"I don't know, but what if he did?"

A spruce branch tangled in Quinn's hair. "Then he'll be caught and put in jail. In the meantime, word of your ice cream cake prowess will spread out like that caramel sauce you make that I can't get enough of." He patted the small pudge around his waist. "See this? Courtesy of that same caramel sauce."

She smiled. "I have one to match."

"All I see is voluptuous perfection. You're gorgeous, every inch of you." His face shone under the streetlights as he looked at her before stumbling and barely catching himself.

She couldn't answer through the happy warmth filling her up from the inside out. This guy was too good to be true.

"Besides, anytime you have to go aboard that steamboat again, I'm signing up to be your catering assistant."

She trotted along in a haze of holiday cheer. In spite of everything, here she was with Quinn at her side and a newly found family waiting inside her very own darling shop. Iris's words circled around her mind.

For me, it's so much more than a business. It's everything.

Not everything, Trinidad thought, listening to Felice's squeal of excitement and the smiles on Bonnie's, Juliette's, and Papa's faces as Quinn plopped the tree on the Shimmy's curb. But Iris seemed to be alone in the world, from what Trinidad could tell. Alone was a sad place to be. There was a flurry of activity as an extension cord was secured and Juliette took charge of wrapping the tree in pink and white lights.

"Your turn." Bonnie offered Felice a box full of ornaments shaped like ice cream cones.

Gabe stood in the shadows, eyes darting up and down the street. Impossible not to notice his anxiety. *Don't make eye contact, Trin.* That seemed to be the way Papa was leaning as he offered cups of hot cider all around. He stiffly held out his tray to Gabe who took the last cup, which surprised her.

"Thank you, Papa."

Papa grimaced at Gabe. "You may call me Mr. Jones. And I will try to refer to you as Mr. Bigley."

She had to be witnessing a Christmas miracle.

"That's a step up from the Hooligan," Gabe said with a laugh.

Papa did not laugh, but Trinidad felt reassured that the evening could continue without too much drama. They'd enjoy the moment, welcome the children attending the cocoa bomb class, and see if Leonard actually did return to discuss an ice cream cake order. Then she'd corner Bonnie.

There was no sign of Cordell, and he wouldn't dare try and rough Gabe up with so many people around. It was even possible he'd gotten tired of hanging around Sprocket and hit the trail. Tiny white flakes dusted Felice's pink cap as she hung the ornaments on the petite spruce. The delicately falling snow reminded Trinidad of the scene at Oscar's house as the police dragged Harry's dead body out of the lake. She swallowed hard.

Accident? Suicide? Murder?

With a deep breath, she pushed the thoughts away.

Tonight would be sweet and smooth, no matter what she learned from Bonnie. Sleuthing could wait for the morning.

But as Scooter warbled from inside the shop, she couldn't help thinking of the dead man who'd offered to keep him.

Poor Scooter. Poor Oscar. Poor Harry.

A grotesque version of the "Twelve Days of Christmas" song played in her head.

One looming wedding.

Two deceased bodies.

Three Barrones in town.

Four creatures stuffed in the tiny house.

What additional chaos would happen when they got to the chorus?

Chapter Seventeen

INSIDE, THE ADULTS MANNED THEIR battle stations, and Trinidad was relieved that Gabe carried himself off to a chair near the back room to observe. The more distance between them the better.

The four kids had increased to six, since two had brought friends along. Trinidad scrambled to produce more muffin tins and made a mental note to prep extras for the next kid's class she might offer. Would it work to do drop-in classes? The first stop for each child was a visit to the "animal corner," which Noodles and Scooter appeared to relish. Scooter even piped up with a "Wowee!" at the perfect moment. Maybe he would turn out to be as much of a shop attraction as Noodles.

With Quinn and Juliette pitching in, they managed to collect payment from the parents and send them on their way for a coveted child-free two hours. Trinidad provided a quick tour of the shop, and Bonnie helped conduct a product tasting that proved to be a thrill for the young ice cream enthusiasts. Felice's favorite, cake batter ice cream, was a clear winner. Doug distributed aprons and hair nets, which elicited a chorus of giggles. Settling down at the table, they started in on the messy process of producing bombs.

Trinidad admired the level of concentration they brought to the task. "You're doing great."

Doug stood well out of the range of any mess, near Noodles and Scooter, ready to dole out the pretty boxes Trinidad had acquired to package the treats, the Shimmy's logo and phone number printed prominently in silver on the top panel. Trinidad explained how the ganache filling was made, and the children stirred their own mini portions with careful attention. Bombs assembled, they were decorated to the nines and nestled in the boxes. *Voilà!* she thought with pride. The perfect Christmas activity and it even produced a one-of-a-kind gift.

Papa had prepared a second batch of bombs for the participants, crammed with special peppermint marshmallows. Class complete, the children took seats while Papa delivered his treats into a set of mugs and Juliette poured in the hot milk. The exclamations made her smile as the bomb transformed the plain milk into a spectacular drink.

As the happy sippers chattered away, Trinidad could not keep her mind from returning to Cordell's Christmas party aboard the Sprocket Steamboat. Those two mugs with cooled milk and unmelted bombs troubled her along with the whole accident on the boat. Two people had been sneaking around to stage that accident that inadvertently got Gabe, hoping to injure or kill…who? Who was the intended victim? Not Gabe, certainly. And which of the party guests had arranged for the mishap? The list of people who had been sitting or passing by that table was long: Cordell, Iris, Renata, Leonard, Harry.

She bit her lip. At least Harry was off the list of suspects now, one way or another.

A squeal of laughter broke her train of thought. Felice smiled shyly and fingered her pink cap as the other girls chattered away. It was good to see her with other children. Bonnie said Felice's peers had been unkind in public school, which was why she'd taken over the instruction at home.

Trinidad looked around to see if Bonnie was pleased with the interaction. To her surprise, she found Bonnie and Gabe had stepped into the back room. Bonnie stood near the threshold with her arms crossed, a full head and shoulders taller than Gabe, who slumped next to her. It wasn't a happy conversation by the look of it. Was Gabe pressuring Bonnie to marry him?

Not on her watch. Trinidad hustled over.

"Come with me," Gabe was saying. "We'll find a place somewhere."

Bonnie shook her head. "No way, Gabe. You can't run from this."

Trinidad slowed. *Run from what?*

"I can't take care of you and Felice in jail." Gabe's voice wobbled.

"I don't need you to take care of me and Felice. I can do that myself."

"Not if the secret gets out. We can run, start over."

The word "secret" made Trinidad stop altogether. Should she listen? Retreat? Barge in?

Bonnie shook her head. "I made a life for Felice and me in Sprocket. We have the inn and we have amazing friends. I'm sorry, Gabe, but if you decide to bolt, you're going alone."

"Bolt?" Trinidad blurted out, making them both jump. "Gabe, you are not thinking about going on the lam, are you? You wouldn't last two days. The one time we tried camping, you were calling an Uber before we got the tent up. And there is no way you can possibly think it's a good idea to pull Bonnie and Felice into your ridiculous plan."

He blinked. "But now that Harry's dead, I'm the only one they can pin it on."

She glared. "And that's a good reason not to get married until this legal trouble is resolved, isn't it?"

Bonnie nodded slowly. "That's a good point and, you know, sooner or later, the trouble will disappear, so maybe if we stall..."

"The trouble will always be a problem unless we take permanent action," Gabe said carefully.

Trinidad scowled. "What is this? Are you speaking in code or something? What trouble are we talking about?"

"Never mind that." Gabe played with the zipper on his jacket.

She turned to Bonnie. "Bonnie, I thought we were friends, sisters. Whatever it is, you can trust me."

Bonnie went pale and she clutched Trinidad's hands.

Trinidad squeezed back. "Please tell me. I want to help."

"I..." Bonnie looked from Gabe to Trinidad and gulped.

"I'm sorry." After one more almost painful squeeze, she dropped Trinidad's hands.

The action sent a pain through Trinidad's heart. Bonnie didn't trust her. Not enough. Trinidad blinked back a film of tears. Maybe they weren't really sisters after all.

Bonnie shifted from foot to foot.

"How about some good news?" Gabe said. "I've already started the ball rolling on the wedding. Figured we'd better get on it before I get arrested." He eyed a newcomer to the shop and waved. Leonard pushed in, a coil of Christmas lights slung over his shoulder.

Trinidad had a sinking feeling as she walked with them to meet Leonard at the front counter. The children's parents were waiting now, and Doug was carefully doling out discount coupons for ice cream and info about the monthly classes Trinidad had decided to host. Juliette and Quinn wiped down the tables and swept up stray sprinkles and flakes of peppermint.

Leonard ignored the children, sidestepping them on his way to the front.

He tapped a palm on the speckled counter. "So it's set for Sunday, then, day after Christmas. Trinidad said she can do an ice cream cake. You can tell her what flavors and stuff you want. If Iris can get off her high horse, the Sprocket Steamboat will provide a bouquet. Cake, flowers, and I can perform the ceremony. Perfect, right? Ship captains don't actually have the power to do that, but I got a certificate because people like the romance of having a captain hitch them. I knew it would come in handy when I expanded the business."

"Hang on." Trinidad looked from Leonard to Gabe. "You want to have your wedding on the steamboat?" She narrowed her eyes at Leonard. "But you were furious at him for crashing Cordell's party."

Quinn and Juliette were now listening too with rapt attention.

Leonard shrugged. "Desperate for good publicity right about now, and I got wind from Cordell that these two love-birds wanted to tie the knot. Boat's already decorated for Christmas. Renata's going to take photos to put up on the website and such. I'm offering up the venue for free, so what's not to like about that? These two get married, I get publicity photos, and everyone wins." He shrugged. "I'll invite a few people to sort of fill in the background spectators, so make enough cake for twenty or so. Coffee too maybe, huh?"

Trinidad looked at Bonnie, beseeching. "This is really what you want? To marry Gabe on the steamboat?"

The moment stretched tight between them until Bonnie shrugged. "It's an inexpensive way to do it, I guess. I mean, I had a wedding back in the day with the frilly dress and a train and all. Believe me, it's not easy to find a dress when you're my height. This will be no fuss for everyone."

"That's what we're striving for in a wedding? No fuss?"

Bonnie shoved her hands into the back pockets of her jeans. "At least I know the ice cream cake will be fantastic."

Trinidad felt like screaming. "Who cares about cakes and dresses? Look me in the eye and tell me you love Gabe and you want to marry him, and I won't bother you again about it."

Bonnie grimaced. "Trinidad..."

"Mommy." Felice held up her beribboned box. "Isn't it pretty?"

"Yes, Fee," Bonnie called back in a soft voice. "That is absolutely gorgeous."

"I'm gonna give some to you and some to Daddy."

Gabe beamed. "That's my generous girl."

Bonnie walked away, and Trinidad was drawn into a conversation with a parent inquiring about birthday parties. Did Trinidad do birthday parties? She'd have to give that some thought. She was already running a shop, conducting classes, and apparently making ice cream wedding cakes. By the time she finished up with a promise to think about it and respond, Leonard was gone. Bonnie, Gabe, and Felice had stepped outside.

Through the window, she saw Bonnie and Gabe standing together by the twinkling lights of the ice cream Christmas tree.

"A steamboat wedding, huh?" Quinn said, putting his arm around her shoulders. "Sounds like we're in for another bash. Let me know when we're reporting for duty and I'll be there."

She didn't answer.

He kissed her cheek. "It's going to be okay. Whatever their reasons, they both love Felice."

As they watched, Gabe put a gentle hand on Bonnie's arm, comfort in the gesture.

Did he really love Bonnie? Was Trinidad letting her own distrustful feelings color her perception of their marriage?

Gabe had changed somewhat since he'd gone to jail, no matter what Quinn thought, and he loved Felice, no doubt about it. But why would he talk about running away and taking Bonnie and Felice with him?

The trouble will always be a problem unless we take permanent action.

What trouble could be worse than Gabe's arrest and return to jail?

The obvious answer was Cordell and his violent intentions toward Gabe.

But that wasn't the whole scoop, Trinidad thought uneasily.

And the time to find out was quickly melting away.

━━━━━━

Chief Bigley caught up to Trinidad as she took Noodles for a brisk morning walk. Noodles, clad in his jacket, wagged his tail. Bigley stripped off her gloves and scrubbed him behind the ears. "Thanks for telling me Gabe was thinking of splitting town. I drove to Quinn's place and explained if he tried anything so dumb, I would hunt him down myself and administer my own form of justice."

Trinidad winced. "I felt bad telling you, but I can't have him dragging Bonnie and Felice into the life of a fugitive."

"I assume Bonnie has sense enough not to listen to my brother."

"Yes, but they're still planning on getting married."

"I heard. A steamboat wedding on Sunday and something

about an ice cream cake. By the way, he said to tell you chocolate and peppermint might be nice for flavors."

Trinidad sighed. "All right. I guess my first wedding ice cream cake will be chocolate and peppermint. The whole thing is pure madness, but neither Gabe nor Bonnie seems to want to stop it. You'll be there, I assume?"

"Right."

She exhaled. At least with the chief of police as a party guest, there couldn't be another incident on the steamboat.

Bigley slapped her gloves against her thigh. "I have some news."

"The good kind or the bad?"

"Neither at this point." She clicked open her phone. "Take a look at this photo. The cop who searched the steamboat the night Harry's body was found took them."

She cupped a palm to reduce the glare, and Trinidad bent to examine the picture. It was the deck of the steamboat, near the front entrance, she gathered. The photo was somewhat dark, shadowed, and the tiniest bit grainy, but she saw a closed cardboard box, a carpenter's tool belt, and a large yellow container with a handle.

"It's Harry's gear packed up on the deck," Bigley said.

"Packed? So he was intending to leave then?"

"I have that confirmed via another source. Stan talked to a disgruntled local who showed up at the Full of Beans Tuesday morning. Guy drives for Uber and says he was supposed to pick Harry up at the dock Sunday night but Harry was a no show and he feels like he got stiffed."

"Bad choice of words."

"Yeah. Anyway, Harry scheduled this Uber. Promised him a great tip."

Her mind zinged along as they continued the walk. "So Harry intended to leave town."

"Yes, so that definitely throws doubt on the notion of suicide. Accident is still on the table but…"

Something niggled at her. "Wait a minute. The nail gun was put away too? It was inside its box?"

Bigley thumbed up another photo, and Trinidad took a moment to view it, the inside of the yellow container with a nail gun neatly packed in its foam compartment.

"Yeah. Photo here shows it stowed away, shipshape. Odd, right? That was the other thing that struck me wrong."

"For sure. Harry had a nail in his ankle. If he'd shot himself, it would have been incredibly painful."

"And it's highly unlikely that he'd have packed up his nail gun neat and tidy like after an injury like that," Bigley finished.

"Not with his reaction to the sight of blood."

Noodles stopped to nose at a clump of grass protruding from under a lacy blanket of snow as the impact of the photo settled on Trinidad.

"So we can rule out accident too?"

Bigley stowed her phone. "In my book, we're looking at a murder."

"And the suspects?"

"Leonard, Renata, Iris. Cordell was there too, but I don't see what he'd have against Harry. That's been the whole fly in the ointment for Oscar's death and now Harry's. Motive."

Hidden motives, Trinidad thought, surprised to find they'd arrived back at the shop. She let Noodles off the leash to help himself to a drink from the bowl of water on the porch.

"What does this mean for Gabe?"

Bigley frowned. "Nothing much, I'm afraid. We can't get a ping on Harry's cell phone so there's no way to prove he was indeed in the car when Oscar was struck."

"Gabe's still the only possible suspect?"

"It looks that way, though I'm still persona non grata in that regard." She slid on a pair of sunglasses. "I have to go to work. Keep me posted on any developments, and I'll do the same."

"Okay. I guess I'd better figure out how to make a wedding ice cream cake."

She rolled her eyes. "Not to make you feel bad, but this is the fourth Gabe Bigley wedding I've been invited too. At some point, you run out of gift ideas."

"Not being arrested would be the best gift Gabe could receive."

She frowned. "Don't think he's likely to get that one."

All Trinidad could do was hope that something happened to clear up the mystery before it was too late for Gabe.

Chapter Eighteen

CARLOS AND DIEGO LET IN a gust of cold air when they arrived for their Wednesday after-school shift. They did a double take at the enormous sheet pan Trinidad had driven into Joseph to retrieve.

Diego goggled at the pan. "Massive. What's it for?"

"A wedding cake. We're making a practice one to try it out. Wash up, okay?"

After handwashing, Carlos grabbed the roll of foil and helped line the pan while Diego slid behind the counter to deliver a cup of pecan pie ice cream to a customer.

"Are we doing cakes now?" Carlos watched as she filled the cake pan with a layer of freshly made chocolate cake, then a layer of chocolate ice cream, and stowed it in the freezer.

"Apparently, we are. Can you look up some ideas for how to decorate this thing?" They spent forty-five minutes scrolling through pictures until the peppermint ice cream was finished churning. Diego chopped up chocolate wafer cookies that she sprinkled atop a lake of fudge filling before the peppermint ice cream layer went on. At closing time, she unmolded the massive cake and smoothed the edges with a warm offset spatula before adding softened ice cream swirls and a ribbon of pink and white peppermint flakes along the bottom.

"What are you going to put on the top?"

"I'm not sure."

"How about a message? Like happy wedding?"

"Wedding cakes don't have writing," Carlos said. "They have little plastic brides and grooms."

"I think we'll break tradition and go with a message." *Why not, since this wedding is a train wreck in the making?* She used a piping bag to add "Best wishes Gabe and Bonnie" with a thin pink icing. They were going to need more than good wishes.

Diego's mouth dropped open. "That's for Gabe? Like he's getting married again? Mom said she heard from Mrs. Mavis that he was going back to jail."

"Well…"

"And Cora at the theater said so too."

"Actually…"

"Oh I get it." Diego nodded sagely. "That's why the hurry-up nuptials. He's hoping to tie the knot before he goes to the slammer."

"It's a wedding on the steamboat the day after Christmas," she said firmly. "I'm sure there will be no arrest to interfere."

"The steamboat?" The twins exchanged a look. "We heard about this wedding." Carlos bubbled with excitement. "So we're gonna help, right? With the service and stuff?"

"I was hoping you might, so I can focus on being a guest." Her hopes that the strained marriage would not come to pass were fading by the hour. She paused her piping work. "Why are you so eager to work the event, may I ask?"

He zoomed the broom under the chairs. "'Cause Cordell Barrone's gonna be there. I heard him talking to his brother while they were filling up at the gas station. He said Mr. Pinkerton invited him to be a guest."

Trinidad felt her stomach squeeze down into a tiny walnut-sized ball. Cordell was going to attend the wedding? She grabbed her phone to make sure the bride and groom knew.

Was Cordell planning to disrupt the nuptials?

At this ceremony, anything could happen.

The shop was quiet for the rest of the week. Trinidad closed the Shimmy Friday afternoon and celebrated Christmas Eve by going to church with Papa and then joining up with Doug and Quinn and the animals. Christmas Day was spent at Juliette's where Trinidad handed out her gifts to Bonnie, Juliette, and Felice. Gabe was almost as quiet as Doug, hoovering up all the chips and dip he could hold. Was he trying to enjoy all the things he thought he'd be missing when he was returned to jail?

They managed to steer the conversation clear of Gabe's impending arrest. Bonnie was reluctant to discuss much in the way of wedding details. She was also clearly avoiding private conversation with her other two sisters. Trinidad was hurt and angry. How had her relationship with Bonnie ruptured without her noticing? Secrets had crept in like the winter cold. Somehow, they stumbled through the awkward Christmas gathering. Quinn was staying as far away from Gabe as possible, but he managed to keep a smile on his face.

His present to her was a watch with ice cream scoops for hands. She buckled on the pink strap in delight.

"Thank you. I love it."

"Good." He looked as though he wanted to say more, but with an audience, he settled on a shy smile. Cheerful as it was, the tiny ticking hands reminded her that Gabe's freedom was winding to a close too. She watched Gabe staring at Felice as she opened another gift, his expression wistful and grave.

How would he and Bonnie explain it to Felice? No matter what they said, she would have to be told her father had taken someone else's life. This might be their first and last Christmas together for a long time.

Trinidad realized Quinn was watching her watch Gabe, but when she turned, he'd looked away.

The Sunday wedding preparations were surreal. Before she and Papa headed to the Shimmy, she'd pulled on a pair of slacks that were only a tad tight around the waist and a blouse Juliette had found her, the palest green with a lacy jacket to top it. She'd pulled her hair into what she hoped was a chic updo and applied lipstick for the occasion. Her smile in the mirror was grim, as though she were going to a funeral, not a wedding. Quinn met her at the Shimmy, sporting a new pair of khakis and a long-sleeved shirt with the price tag still dangling from the side. Doug was similarly dressed, his dark hair plastered down.

"Well, don't you two look handsome." Trinidad snapped the price tag off Quinn's shirt.

He flushed. "Oh, is that what was scratching me?" His gaze was appreciative and made her own cheeks warm. "As Papa would say, you are a picture."

"So true." Papa straightened his tie. She'd told him the occasion probably didn't call for a necktie, but Papa would not be dissuaded. Felice had requested Noodles be present and Leonard hadn't objected, so Noodles sported his own formal wear, a spiffy red-and-green bow tie. He danced agitatedly around Scooter's cage.

"No birds allowed, Noo. You can see your friend when we come back to the shop."

Papa had arranged to help Stan transport the coffee urn since he did not drive. Juliette would be meeting them at the dock.

"Hold on." Papa gestured for them to stand close while he readied his old Polaroid camera and pressed the button. "Got it. A striking couple."

Is that what they were? A couple and a striking one at that? Quinn's touch on her lower back made her thoughtful. His hands were nothing like Gabe's. They were calloused from long days of manual labor, the nails stained by nut oils. Quinn hardly noticed what he wore and Gabe was a clotheshorse. How had she been coupled with two men over the course of her life who were so completely different? And was she actually about to attend Gabe's *fourth* wedding? To Bonnie? It was too much to wrap her brain around.

"Is it weird that we're going to arrive at a wedding in a food truck?" She, Quinn, Noodles, and Doug climbed aboard the pink behemoth. She'd figured it was the best way to keep the fresh ice cream cake she'd put together the night before ultracold on the way to the venue. Doug strapped into the small seat in the back, and Noodles dutifully climbed into the doggie crate she'd provided for extra safety.

"The way I see it, we've got a groom on the cusp of an arrest, a bride who is remarrying a guy who just got sprung from jail, and the venue is a boat on which someone probably got murdered. The food truck vehicle hardly rates a blip on the weird-o-meter."

"Mm-hmm," she said absently, guiding the truck along. "There's still this secret trouble issue he was talking about with Bonnie."

"Gabe is one giant walking trouble issue."

She laughed. "At least you'll be getting him out of your office."

"I suppose. We haven't discussed his postwedding living arrangements. Do you think he'll stay in Sprocket if he doesn't get carted off to jail?"

"That's the point of getting married, isn't it? To be a father to Felice?"

He frowned. "Honestly, the thought of him living here gives me the willies."

Trinidad considered as she drove. To her surprise, she found her feelings had changed. "You know, I think it might be a good thing."

"Good?" Quinn blurted. "For Gabe to stay here?"

"Yes. I have no delusions that he and Bonnie love each other, but he'll be involved in Felice's life again."

"He's a human dumpster fire."

"This time, I think he might have grown up a little. At least I hope so. He seems willing to sacrifice for Felice. I respect that."

Quinn's brows knitted. "He'll never change, Trin. It's a matter of time before he starts down another crooked lane and messes up their lives again."

"Bonnie is wiser too, about parenting, not romance, anyway, and Juliette and I will be looking out for her and Felice."

His nostrils flared. "So you'll be staying close to Gabe then too?"

It was time to put the cards on the table. She took a breath. "If he's in Bonnie and Felice's life, he's in mine too."

"This is crazy."

"That's what's really bothering you?" She gripped the steering wheel. "That Gabe and I might get close again? He'll be married, remember? And I wouldn't want him even if he wasn't."

"I know, but he's got this power over women." Quinn's tone was acid. "I mean, the guy's getting married for the *fourth time*."

She spoke slowly. "Quinn, this isn't an issue between me and Gabe. It's between you and me. I am an intelligent, independent woman. Gabe doesn't have any power over me, like he's Svengali and I'm helpless to resist or something. If you can't understand that, I guess you don't trust me very much." It took all her courage to say it, but she knew she had to.

He didn't answer, arms folded. The atmosphere had gone from cheerful to morose in the space of five minutes. Her heart ached. She'd suffered through her divorce and rebuilt her life brick by painful brick and morphed into a strong, resilient woman who could make smart choices, her choices. If Quinn thought she was weak willed enough she'd forget all that simply because Gabe was in the same town…

Her fingers were clammy on the steering wheel. She was offended, disappointed, and her insides pulsed with sadness. She'd thought he knew her better. She'd thought she knew him.

Just at the point where the silence was becoming unbearable, Quinn spoke. "Let's just try and get through the ceremony without any further catastrophes."

On that ominous note, they pulled into the lot and Quinn hefted the ice cream cake on its crystal platter. In its rock-hard state, she figured it would be a good hour before it was soft enough to slice, which would work out perfectly since the short ceremony would not kick off for forty minutes. Doug freed Noodles from the crate, and he hustled to Trinidad's side to give her an encouraging nose poke. He sensed her emotional turmoil.

"It's okay, Noo. Let's go attend a wedding, shall we?" Tears pricked her eyelids but she willed them away. It would be her gift to Bonnie, supporting her choice as best she could. Plastering on a smile, she strode up the gangplank, passing by the massive red paddle wheel, which had been turned on. It was churning up lake water in a merry cloud, and Doug stopped to stare in awe at the clanking pistons that powered the structure. There was a waist-high security gate to prevent visitors from getting too close. No telling what would happen to someone falling in the spot where water and paddle wheel crashed together.

A spark of green caught her eye as the wheel plunged along. Maybe a piece of trash sucked up from Big Egg? For a moment, she flashed on Harry's body spread on the water, dead eyes staring at the lake bottom. Murdered, there was no question in her mind. By one of the people attending this very wedding?

Snap out of it, Trin. Bonnie has decided to marry Gabe for whatever bizarre reason. The least you can do it plaster on a smile and stop thinking about corpses. And with a police chief attending, there would be no trouble in spite of Quinn's dour warning.

The lobby Christmas tree, decorated with ships of all types, sparkled in the corner, and the hostess desk was still twined with lights as they had been for Cordell's party. As they entered the dining room, it seemed almost cavernous without all the tables. There were only three, but each sported a basket of plump white roses. Stan and Papa arrived with the coffee urn, and Juliette, svelte in a cream dress, helped set up the beverage station. There were two rows of twelve. Twenty-four chairs? She wondered if Leonard was following the method they used at the Academy Awards, roping people in to fill empty seats.

He wore an ill-fitting suit and some sort of captain's hat, and he was leafing through a yellow legal pad.

There was no sign of the groom, but Bonnie appeared with Felice. The little girl skipped instead of walked, telegraphing her excitement. Trinidad's heart swelled. At least Felice was thrilled to witness the wedding of her parents.

"Look, Auntie Trinidad." She twirled to puff out her pink satin dress to best effect.

"I love it and your hat is a perfect match."

Felice fingered the silk roses that adorned her fascinator along with a fountain of ribbon and lace so poufy that it covered the entire crown of her head. "Mommy made it for me."

Bonnie laughed. "I've already taken a million pictures of her."

Trinidad took a breath and hugged her friend. "And your ensemble is stunning too."

Bonnie smoothed the sleek pants and single-breasted jacket in a muted pearl color. She wore only a touch of gloss on her lips, pearl studs on her ears, and metallic flats. Even with no heels, she'd tower over Gabe in the photos. Trinidad let her hand rest on Bonnie's arm, seeking to catch her eyes.

"Are you…sure about this? Really, really sure? I won't press you for your reasons anymore. I…"

Bonnie took Trinidad's hands in hers. "I'm sorry I hurt you by keeping secrets. You and Juliette are my sisters and I love you."

Trinidad clutched her back. "We love you too. No matter what. If you're certain this is what you want…"

"I am." Bonnie's eyes were bright with tears. "This is the right decision for all of us."

Trinidad applied pressure for one more moment. Quinn didn't trust her, and it crushed her to the core. She would not do the same to this sincere, loving woman who'd become a sister to her. She smiled. "All right. I am honored to be here for you both."

Bonnie patted her hand and let out a breath. "Thank you, Trinidad." Stan and Juliette came over to offer their regards to the bride.

Renata trundled in, a candy-cane-printed scarf around her neck, taking photos of everything and everyone. "Oh my gosh," she said to Felice. "You are the most adorable thing ever. And that hat? *Très chic.* Can you pose with the dog?"

Felice obliged, kneeling next to Noodles. Trinidad took a photo with her phone as well for Bonnie's album. Bonnie's eyes narrowed as Cordell and Reg strolled in. She crossed the room in five long strides.

"Cordell, I don't understand why you're here. It'd better not be to make trouble."

He raised his palms in a gesture of surrender. "Hey, Bon Bon. The captain requested I attend. Though I still can't understand why you'd—"

She poked him in the chest. "I don't want to hear it. I'm marrying Gabe. It's my choice. Stay out of it and don't make waves, do you hear me?"

Trinidad and Quinn took positions on either side of Bonnie in a show of moral support.

"He's a crook," Cordell said, face hard. "And he stole money from my mother. He hasn't paid his debt for that."

Reg nodded in silence.

The whole "debts must be paid" motto was apparently shared by all the Barrones.

Gabe entered in a suit he must have borrowed from someone. The chief was at her brother's side. Trinidad was surprised to see her in uniform. Probably to send a message to Cordell and company. Gabe's radiant smile dimmed as he took in the tableau.

"Come on," Renata said. "First, we need photos of the men. Cordell, how about you first? Incredible jacket, by the way."

Cordell looked at Bonnie. "Wore my best for you, Bon Bon. How about we get a photo together?"

Stiffly, Bonnie stood next to him. He leaned close and wrapped an arm around her, all the while glaring at Gabe. Renata took the picture. Leonard smiled from across the room, pleased to have his celebrity photo.

Bigley walked Gabe well away from Cordell. "Stick by me and he can't do anything."

The tension was ridiculous. Trinidad took a breath and spoke louder than she'd intended. "Gabe, I wish you and Bonnie every happiness."

He crooked a smile. "I'm going to do it right this time, Trin. I, uh, I'm sorry for how I treated you three." He paused. "Um, if I, you know, go back to jail, can you look out for Bonnie and Felice?"

"I will do my best."

He sighed. "I messed up in the marriage department, but at least it brought you and Juliette and Bonnie together, right?"

Something she'd always be grateful for. "Right."

Bigley was still scanning the room. "How about we don't talk about arrests, at least until the wedding is over, okay?"

"Deal." And Trinidad would try not to think of Quinn or Harry's murder or poor Oscar's either.

Leonard looked up from the printed notes he was reading and frowned. "Iris, can you put some flowers or something by the door? I want it to look as Christmassy as possible. We gotta sell this as a year-round venue."

Iris shot him an annoyed look, but she turned on her heel.

Renata photographed the ice cream cake in all its glossy glory. "Trinidad, can you grab the guest book from my hostess stand? I forgot to bring it in."

Trinidad hurried to retrieve the item. The irony struck her. There had been more than a hundred people signing the guest book at Trinidad's wedding to Gabe. At this event, they'd be hard-pressed to get two dozen. Big or small, marriage was a leap into the unknown. She passed Iris, bent over retrieving the poinsettia basket from Cordell's party.

Iris grumbled. "I'm going to repurpose this in the dining room as wedding decor, since cheapskate Leonard is only paying me one hundred bucks for the bouquet and head table spray. He has no clue what fresh flowers cost."

"He's a skinflint, that's for sure." Trinidad rummaged around the hostess stand and registration desk without finding the guest book. She'd have to ask Renata for better directions. She caught a white gleam from the glossy foliage in Iris's basket when she started back to the dining room.

"Hang on," she said.

Iris straightened. "What?"

Trinidad peered at the plant. "The night of the accident, Harry knocked the basket over, and I uprighted it and shoved everything back."

"That explains why it looks terrible," Iris said.

"I thought there was an ornament peeking out of the leaves."

"I didn't use ornaments in the poinsettia baskets."

It wasn't an ornament she'd seen. Trinidad reached in and extracted a light bulb. They both stared at it.

"What's *that* doing in my poinsettia plant?"

She thought back to the moments before Gabe had been shoved into the lake. "Leonard said he'd gone upstairs to replace the burnt-out bulb in the women's room the night Gabe went over the side. I checked. The bulb in the bathroom that night really was burned out and the fixture was old and rickety."

"And the switched-out bulb was hidden in my plant?" Iris's eyes flew wide behind the lenses of her glasses.

"I think so." Trinidad grimaced. "Oh man. I don't think I should have touched it." She paused. "But since I already have…"

She grabbed a paper napkin from her pocket and held the bulb gingerly, hoping not to mess up any fingerprints. Spying the old torchiere lamp in the corner, she hastily removed the existing bulb and screwed in the recently discovered one. Turning the switch, the lamp sprang to life.

"Still works perfectly," Trinidad said.

Iris frowned. "You're saying someone removed a good bulb and replaced it with a dud so Leonard would have to go upstairs to fetch a new one. They stuck it in the plant to get it out of the way. Who?"

"Could have been Harry or Renata."

Iris hefted her poinsettia. "Or Leonard to give himself a reason to go upstairs. Maybe he was trying to kill Iris or Gabe or Harry." She looked stricken. "Or me. That guy is a reprobate, and I wouldn't put anything past him."

"Sorry, Iris, but you should probably leave that plant here. I'll send Bigley in to fetch it."

"Guess Leonard will have to do without." Hesitating, she lowered the plant down. As she straightened, her expression was wary. You might want to be careful, Trinidad. Oscar's dead and now Harry. Getting mixed up in whatever this is... might land you in trouble you can't get out of."

There was no coming back from dead, Trinidad agreed. Iris turned and left.

Was Iris's warning to alert Trinidad to the danger?

Or was there a deeper reason?

Shivering, Trinidad hurried to fetch the chief.

While Renata continued photographing and the guests remained oblivious, Bigley dutifully retrieved the evidence, photographed it in place, and called Chang to pick it up for the tech people to process. Bigley listened to Chang for a moment before ending the connection.

"Chang said the lab team got the boat finished. Some partial prints from Leonard and dozens from who knows whom, since he lets it out for rentals to people who want to go fishing. No blood traces that we can find."

"What about Harry's cause of death? Was he, er, alive when he went into the water?" The thought made Trinidad queasy.

"Nothing to report yet," Bigley said.

Harp music suddenly blared via the sound system. Murder in the lobby and marriage in the dining room. What a dichotomy.

The chief frowned. "We'll keep this on the down-low until after guests leave, okay?"

Guests. Trinidad remembered her failed errand and went in search of Renata. She found her still photographing.

"Sorry but I couldn't find the guest book."

Renata brushed the hair from her forehead with the back of her hand. "It's okay. I'll get it. The cake looks great, by the way."

"Thank you," Trinidad said, but Renata had already hurried off.

The twins arrived, immaculate in their Shimmy catering outfits, and took their places behind the cake and coffee table. They were already eyeing Cordell and whispering to each other. He'd taken a seat in the back row next to his brother Reg.

Juliette slid neatly into the chair next to him, and they were soon chattering and laughing. Trinidad had to admit they looked good together. Cordell was somehow softer when he was around Juliette, but it still made Trinidad worry. She hoped her friend was not following her trend of picking one bad love match after another.

"Carlos," she said sternly. "Put your phone away."

"I gotta get a quick video for TikTok."

She stood blocking his view. "We're not doing that. This is a wedding, not a celebrity stalking. Renata said she would send us what she's taken, so that will have to do."

Both boys groaned. She held out her hand. "I'll hold on to your phones until the wedding's over."

They gave her identical looks, incredulous. She might as well have been telling them they were being marched off to the guillotine.

Carlos looked past her and cocked his head. "What's the matter with that lady?"

Renata was standing zombielike in the doorway, her bottom lip caught between her teeth. Trinidad hurried over. "Are you all right?"

"I...I found something."

Trinidad groaned inwardly. Another something? Wasn't the light bulb enough?

The tension around Renata's mouth made it clear, this something was definitely not nothing.

Chapter Nineteen

BIGLEY WALKED OVER AND PEERED at the paper between Renata's fingertips.

Renata found her voice. "It's a note…from Harry."

"Harry the dead guy?" Carlos said before his brother socked him in the shoulder.

Renata's eyes were round, dark pools. "It was in my inbox under a bunch of receipts. I was looking for the guest book."

Trinidad drew close enough that she could read the scrawling pencil-written note over Bigley's shoulder. She read aloud.

I'm sorry, Renata. I loved you since high school. We talked at the reunion and I knew Leonard was keeping you chained to this old boat. When you hired me as a carpenter, I made a plan. I thought if I killed him, we could be together, maybe live on the steamboat, or travel or something. I bummed a ride with some guy named Gabe at the diner. Knew Leonard did his dumb birdwatching thing every day at the same time. Conked Gabe over the head and took the wheel. I didn't know I was killing the wrong guy. Honest. And that little bird. I can't forgive myself. Tried again to push Leonard over but that didn't work out either. He's a hard man to kill. Sorry. It's all over for me. Gonna go take a long walk off a short pier. You can resell my tools and make a few bucks. I hope you are gonna be happy somehow.

Harry

Juliette gripped Trinidad's shoulder. She hadn't even realized her friend had drawn close. "That's a confession... from Harry?"

Renata shook her head. "That poor man. I had no idea."

Bigley took the paper between her fingertips.

Trinidad tried to assimilate the information. She'd been so sure Harry had been murdered, but the posthumous confession changed everything. Oscar's death made sense now. He'd been killed by mistake. But something refused to add up in her brain.

"Wait one red-hot minute." Leonard dropped his legal pad. "Harry wanted to kill me?"

"But he got the wrong guy," Quinn said.

Stan groaned. "Poor Oscar."

"Poor Oscar? What about me? I've been living on the same boat as a guy who wanted to kill me."

"You're fine," Renata snapped. "It's Oscar and Harry who are dead."

Leonard shook his head, eyes bugging. "Harry was an even worse killer than he was a carpenter. Ran over the wrong guy. Pushed Gabe over the railing instead of me. A complete clown."

Renata glared at him. "This isn't the time for jokes."

"Who's joking?" Leonard guffawed loudly. "Serves him right that he's dead and I'm still kicking. Just too bad Oscar got the brunt of it."

"Yes, it is." Iris shoved her glasses up higher on her nose. "Oscar was a good man who happened to be in the wrong place at the wrong time, and he didn't deserve what happened to him."

Leonard arched a brow. "Are you implying it would have been better if Harry killed me?"

Iris didn't reply, which was answer enough. Leonard muttered to himself.

Renata sank onto a chair. "At least it's over. I can't take any more. I'm practically unraveling."

Trinidad caught Bigley's eye. It was clear she thought there was something fishy about the suicide note too. The confession created more questions than answers. Harry had ordered an Uber, intended to leave town; that didn't sound like the actions of a man who'd decided on suicide. It might have been an impulsive decision made at the spur of the moment, of course, but the details that still made no sense to her were the neatly packed tools and the nail in Harry's ankle. Perhaps he'd meant to end his life with a properly placed nail and he'd missed, which would be in character, but she couldn't envision him stowing his equipment afterward.

And he couldn't swim, so how had his body gotten clear across the lake?

"Wait." Gabe's mouth worked for a moment before he got the words out. "This letter is a confession, right? Harry is the killer. So…I'm in the clear? I'm not going to be arrested for what happened to Oscar?"

"I'd say it's too early to tell, but it can't hurt your case, I don't think." Bigley tucked the note into the plastic bag. "There are still a few things to work out."

Cordell had moved close with the other visitors. Reg stood beside him, glowering.

"Hold up." Cordell thrust his chin out at Bigley. "You don't believe this, right? That Harry confessed to killing this Oscar guy? The whole confession note is pretty convenient."

Bigley shot him a curious look. "Nothing's certain, but that is what it would appear to be, a confession."

Cordell grew in height. "No way. There is no way that can be right. Someone faked that to get Gabe here off the hook." Cordell stabbed a finger at Gabe. "Did you write this, huh? Or get your sister here to do it?"

Bonnie cocked her head. "That's ridiculous. Calm down, Cordell."

"Not going to calm down. Someone is making stuff up so your loser groom is going to get off without any jail time for what he did."

"I didn't kill him." Gabe frowned. "I'm ninety-nine percent sure."

Cordell's chin jutted. "You belong in jail."

Gabe straightened. A flicker of defiance appeared in his

demeanor. "I've been to jail. I broke the law, hurt people, and I served my sentence. Then I got out."

"You shouldn't have gotten out," Reg said. Trinidad jumped at his gravelly baritone. "You should have died in jail."

"Stop it," Bonnie said desperately. "Both of you."

Gabe squinted. "You had inmates try and beat me up, didn't you? If they hadn't moved me to a solo cell, I'd probably be dead. You hate me that much? Because your mother didn't get her fried chicken restaurant chain?"

"Yes," Cordell and Reg said in tandem.

Bigley had drawn herself up to her full height, hands on her hips. "Sorry, boys. That's how the justice system works. We have trials and juries and sentencing, not vigilantism. Deal with it."

"We have our own kind of justice." Cordell sprang like a cat toward Gabe, uncoiling as he moved. Gabe stumbled back. Quinn shot out a foot, catching Cordell's ankle and sending him stumbling into his brother. The action startled Noodles, who bumped into Felice and knocked her over.

Bigley dove in to wrestle Cordell upright and twist his hands behind him. It took Quinn and Stan together to do the same with Reg. Trinidad hurried to Felice. Noodles was attempting to tug the child to her feet.

"All right." Bigley's cheeks were crimson. "Now guess who's going to jail this time, Cordell? You can see how the justice system works from the inside."

But Cordell was no longer staring at Gabe. His gaze was riveted on Felice.

Trinidad had been tending to Felice while eyeing the fighting, but now she too got a good look. Felice's pink fascinator had fallen off and was dangling below her ear. Her hair on the crown of her head was interrupted by small bald patches, round and shiny. She patted her head in a panic.

Trinidad stepped between her and the others and quickly repinned the fascinator into place. "There you go, sweetie. Did you hurt yourself when you fell?"

Felice shook her head, lips trembling. The chagrin on her face made the pieces snap into place for Trinidad. Felice's ever-present pink cap. The sudden switch to homeschooling. Bonnie's remark that the children had been unkind. A memory of Cordell at the Shimmy scrolled through Trinidad's mind, when he'd knelt to examine the raggedy bird with no feathers.

"What's the matter with that birdie?"

"His feathers fell out," Felice said.

"Aww. I can relate. When I was a kid, all my hair fell out and everybody laughed at me."

A wedding Bonnie didn't seem to want...for the one person she would give up everything to protect: her daughter.

Trinidad looked at Bonnie. Her mouth was screwed into a tight knot. The silence hummed with tension.

Cordell was no longer looking at Felice but straight at Bonnie. "It's alopecia, isn't it?"

She didn't answer.

"Isn't it?" he repeated, louder. "Alopecia, like I had as a boy." His gaze traveled to Felice. "The kids made fun of me. How about you?"

Felice nodded.

Cordell grimaced as if reliving a painful memory. "Called me baldie and giraffe because I was super tall. You're tall, aren't you, Felice? Taller than most of your friends?"

"Yes," Felice said.

"Juliette." Bonnie's words came out in a croak. "Would you take Felice on the deck for a walk, please? I need to talk to Mr. Barrone for a minute."

"Yes, you do," Cordell said darkly.

Juliette nodded and took Felice's hand. "Come on, Fee." She led the girl from the room.

Bonnie stood ramrod straight as if preparing for a blow. Bigley still held Cordell's wrists behind him. Trinidad knew she should probably leave, but she could not make her feet walk away from what was about to happen.

"Please," Bonnie said to Bigley. "Can you let him loose for a minute? I need to talk to him, and I'm sure he's not going to try and hit anyone else."

Trinidad wasn't so certain but Bigley pushed Cordell into a folding chair, and Stan and Quinn did the same with Reg.

Leonard flapped his meaty arms, waving a hand around the venue. "This isn't the way a wedding works. Why don't we put all this behind us and carry on? I got the officiating stuff all written down here. We can still get some good pictures and eat ice cream cake and stuff."

Renata sagged with weariness. "Sit down, Leonard. This isn't about you."

Gabe started over to stand next to Bonnie, but she held

up a palm to stop him. He halted, glancing from Bonnie to Cordell and back again as if he was watching a tennis match. She glared at Cordell. "This is what should have happened the moment you messaged me that you were returning to Sprocket. Maybe it's what I should have said to you six years ago, but you gave me plenty of reasons not to."

"Quit stalling. Felice is my kid, isn't she?" Cordell said. "And you never told me, Bon. You lied to me."

Bonnie rolled her eyes. "And you sit there wondering why? When we were together in college, you were out of control. You played dirty on the court, and if people crossed you outside the arena, you'd rough them up or have your family do it."

He shrugged. "No big deal."

"It was a big deal to Germain. Remember him? The guy who took you to task for being a ball hog? You hurt him, broke his rib so he was out for the season."

Cordell shifted on the chair, silent and sullen.

"When I got pregnant, I knew I didn't want my baby to be raised around that."

"Our baby," Cordell growled.

Trinidad thought of Queenie and shuddered.

"You'd already moved on to other women. I did what was best for Felice. That's what you do as a parent."

"So you married Gabe?" Cordell's expression looked as though he'd taken a swallow of spoiled milk. "And you let him take my kid? A loser like that?"

Cordell would have leapt to his feet if Bigley hadn't restrained him.

Bonnie didn't flinch. "Gabe was the only person I could trust, and he offered to marry me. He took care of me and Felice. I had to drop basketball and I lost my scholarship. He paid for my medical care and tried to be a good father to her while I finished college. You should be thanking him."

Papa outright gaped at Gabe, muttering under his breath in Spanish.

"A good father? The guy's a crook," Cordell spat.

"He became a crook, but you know what? I'd take the mistakes Gabe made any day over a bully, and that's what you are, Cordell."

He was staring daggers at Gabe. "It's not bullying if a guy deserves it."

Trinidad noted that the rapt twins were nodding in agreement.

Bonnie stared him down. "You're proving my point exactly. There is no way I want Felice to hear things like that or learn from a man who is motivated by one thing... winning."

"I..." He closed his mouth, deflating slightly. "All right. I can see your point, but I should've been given the chance to be a father to my own kid."

"Would you have wanted to?" Bonnie's volume dropped into the softer range. "Made time for her? Prioritized what she needed over your career? All the traveling? The women? The partying?"

He shrugged, shoulders slumped, and Trinidad saw a change come over him.

"I dunno. But that doesn't excuse your lies. You thought

I'd find out so you decided marrying Gabe would throw me off the trail."

"It was a bad idea and I should have said no." Bonnie shot Gabe an apologetic look and blew out a breath that puffed her bangs. "But you kept pushing to hang around me and Felice. You even mentioned buying a cabin in Sprocket. She looks more like you every day, her eye color, her height, and the alopecia. I was afraid you'd find out. Gabe wanted to get married and officially adopt her."

Papa actually patted Gabe on the shoulder, which seemed to surprise them both. "This was an honorable thing for a hooligan to do."

"Thank you," Gabe said.

Cordell almost rose from the chair again. "Adopt her? No *way* is that gonna happen."

"I'll tell you what's gonna happen." Bonnie mimicked his macho tone. "Felice is going to stay with me here in Sprocket, and Gabe will have as much contact as he likes because Felice cares for him. I will explain, somehow, that you are her biological father if you're going to act like one. If you wish to have visitations, we can talk about that, as long as you behave like a loving, civilized adult."

Cordell's eyes slid to Gabe, narrowing in disgust. "Maybe I'll just take you to court. Let my mama raise Felice."

The change was instantaneous, a cat morphing into a tiger. Bonnie marched close and stuck her face within inches of Cordell's, fury radiating from her in hot pulses. "If you try to take my child away from me, I will march straight to the newspapers and tell them everything about your past and I mean every last dirty stunt you pulled. Your fans won't be so loving then." She was shaking with rage. "And I will fight you with the last breath in my body, Cordell. You. Will. Not... take Felice. Do you hear me?"

"All right, Bon Bon," Cordell said, palms up. "I wasn't really going to do that. You're right anyway. I don't want the whole kid responsibility thing in my life."

Bonnie heaved out a breath. "Fine then. Glad that's settled."

Trinidad noticed that Juliette was positioned perfectly near the open window, listening in. Her eyes were wide as gingersnaps.

"So, Gabe," Bigley said. "That leaves one question. Are you going to press assault charges against Cordell and Reg here?"

Gabe blinked. "Uh, no. Cordell is Felice's father. I think we'll call it bygones, huh?" He stuck out his hand.

Cordell didn't take it, but neither did he punch Gabe in the nose. He looked chagrined, muttering to himself. Juliette reached through the open window and gave Cordell a brilliant smile and an encouraging thumbs-up. She hefted Felice and said something that made the girl giggle.

Cordell shot out his palm for one brief shake with Gabe, dropping Gabe's fingers quickly as if they were slimy.

Progress, Trinidad thought.

Leonard sighed. "Does this mean there isn't going to be a wedding?"

Trinidad almost laughed.

Bonnie exchanged a look with Gabe. "I appreciate what

you were willing to do for us, but there's no need for a wedding. Ring or not, you'll always be a father figure to Felice."

Gabe beamed. "I'll do my best, even though I'm not a pro athlete or anything."

"That's for darn sure," Cordell said.

Trinidad gripped Bonnie's shoulder. "I'm sorry you went through all this worry alone."

Bonnie smiled and hugged Trinidad. "Me too. But I'm glad it's over. All the sneaking around's been killing me."

"Us too. Juliette and I have been worried sick."

"No more," she said with a sigh. "But I have to figure out how to explain it all to my daughter."

"We'll help. Any way we can."

Trinidad noticed that Quinn was staring fixedly at his own feet. Had the revelation of what Gabe had done made him feel bad? Or was he stewing about Gabe returning to a single life in Sprocket, near Trinidad? Her heart quivered as she considered it might be too much for Quinn's ego to live with. Suddenly she craved a breath of fresh air. "I'll go get Felice and Juliette."

The two were no longer at the window. Maybe they'd gone to watch the paddle wheel in action. She strolled along toward the stern, thinking as she went. Her mind was a muddle. Cordell was Felice's father? Wild. And Gabe had been willing to remarry Bonnie and adopt Felice after caring for them for years? Even wilder. It was like learning you'd been living on a different planet than Earth your whole life.

Gabe, maybe still a hooligan, but with a truly noble streak. The cold air slapped her into another thought. Would

Gabe be able to escape jail now? The newly discovered confession would perhaps put him in the clear, but there were things that still bothered her. First was the packed nail gun. It was possible that Harry had shot himself with a nail, bandaged the wound somehow, and neatly packed his tools before he swam to his death or he'd jumped in the lake from another spot they'd not considered that would carry his body to Iris's. It just didn't feel right for a man who'd almost keeled over when Renata endured a small cut on her finger.

The cut. She thought back to that moment. It had happened on the night of Gabe's accident, which she believed had been intended to kill someone else. Today they'd found the light bulb hidden in the poinsettia plant. What if the person who'd removed it from the "rickety fixture" had cut their finger in the process? She walked closer to the rumbling paddle wheel.

The water churned and cycled with a soft roar. Trinidad noticed a flash of color on one of the struts as it flashed by, the streak of green she'd seen when they boarded for the wacky wedding. An emerald strip, silky and smooth, speckled with dots. What if…? Her imagination poked her.

It was a ridiculous idea, an outside chance, but if someone had shot Harry with a nail on the boat, he would have bled. Might the murderer have bound up the wound to keep things tidy before they rowed him out in the lake? The killer would have gotten rid of the cloth quickly to prevent the police from finding it. Or maybe the cloth had accidentally come loose when the murderer was trying to dispose of the body?

As if in a daze, she eased closer to the massive spinning wheel. Again she saw the flash of green before it plunged into the water. She thought about turning around and asking Quinn to join her, but what she thought she'd seen was probably something completely innocent. And he was angry with her, their last conversation still stinging.

She moved to the low metal gates that provided a safety barrier to keep guests away from the massive machine. No way was she going to put herself in danger on that icy deck by pushing past the gates, but she was desperate to know. Maybe she could get a quick photo to show the chief. Again she caught only a flash as the wheel completed another cycle, too quickly for her to ready her phone camera.

Steadying her elbows on the metal barrier, she zoomed in through the spray. The red wooden slats kicked up puffs of vapor. The wood rumbled under her feet, drops of lake water spraying her hair. One rotation as the wheel circled through the water and…there! She almost missed it, but for a moment, there'd been a peek of fabric, caught on the giant wooden spoke. Again she waited for the wheel to make a noisy revolution before she got a better look, this time capturing the image on a video.

She paused to watch what she'd recorded. Twice. Her breathing grew shallower with each viewing.

The fabric wasn't patterned; it was stained with an ominous dark patch. What if the cloth had been used to mop up Harry's blood?

Trinidad's own blood ran cold. Harry killed Oscar instead of Leonard. She felt that much was true. Leonard

was right. Harry was a terrible hit man, and he'd been murdered when he'd not been able to dispatch the right person.
But who hired him? Who had a steamboat-sized reason to
wish Leonard dead?

The green scarf. The fake suicide note.

The person who desperately wanted him to sell the
Sprocket Steamboat.

His sister, Renata, who'd cut her finger tampering with
the light bulb.

A huge shove from behind sent Trinidad tumbling over
the locked gates.

Chapter Twenty

SHE LANDED ON HER FACE, her body swooshing across the wet wood decking like a penguin on an ice floe. As she struggled to her knees, another push forced her farther toward the edge, mere feet from the enormous wheel. There was no safety railing here, only the relentless wheel, a narrow strip of decking, and the roiling lake.

This time, Trinidad did make it to her feet to find Renata behind her, a baseball bat poised and ready to tee off on her head.

Feet slipping on the wood, she tried to stay upright, shouting, but her voice was drowned out by the water. Renata's face was hard with hatred, a killer's face. Never had Trinidad been so sorry to be right.

Offense was the best defense, Quinn had told her as they watched a basketball game together. She shouted over the noise. "You killed Harry, didn't you, Renata? The suicide note was faked."

The woman ignored the question, swaying from side to

side. "This has been a comedy of errors from the get-go." Without warning, she bashed madly at Trinidad.

She was barely able to jerk back and avoid the blow that almost unbalanced Renata.

"The dumbest thing I did was hiring that idiot Harry to kill Leonard. I figured even a dope like Harry could manage to off my brother. How hard could it be? Leonard is a lump. I figured he'd hit him with a brick at night or tie him up and drive him to a quarry somewhere. But no, Harry had to go and be clever, figuring he'd ambush Leonard while he was bird-watching. Did that go to plan? Of course not. The half-wit conked Gabe and ran Oscar down instead. Couldn't even push him off the boat when I set up a foolproof plan to get Leonard up there."

As Trinidad had suspected, the shove on the boat had been meant for Leonard, but Gabe had inserted himself first. Renata must have switched out the light bulb, which was how she cut her finger. Harry was lying in wait to shove Leonard overboard, but when things went wrong, he snuck down the back staircase. That was why his and Renata's hot cocoa bombs weren't melted. They'd both been away from the table to carry out their plot to kill Leonard.

Trinidad crab walked away from the paddle wheel and tried to get to her feet. "Harry loved you."

Renata's hair was curling in the spray. Mascara streaked her face as she rolled her eyes. "Oh please. I was his paycheck. He felt more guilt over orphaning that bird than killing Oscar. Scooter jumped out while he was trying to turn Oscar over and check his ID. Idiot tried to find him but he heard someone coming and he had to quickly shove the car in the creek."

Trinidad could only gape. "Gabe is innocent. Just like he said."

"For a hot minute, it looked like Harry might actually be able to pin it on Gabe, but that didn't go right either and Gabe survived." Renata swung the bat again, and only Trinidad's last-minute jog to the left saved her.

"Renata, we're on a boat with two dozen people. You can't kill me without being found out."

Renata swiped at the moisture collecting in her hair. "I'm not going to kill you. You're going to fall into the paddle wheel. You're curious and annoying. Everyone will totally believe it. I'll find another way to kill my brother when things have died down around here, no pun intended."

"You'll be caught," Trinidad yelled over the noise. "Sooner or later."

Renata squeezed the bat. "This isn't how my life was supposed to work out. Do you think I *wanted* to be a killer? No, I wanted to find a nice man, get married, and spend summers in the Poconos like normal people, but Leonard will never give up this boat, and all our money is tied up in it. He's been a pain in my backside since we were kids." Her face was blotched and twisted with emotion. "I only wanted to get off this nasty tub and start a life. Was that too much to ask?" Her tone rose to a shriek.

There was no way to get around Renata and back to safety. Trinidad had to keep holding on, using the no-nonsense tone she took with the twins. "Stop this, Renata. Right now. You're not a murderer." But in fact Renata was responsible for more than one death.

Renata exhaled with an elaborate eye roll. "Thanks for the vote of confidence but that ship has sailed. I never thought I could kill someone myself until I did. I should have done it right after the Oscar fiasco. After Leonard fired Harry, he got drunk in town. Blabbering about marrying me and finishing off Leonard but I knew it was a matter of time before he let something slip or killed the wrong person again. I texted him, and when he showed up, I grabbed his nail gun and meant to shoot him in the heart, but I got his foot." She laughed, gripping the bat like a major league hitter. "Worked fine anyway because when he got a look, he fainted at the sight of his own blood. Why? Because he was an *idiot*," she shrilled. "I loaded him in a luggage cart and took him to the dock to dump him over, but he started to come to."

"So you rowed him out into the middle of the lake and tossed him in?" Horrifying.

"Yeah." She laughed. "He didn't suffer. You won't either. Terrible accident. So sad."

This time, Renata's swing came close enough that Trinidad grabbed the end of the bat.

"Leggo," Renata screamed as they twisted around. Connected by the bat, they circled in a violent dance. *I've got to get past her, run back to the lobby.* Finally Trinidad forced her weight forward, sending Renata sprawling hard onto the deck, dazed, but Trinidad lost her footing too. She tumbled backward toward the crushing paddles, a scream frozen on her lips.

Through the mist, she saw Noodles dash up and snag her sleeve between his teeth. But her weight was too much for the old dog. She teetered there.

She tried to scream. "Noodles, let go." But her valiant friend would not. They both skidded toward the roaring paddle wheel where they would certainly drown. How many people would grieve? Her dear Papa, Quinn, her sisters, Felice. It was not fair, not fair at all. Most of all, it was not right that her noble old dog should die trying to save her. She tried again to push him away, but he would not let go, his forelegs juddering with the effort of bracing himself.

When her skull was inches from the battering wheels, two more figures appeared through the pummeling water. Gabe and Quinn each seized one of her arms and hauled her away. Bigley appeared and yanked the bat from Renata's grip, wrestling her to her belly. Panting, crying, and clutching Noodles to her, Trinidad allowed Quinn and Gabe to support them as they returned to the dining room.

Quinn guided her into a chair, Noodles on her lap. Bonnie came running with a blanket to throw over them, and Juliette found another for Noodles. Leonard stood staring, shocked.

Quinn knelt next to her and stroked her hand. "Are you okay, honey?"

His words only made her blubber harder. "If you hadn't..." Her eyes found Gabe, who stood staring. "If...if you and Gabe and Noodles hadn't..."

Quinn squeezed. "I looked everywhere for you. Doug climbed to the sun deck and texted me that you and Renata were near the paddle wheel."

"Th...thank you, Doug," Trinidad said.

Doug nodded.

Papa was right by her side, adding another blanket. "I

cannot fathom it. At my very core, I cannot fathom a sister wanting to kill her brother and almost killing my Trina."

Leonard slumped into the chair next to Trinidad. "I thought we had plain old sibling rivalry. Who knew she legit wanted me dead?"

Noodles licked the water from Trinidad's chin and she cuddled him close. "And you are my hero, Noodles. Forever and always." She pressed her face to his damp fur, heart full to the brim.

The twins had their phones out, eyes ping-ponging. She was too tired now to correct them.

"Oh man," Diego said. "This ice cream job is the best thing that ever happened to us. We got to see a murderer nabbed in real time, and like a whole secret paternity thing come to life. This is way better than Netflix."

Felice ran over, tears streaming down her cheeks.

"Auntie, Noodles."

Trinidad clasped her tight while Noodles licked the tears away. "I'm okay," Trinidad reassured her. "Not hurt. Noodles is safe too. Everything is okay."

Felice sobbed, great big shuddering gasps.

Cordell appeared pained, watching his daughter cry. "Hey, um, don't worry, Felice. Everything's gonna be okay now, right?" He shot Bonnie an uncertain look.

She rubbed Felice's back. "Right."

Juliette gave Cordell an approving smile. "You'll get the hang of it," she whispered, taking his hand.

The look he gave her was tender. He lifted her knuckles to his lips. She looped her arm through his and squeezed.

Felice continued to cry in spite of the comfort from her auntie, mother, and Noodles.

"I don't wanna be on this boat anymore," she wailed. "I don't like it here."

"I'm with you, Fee." Trinidad looked at Chief Bigley standing in the doorway, holding a cuffed Renata by her elbow. "Can we please go?"

Bigley nodded. "Chang's on his way. I'll catch up with you later."

"Okay." Trinidad spoke firmly. "And we're taking the cake with us."

Leonard did not argue as the twins repackaged the slightly melted dessert. Noodles shook the water from his coat when she set him down. Her darling friend, ready for the next adventure. *I love you, Noodles.*

Papa trapped her arm in his. "Where to?"

After she'd nearly been killed? There was only one answer...to the place where she felt like she belonged, a store of her very own that she'd survived to return to once more. "To the Shimmy."

"Not the tiny house?" Quinn's tone was subdued.

"No, the store. I have dry clothes there. Scooter will be missing Noodles, and I'm going to drown my sorrows in ice cream cake." She gestured to them all. "Everyone is welcome. We'll have a...I don't know, reverse wedding reception."

Diego raised a brow. "Is Crusher going to come?"

She turned around and saw Bonnie shoot a look at Cordell, who was standing arm in arm with Juliette.

Cordell swallowed. "Your call, Bon Bon. If you don't think it's the right thing for Felice…"

Bonnie only hesitated for a moment. "You're going to be part of Felice's life now, for better or worse. Come and have cake with us. Reg too, if he's got his act together."

Cordell's smile was as warm and gentle as the squeeze he got from Juliette.

They all walked, squelched, and trudged their way to the gangplank.

Iris accompanied them, carrying a big pot of poinsettias, and Trinidad repeated the invitation. She'd been suspicious of Iris, and she felt the need to make amends.

Iris declined. "I'm going home, but thanks anyway."

Trinidad wondered if "home" for Iris would be Oscar's house or the tiny apartment over the floral shop. Time would tell.

Leonard sat glumly waiting for Officer Chang. The rest made their bedraggled way off the boat. Felice's fascinator was missing a feather. Trinidad, Doug, Quinn, and Noodles had damp hair, and Bonnie's mascara was smudged. Even the creases on Papa's perfectly pleated pants looked less crisp. It was an afternoon they'd never forget.

Papa held Trinidad's hand. Every footstep sapped her of energy and the cold pressed into her bones. Two murders and a wedding cover-up was plenty for one day.

They made it to the truck and Quinn unlocked it. "I'll drive." She was happy to let him. Doug loaded the cake into the truck's freezer and secured Noodles.

Before she climbed in, she felt a tap on her shoulder.

Gabe stood uncertainly, dark hair curling. "I guess maybe I should say my goodbyes now that there's no wedding."

No wedding and no more reason to hold grudges like the one that led Renata to murder. Trinidad spoke calmly, plenty loud enough for Quinn to hear. "I don't know what your plans are, Gabe, but you're invited to come eat ice cream cake with us."

He blinked. "I am?" Gabe yanked a look at Papa, who stood a few feet away near his Bel Air.

"If you aren't too wet," Papa said after an audible swallow, "you may ride with me to the Shimmy."

"I can?"

Papa answered with a nod.

She couldn't read Quinn's expression, but Gabe's was like a dog who'd found a beam of sunshine on a winter day.

"I'm practically dry." He hustled to the Bel Air and climbed in. Papa waved and drove off.

Quinn opened the food truck passenger door for Trinidad and they set off. They'd made it several silent miles before Quinn cleared his throat.

"I…"

She waited until he started again.

"I was a jerk."

Though her heart thrummed hard, she did not interrupt.

"You are an intelligent, self-determined woman, and I treated you like you were a child. Jealousy got the better of me, and I apologize." He swallowed. "If Gabe is going to stay in town, that's fine. I'll try to keep my immature side in check. I…I hope you can forgive me because you're the most amazing woman I have ever met."

Eyes on the road, he offered a palm. And there it was, another decision to be made.

Take Quinn's hand, step back into life with a good, flawed man, or keep still and let the moment pass and move forward with only her life's ambition for company, to make the Shimmy thrive? Ever since she'd arrived in Sprocket, it had been one set of momentous decisions after the next.

Keeping her own eyes fixed on the town of Sprocket, she reached between them, knotted their fingers together, and squeezed. Decision made. Risk taken.

The Shimmy was officially closed to the public, so the twins drew the shades before they set out the drippy ice cream cake. The strange gathering—Reg, Cordell and Juliette, Bonnie and Felice, Quinn, Doug, Papa, Gabe, and Stan—settled into chairs with plates of oozing dessert.

"This is really good," Bonnie said. "Even better when it's half melted."

"Yummy." Felice licked her fingers.

It had been the strangest night of her life, but Trinidad realized the ending was perfect. The people she loved, the store she adored, an odd town she called home.

"Wowee," Scooter said.

Noodles barked.

And everyone laughed.

Epilogue

THE WEDDING WAS AS FARAWAY from a boat as possible. Bonnie's train-car inn was surrounded by a new carpet of spring grass. The centerpiece of the old dining car was a long table, covered in white linen, sparkling with china, silver, and lush blush-colored roses entwined with ivy, Iris's best work.

"You look nervous," Quinn whispered in Trinidad's ear.

She felt the tingle of their private communiqué. "Not nervous, excited. I never imagined it would work out, but now that it's here…" She shivered and he put his arm around her silk-clad shoulders.

Felice twirled around in a shimmering pink dress with a tulle underskirt. The new fascinator her mother had made featured fresh roses to match the centerpiece.

"Our very first wedding reception at the Station." Bonnie beamed. "I couldn't be prouder."

"And you're confident this is going to work out?" Trinidad said.

"No, but life's all about risk, right? I wasn't confident

when I had Felice, but she's the best thing that's ever happened to me."

"I get that." Quinn kissed Trinidad's temple and whispered in her ear. "And you're the best thing that's ever happened to me." The small diamond solitaire on her left ring finger winked at her in the warm light. "Shall we find our spots?"

"Yes, let's." With Quinn at her side, they slid into a seat in the single row of chairs at the rear of the car. The arch made of twined branches was plain except for a simple spray of roses that perfumed the air. Papa and Gabe sat on the end. Noodles was curled at Papa's feet, eyeing his friend. Scooter had been brought at Felice's suggestion and he tippy-toed up and down his perch, admiring the shiny white bow festooning the top of his cage.

Pastor Phil cleared his throat as Cordell strolled up to his spot under the arch, perfectly groomed to match his expensive suit. He stopped and took Felice by the hand. Shyly, she followed him to meet the pastor as Juliette stepped into the dining car, radiant in her tea-length bridal gown.

"She's gorgeous." Trinidad took in the elegant, fitted dress and wisp of veil stylishly pinned to her upswept hair.

"Almost as beautiful as my fiancée," Quinn whispered.

As Juliette floated to meet her groom, Queenie grimaced from her chair. Reg gave her a consoling pat on the knee.

"How's Juliette going to do with Mama Queenie for an in-law?" Bonnie murmured.

Trinidad whispered back. "She told me she'd survived jail time so she figured she could handle any cranky relative the Barrones mustered up."

Bonnie stifled a giggle.

"Oh. I almost forgot. She said to give you this." Bonnie pulled a velvet bag from her pocket.

Trinidad opened the drawstring, and a small magnifying glass fell out with a note. "For your next case."

Trinidad laughed. "Right. I guess I'm all primed and ready for another murder investigation."

"*Más vale pájaro en mano que cien volando,*" Scooter crooned in perfect Spanish. Trinidad gaped and Papa smiled proudly.

"A bird in hand is worth more than one hundred flying," she said with a laugh, squeezing Quinn's hand. The Shimmy would survive. She had a partner for life. "I think I'll stick with what I've got in hand." She put the magnifying glass in her pocket.

Tucked into the crook of Quinn's arm, she settled back in her seat to enjoy the wedding, ideas churning for her next ice cream creation.

Dear Reader,

In the words of Scooter the parrot, "Wowee!" I have had a fantastic time writing these three Shimmy adventures. This installment had bits from my own world, notably Scooter the parrot. My amazing sister owns an eclectus named Jonah who was born minus one eye. Jonah is a "plucker" so he looks as though he's wearing fuzzy gray pajamas. He is absolutely hilarious and sounds JUST like her when he talks. A few of his favorite phrases are "Are you okay?" and "Love you." Jonah's joie de vivre reminds me that though life is full of imperfect situations, health challenges, aging struggles, relationship issues, and on and on, there are joys to be had, treats to be eaten, wings to be spread, and love to be given.

I hope that you have enjoyed the series and it has given you a spot of sweetness!

Fondly,
Dana

Shortcut Hot Cocoa Ice Cream

This is an easy recipe that doesn't involve cooking and can be ready in a snap if you want a "soft serve" dessert. You can make it extra decadent by serving it with marshmallow topping!

Ingredients

    1 (5-oz.) package instant vanilla pudding
    1 cup whole milk
    6 tablespoons sweetened hot cocoa mix (I use
        Swiss Miss)
    2 cups heavy whipping cream

Directions

Whisk together pudding mix and the cup of whole milk until the pudding is dissolved. Add hot cocoa mix, and whisk thoroughly. Then whisk in the two cups of heavy whipping cream. Pour into your ice cream maker, and churn for 15 minutes.

Hot Cocoa Bombs

Hot cocoa bombs are lovely delicate orbs filled with cocoa mix that dissolve in warm milk, but they are tricky to make at home. I wanted to find a way that people could mimic those fancy items with household items and a lot less work! Here is a fun recipe that's easy to make and produces a delicious, rich chocolate drink. Plus, it's really fun for the kids to make, decorate, and enjoy.

Ingredients

3 ½ cups semisweet chocolate chips
1 (14-oz.) can sweetened condensed milk
½ cups heavy whipping cream
Assorted toppings: sprinkles, peppermint flakes, marshmallows, etc.

Directions

Place chocolate chips in a heat-safe bowl. Lay out mini muffin tins, and spray with a light coating of cooking spray. You can also use mini muffin liners if you'd prefer.

In a saucepan over medium heat, whisk the sweetened condensed milk and the cream in a saucepan over medium heat, stirring frequently to prevent scorching. Just when it starts to bubble, remove it from the heat. Pour the heated mixture over the chocolate chips and stir until smooth. This is called a ganache.

Pour the ganache into the mini muffin tins until level. Refrigerate for 10 minutes to harden slightly, and then add your decorations*. Let them harden fully before use. They can be kept in the refrigerator or at room temperature.

When you're ready to use, bring 6 ounces of milk just to a boil. Peel off muffin liners if you used them. Put in one bomb or two. (We preferred two.) Stir with a candy cane to make it extra festive. Enjoy!

*Be aware that if you overload the bomb with decorations, they sometimes sink to the bottom of the cup after the bombs are melted.

Lactose-Free Gingerbread Ice Cream

We've experimented with many different versions of this ice cream, and this is the winner. The gingerbread recipe itself yields more than you'll need to mix into the ice cream, but Trinidad will tell you that the surplus can be eaten for a snack and even, possibly, toasted with butter for breakfast.

Old Fashioned Gingerbread
  ½ cup butter (you can use margarine if you want the gingerbread to be nondairy)
  ½ cup white sugar
  1 egg
  1 cup molasses
  1 ½ cups flour
  1 ½ teaspoons baking soda
  1 teaspoon ground cinnamon
  1 teaspoon ground ginger
  ½ teaspoon ground cloves
  ½ teaspoon salt
  1 cup hot water

Directions
Preheat the oven to 350 degrees. Grease and flour a 9-inch loaf pan.

Beat butter and sugar together in a large bowl until smooth. Add egg. Beat until light and fluffy. Stir in molasses.

Combine flour, baking soda, cinnamon, ginger, cloves, and salt. Add the molasses mixture, stir in the hot water, and mix until the batter is smooth. Pour into the prepared pan. Bake for 60 minutes.

Allow the cake to cool completely. Cut approximately 1 cup of gingerbread into ¼ inch cubes, which you will add to the ice cream later. Enjoy the extra!

Spiced Ice Cream

    1 (13.5-oz.) can coconut cream
    1 (13.5-oz.) can coconut milk
    ½ cups almond milk
    2 tablespoons molasses
    1 tablespoon vanilla extract
    1 teaspoon ground cinnamon
    ¼ teaspoon ground ginger
    Two shavings of fresh nutmeg

Directions

Blend the ingredients together. Pour into your ice cream maker, and churn for 20 minutes. Then mix in the cubed gingerbread, and freeze for several hours or until you're ready to use.

Congri (Black Beans and Rice)

When I make a pot of this simple recipe, the fragrance brings me back to my youth when my mom would cook up a batch. Mouthwatering! There are many versions of this hearty meal, but this is closest to the family recipe and it's the easiest too! You can add chopped onion when you're frying the bacon if you'd like as well.

Ingredients

3-4 slices bacon
1 (13.5 oz.) can black beans (not rinsed)
1 cup long grain rice
2 bay leaves
1 teaspoon garlic powder

Directions

Fry up the bacon, drain, and chop it into small pieces. Put the undrained beans into a large pot. Add enough liquid to make three cups. Add the rice, bay leaves, bacon, and garlic powder. Simmer for 20 minutes. Discard bay leaves, and serve with salt and pepper.

Check out Trinidad's first sweet mystery in
PINT OF NO RETURN

Chapter One

IT WAS AN ABSOLUTE MONSTER.

Trinidad Jones rubbed at a sticky splotch on her apron and slid her offering across the pink, flecked Formica counter. The decadent milkshake glittered under the Shimmy and Shake Shop's fluorescent bulbs, from the glorious crown of brûléed marshmallow down to the candy-splattered ganache coating the outer rim and the frosted glass through which peeked the red and white striped milkshake itself. Her own reflection stared back at her, hair frizzed, round cheeks flushed. Something this decadent just had to be a crime. "What should I call it?"

Trinidad's freshly minted employees, twins Carlos and Diego Martin, were transfixed, eyes lit with the enthusiasm only fifteen-year-old boys with bottomless appetites could attain. They might have been staring at a newly landed spaceship for all the wonder in their long-lashed brown gazes. She still wasn't entirely sure which twin was which, but they were doing a bang-up job helping her ready the shop for its launch in a scant seven days' time.

Noodles, her faithful Labrador, cocked his graying head from his cushion near the front door and swiped a fleshy tongue over his lips, which she took as approval. He had already been consulted on a pup-friendly shake she'd dubbed the Chilly Dog, determining it to be more than passable. Noodles was an encouraging sort, which made Trinidad doubly glad she'd decided to adopt a senior citizen companion six months earlier instead of a younger pup. Besides, he had a wealth of skills she was still discovering.

Carlos whistled, running a hand through his spiky hair, sending it into further disarray. "It's like a Fourth of July Freakshake." He gripped the pink-coated paint roller he was holding as if it was a Roman spear. "Like, an eighth wonder of the world or something. You should put a sparkler on the top, you know, for the holiday. People would dig that."

Diego shook his head. "Bad move. Those things can burn at two thousand degrees Fahrenheit, depending on the fuel and oxidizer. Of course, temperature is not the same as thermal energy, which is going to relate to the mass, so…"

"Dude," Carlos said, punching his brother's arm. "You're such a dweeb. I mean, turn off your bloated brain and just admire it, wouldja?"

Diego ceased his impromptu physics lecture to join his brother in their mutual appreciation fest. He pulled a clunky video camera from his backpack, and his twin immediately grabbed a spoon and began speaking into it as if it was a microphone.

"This is Carlos Martin reporting live from the Shimmy and Shake Shop where an ice cream phenomenon is about to be revealed to the world," he pronounced in a booming baritone.

Trinidad laughed. "I didn't think people used video cameras anymore."

Carlos grinned. "They don't. We saw it at the flea market for two bucks along with a bunch of old history stuff and home videos no one will ever watch. We just thought it'd be fun to mess around with it since Diego wants to be a news reporter someday."

"And a physicist," his brother added.

"It's good to have goals," Trinidad said. "So, the shake gets a thumbs-up from the news crew, then? We'll skip the sparklers and call it the Fourth of July Freakshake. What do you think about adding a hunk of a red, white, and blue nutty brownie star in the marshmallow?"

Diego smirked at her. "Is adding brownies a bad thing, like…ever?"

All three of them considered.

"Point taken," Trinidad said. "I'll bake them when I get back from my errands and freeze them for the opening. I have to run to the storage unit and pick up a few final things. Go ahead and lock up the shop if I'm not back when you finish for today, okay?" She knew Carlos had afternoon football practice, and they'd chatted about doing some additional odd jobs around town in their effort to bankroll a used Plymouth while they were both studying up for their driving permits. She eyed the fresh coat of pink paint the boys had been applying to the walls. "Looks like you're almost done."

Diego pointed to the longest wall. "We calculated the volume of paint just right, considering we had to apply a third coat. Weird how your husband's name keeps showing through. Reminds me of a horror movie I watched, like he's rematerializing in town again since all his ex-wives are living here now…" Carlos broke off as his brother elbowed him in the ribs.

"Ex-husband," she said, "and that would be a good trick for him to rematerialize himself out of jail." She swallowed down a lick of something that was part shame, part anger, as she considered the spot where "Gabe's Hot Dogs" was once emblazoned in blocky letters. Moving to the tiny eastern Oregon town of Upper Sprocket, hometown of her cheating ex-husband Gabe Bigley and his two other ex-wives, was her most mortifying life decision to date. At age thirty-six, she should have been settled, married, and raising a family, not jumping into a highly risky entrepreneurial endeavor in her ex-husband's hometown, no less. Funny how pride took a back seat to survival. The faster her money ran out, the more palatable the notion of taking over the building Gabe had deeded her on his way to jail became.

Her grandfather, Papa Luis, used every derogatory word in his Cuban Spanish arsenal to convince her that Gabe "The Hooligan" Bigley should be obliterated from her mind and that moving back to Miami with him and her mother was the prudent choice. He was probably correct, but here she was in Sprocket anyway.

Now "Gabe's Hot Dogs," a store Gabe had never actually helped run, was being reborn as the Shimmy and Shake

Shop, and it was going to be the most successful establishment in the entire Pacific Northwest if it killed her. Upon
arrival in Sprocket, she knew the small town tucked in the
mountainous corner of eastern Oregon would be the perfect
home for her shop. A gorgeous alpine backdrop, sweeping
acres of fields, a constant stream of tourists arriving to witness the wonder of Hells Canyon and participate in various
festivals… It could not fail. Especially since it wasn't a paltry
run-of-the-mill ice cream parlor. Shimmy's would specialize
in extravagant, over-the-top shakes that would take Sprocket
and the dessert-loving world by storm. Unless it had all been
a massive mental misfire on her part. She swallowed a surge
of terror.

Noodles shook himself, his collar jingling in what had to
be a show of support. He gingerly pulled a tissue from the
box on the counter and presented it to her, a throwback to
his service dog training. "It's okay," she said, giving the dog a
pat. "No tears right now." She realized both boys were staring at her.

"That's an awesome dog," Diego said.

She nodded her agreement.

"Um, sorry, Miss Jones," Carlos said. "Mom said we
weren't supposed to mention anything about, I mean,
you know, your ex or the other exes or…uh…" His face
squinched in embarrassment.

"No worries. I know the situation is a bit unorthodox."
And delicious fodder for the local gossips. Somehow, she'd
managed to be in town for six weeks and had not yet run into
Juliette or Bonnie, Gabe's two other ex-wives, the ones she'd

had no clue about until her life fell apart, but it was only a matter of time before their inevitable meeting; her own rented residence was only a short distance from Bonnie's property. She put Carlos out of his misery with a bright smile. "You didn't do anything wrong. It's a weird situation."

"Downright freaky," Carlos said, earning another elbow from his twin.

"Right. Well, I'll just go see to those errands." On the way to the door, Noodles stretched his stiff rear legs in the ultimate downward dog yoga pose and trotted after her.

"By the way, boys," Trinidad called over her shoulder. "I left two spoons on the counter. Someone has to taste test the Fourth of July Freakshake, right?" The door closed on the boys' enthusiastic whoops. She chuckled. There should be some perks to a job that only paid minimum wage and took up plenty of precious hours of summer vacation. If only she could pay them entirely in ice cream.

On the way to her car, she admired the whimsical pink and pearl gray striping on the front of her squat, one-story shop. The awning the three of them had painstakingly put up would keep off the summer sun, and some artfully arranged potted shrubs enclosed a makeshift patio with a half dozen small tables. Noodles had already staked out a location in the coolest corner as a designated napping area. She plodded down the block to spot where she'd parked the Pinto beneath the shade of a sprawling elm. What she wouldn't give to rest her aching feet. The doctor reminded her with ruthless regularity that losing thirty or so pounds would help her complaining metatarsals. Probably a nice vacation to Tahiti would do the same, but it was just as unlikely to happen. Her metatarsals would have to buck up and quit their bellyaching.

Trinidad regarded the shady main drag. Working from sunup to well past dark on a daily basis, she hadn't had nearly enough time to explore the charms of Upper Sprocket.

Somehow the quirky name suited the town settled firmly in the shadow of the mountains, with old trees lining the streets and people who still waved hello as they drove by. Five hours east of Portland, surrounded on three sides by the Wallowa Mountains, Sprocket was plopped at the edge of a sparkling green valley, with soaring peaks as a backdrop and air so clean it almost hurt to breathe it. The mountains were considered the "Swiss Alps of Oregon," and the nearest neighbor, Josef, hosted numerous events like the popular Alpenfest fall bash. Visitors had opportunities to take the Wallowa Lake Tramway to the top of Mount Howard—3,700 feet of eye-popping splendor. The multitude of outdoorsy activities and sheer loveliness brought plenty of visitors to the larger towns, and Sprocket, though more out of the way and shabbier than chic, pulled in its share of tourists too. Enough to keep Trinidad scooping ice cream in the warm weather months. Winter would be another challenge.

"One season at a time," she told herself. She passed a trailer and exchanged a friendly smile with the driver. The RV was one of many in town to enjoy the upcoming celebration. There would be plenty to do before the Fourth of July. Sprocket featured its very own lake, an annual apple festival, and even a third-generation popcorn stand that was a favorite of snackers far and wide. She'd also heard tell of hot springs in the area, though she'd not yet clapped eyes on them. It amazed her how much sunnier this little town was compared to her previous home in Portland with Gabe.

Her spirits edged up a notch. Sunshine, a fresh start, and a darling shop all her own. Rolling down the window, she let the air billow in, bringing with it the scent of dry grass and sunbaked road. On the way, she ticked off the items she needed to retrieve from her storage unit—something she hadn't yet had the time to tackle. There were three more plastic patio chairs she'd have the twins spray-paint a subtle shade of gray to offset the pink theme and her prized antique cookie cutter collection, passed down from her mother who had never so much as laid a finger on them.

Cruising away from the town's main street, she waved to the gas station owner who'd erected a card table on the sidewalk with a cooler on top and a scrawled sign that read BAIT WORMS, FIVE DOLLARS/PINT. As she drove along, she wondered exactly how many worms one got in a pint. The turn onto Little Bit Road took her to what passed for Sprocket's industrial center. It was comprised of an aged feed and grain store, a weedy property that used to be an air strip, and the Store Some More facility, a set of tidy white buildings with shiny metal corrugated doors. One lone tree in the lot next to the structure offered a paltry speck of shade and, nestled underneath, was a bird bath where a small brown wren was splashing with gusto. Parking the Pinto by the closest unit, she pulled out her key and unlatched the padlock that secured her space. The same young man who'd helped her sign the rental papers when she moved in was sweeping the walkway in front of the empty unit next to hers.

She waved. "Hi, Vince. Just back for a few supplies."

He nodded, hiking up the jeans that hung loose on his skinny frame. He was probably in his early twenties, by the look of him, a cell phone poking from his back pocket.

A woman with long blond hair stepped out of the office and pulled his attention. She held a bucket. "Call for you, Vince. Your mom needs you to deliver a half dozen pepperonis and two veggie combos."

Trinidad felt her pulse thump. Everything about the woman was long and lean, including the delicate gold earrings that gleamed against the backdrop of her hair. She appeared to do a double take as she spotted Trinidad. After a pause, she walked over. "I'm Juliette Carpenter. Formerly..."

"Juliette Bigley," Trinidad filled in. She'd known that Juliette owned the storage place, but she didn't imagine the woman was engaged in the day-to-day running of it. She'd only ever dealt with Vince. The hour had arrived. She could practically hear the bells tolling as she cleared her throat. "And it seems like you recognize me, too."

Juliette's face was seared into her memory even though she'd only spoken with her briefly at the trial where Gabe was found guilty of embezzling money from various companies as their accountant. It had been a tense conversation. After all, Gabe had still been married to Trinidad when he'd started the relationship with Juliette, and neither of them had suspected a thing. When Trinidad had discovered Gabe's cheating, and their divorce became official, it was followed quickly by Juliette's whirlwind marriage and divorce. Juliette had not even known of Trinidad and their defunct marriage until a few weeks after Gabe was arrested. He was an accomplished liar. The final shoe had dropped at the trial, when they had not only met each other but also learned of another wife, Bonnie, Gabe's first.

The turbulent storm of memories resurfaced as Trinidad stared at Juliette. She tried not to notice the generous five or ten years between their ages. *You're the older model. Gabe traded you in for one right off the assembly line.* How was it possible to feel old at the age of thirty-six? Trinidad cleared her throat.

"I rented one of your storage spaces. I'm…uh…opening a store in town."

"I heard. I meant to come by and reintroduce myself, but…"

But the whole situation was just *too* ridiculously awkward.

Juliette stared at the bucket, then continued. "I was, um, just filling the bird bath. It's been so dry this year. You wouldn't believe the animals that drink out of it: birds, deer, raccoons." Her stream of conversation dried up.

Trinidad was desperate to fill the silence. Noodles, perhaps picking up on her tension, nosed her thigh, leaving a wet circle on her jeans. "This is Noodles. He's very easygoing. His real name is Reginald, but the shelter workers named him Noodles since he has a thing for them. The noodles, I mean, not the shelter workers."

Noodles offered a hospitable tail wag. Juliette put down the bucket, crouched next to the old Lab and rubbed his ears. "Bet you would be a great watchdog. We could use one around here. More effective than the new padlocks I had installed, and way cuter, too."

The conversation sputtered again. Trinidad tried to think of something to say, but Juliette rose to her feet.

"Let's just clear the air here. This is strange, running into each other, but it shouldn't be. It's just…I thought you said during our talk at the trial that you didn't want anything to do with Sprocket."

Trinidad went cold with shame. "The truth is I had to swallow my pride and take what Gabe deeded me." She didn't add more humiliating details, that her stenographer work had all but dried up and she could no longer make the rent for the Portland apartment she'd shared with Gabe. "It was move to Gabe's hometown or return to my family home in Miami, and I really wanted to prove to myself that I could make it on my own." It was more than she'd meant to say.

Juliette's expression softened, and she surprised Trinidad by gently touching her shoulder. "Hey, I get it, believe me. Same reason I moved here last year. I figured Gabe owed me something, and he had signed over his storage unit business to me, the rat." She shrugged. "It was doing better than my hotel manager gig, so here I am. New life, fresh start, just like you."

Trinidad nodded. "And, besides, who wouldn't want to move to a charming town called Sprocket?"

Juliette blinked, then grinned, and the tension dissipated

into the blaze of golden sunlight that edged over the rooftop. "Upper Sprocket."

"Is there a Lower Sprocket?"

After a moment, Juliette let loose a silver peal of laughter. "Not that I know of. One Sprocket is enough." She lifted a slender shoulder and tossed back her curtain of blond hair, which looked like it had not come from a bottle. Trinidad had always daydreamed about being a sleek blond, but her curly frizz of dark-brown hair, inherited from her Cuban father, would never be smooth, nor fair. She'd be content if it stayed brown for a while, though that was unlikely since she'd caught the glimmer of a silver strand in the bathroom mirror. Gray before forty? Another curveball.

"The ice cream place is a bold idea. Good for you."

Bold or boneheaded? The doubts crept in again. Sprocket's charms notwithstanding, would her wacky business idea fly in a town of less than three thousand people? A place where the locals specialized in raising goats and tending apple orchards, who rolled up the sidewalks promptly at six o'clock p.m.? But Sprocket was reinventing itself as a bona fide tourist stop for the hordes looking for their "alpine experience." They'd even constructed a railrider excursion, pedal-powered carts that tourists used to ride on old train tracks as they took in the countryside. Sprocket was aiming to get its share of the tourist dollars, and Trinidad meant to do the same.

"The funny thing is, I've never been much of a risk taker, but, after Gabe…" Trinidad trailed off. After Gabe, she'd felt snipped from her moorings, like she'd left her old self adrift in still water. The trouble was, she wasn't sure who the new Trinidad Jones was supposed to be. And why was she sharing her innermost thoughts, anyway?

"I understand. My life is sort of divided into B.G. and A.G., before and after Gabe." Juliette tipped her chin up, mouth in a hard line. "No one should have that much power over our lives, Trinidad." After a fortifying breath, she stuck out her palm. "Welcome to Sprocket. Hopefully this is the place where we will both find new beginnings."

Trinidad solemnly shook. "Here, here."

Juliette smiled. "I am glad to extend an official welcome. Come into the office for a minute. It's already too hot out here, and I want to get the rest of your contact info. Vince was supposed to do that, but sometimes his head is in the academic clouds." Juliette's cell phone rang, and she stepped away to answer it.

Trinidad gathered up her items and stowed them in the Pinto before she and Noodles made their way to the office. Juliette was still on the phone, standing with her back to her, tall and statuesque, like a dancer. Trinidad felt acutely aware of the extra pounds her doctor harped on as she noted Juliette's willowy frame. She considered sneaking away. It seemed entirely too painful to extend her visit with the woman who had been her replacement. However, she felt a strong connection to this other wife who had been a stranger only moments before. Of all the zillions of people on planet Earth, no one else could possibly understand how she felt better than Juliette and, perhaps, Bonnie, if she ever should happen to meet her.

Only eighteen months had elapsed since Gabe went to jail for embezzlement and assorted other frauds, but she was determined to make a way for herself in Sprocket, a life after Gabe. A.G., as Juliette put it.

After another hesitant step forward, her shoe crunched on something. Juliette whirled, phone at her ear, and took in Trinidad as she inspected her foot. "Sorry. I was throwing something away, and I didn't get time to clean up properly. Somebody's feeble attempt at a peace offering." Her eyes flashed with anger for a moment as she disconnected the call before summoning a smile. "The hours here are getting to me, and the storage unit business can be ugly. Can I get you some coffee?"

"No, thank you. Why ugly?" Trinidad scraped the sticky bit from her shoe. She realized after the fact that her question had probably been nosy, but Juliette did not seem to take offense. Trinidad, a natural introvert, realized she didn't have a whole lot of practice making chitchat, a problem she'd have to remedy living in Upper Sprocket.

Acknowledgments

Thanks especially to my darling cyber family who has encouraged me greatly in my new series. Also, much gratitude to Super-Agent Jessica for finding a home for this series and to top notch editor MJ for whipping this concoction into shape!

About the Author

Dana Mentink is a USA Today and *Publishers Weekly* bestselling author and the recipient of a Holt Medallion for excellence in mystery/suspense. She was honored to receive the Author of the Year award from West Coast Christian Writers. A California native, she's written over fifty titles in the suspense and mystery genres. She is pleased to write for Harlequin's Love Inspired Suspense and Poisoned Pen Press. You can connect with Dana via her website at danamentink.com. You can also find her on TikTok (danamentinkauthor) and Instagram (dana_mentink) if you'd like to learn more.